D0880595

IN THE WOODS OF MEMORY

IN THE WOODS OF MEMORY

Shun Medoruma

TRANSLATED FROM THE JAPANESE
AND WITH A PREFACE BY TAKUMA SMINKEY

AFTERWORD BY KYLE IKEDA

Stone Bridge Press ◆ *Berkeley, California*

Published by
Stone Bridge Press
P.O. Box 8208, Berkeley, CA 94707
sbp@stonebridge.com • www.stonebridge.com

This work is a translation of 眼の奥の森 [*Me no oku no mori*] by Shun Medoruma, published in Japanese in 2009 by Kage Shobo Publishing Co., Tokyo, Japan.

Front cover background photograph "Wild Iriomote," © Sam Spicer. Villagers photograph by Reinhart T. Kowallis, used by permission. Photograph of American GIs on Iejima is believed to be in public domain.

Chart on pp. 18–19 based on an original concept by Sayuri Shimanaka.

Book design and layout by Linda Ronan.

First edition 2017.

Printed in the United States of America.

Library of Congress Cataloging-in-Publication Data on file.

p-ISBN: 978-1-61172-037-2

e-ISBN: 978-1-61172-924-5

CONTENTS

TRANSLATOR'S PREFACE

I knew little about Okinawa when I was hired by Okinawa International University in April 2004. Like others living in Japan, I knew there were many US military bases here but viewed Okinawa as being something of an idyllic paradise, akin to Hawaii. That all changed on August 13, 2004, shortly after the end of the first semester. Early in the afternoon, I was entering my office when I saw a US helicopter moving across the window. Obviously in distress, the helicopter was spitting smoke and twisting out of control. I ran to the window and saw it disappear behind some trees. From the angle, I assumed that it had crashed into the street. Without thinking, I dashed down the steps and ran toward the huge clouds of smoke. I was there in a minute, before hardly anyone else. The first thing I noticed was that the helicopter had actually crashed into our main administration building! I saw one of the pilots being helped to his feet. Within minutes, a group of Marines from Marine Corps Air Station Futenma, which is located directly next to my university, came running up, and I was asked to move back.

Later, I chatted with one of the Marines stationed at the perimeter. "Yeah, these people always want to see what's going on," he said. I nodded noncommittally, but he seemed to see me as being on his side. Then I noticed that smoke was pouring over a group of students gathered in front of a nearby building. So I said, "This smoke could be dangerous to breathe, don't you think? Maybe you should do something." The second I said that, his attitude toward me abruptly changed, and he officiously stated, "I'm sorry, sir. I'm not supposed to be talking to you." It became clear that his job was to secure the perimeter, not to protect the local people.

In the weeks that followed, my quiet university became the site of daily protests, investigations, and intense media attention. On September 12, in the largest protest in nearly a decade, approximately 30,000 people gathered on campus to protest the presence of M.C.A.S. Futenma. Not surprisingly, the crash intensified the pressure on closing this dangerous base, which is situated in the densely populated city of Ginowan. Actually, the Japanese and US governments agreed to close the base back in 1996, but the plan has never been implemented due to the inability of the two governments to find a replacement facility. In 2017, the problem remains unresolved, and local protests have only intensified, as the Japanese government has become determined to proceed with construction of a new base in the seaside village of Henoko in northern Okinawa—in complete disregard of Okinawa's reasonable request to have the base relocated outside the prefecture.

The helicopter-crash incident completely changed my view of Okinawa. As an American living in a place that my country had invaded and occupied, I couldn't help but feel somewhat awkward and self-conscious. Not only did I become keenly aware of how the legacy of the Battle of Okinawa impacts the daily lives of people living here, I also became more motivated to educate myself about the prefecture's history and culture. Of course, reading as much Okinawan literature as possible has been an important part of that education, as I've always believed that literature is the best way to understand the heart and soul of a people. After reading works by Tatsuhiro Ōshiro, Mineo Higashi, Eiki Matayoshi, Tami Sakiyama, Shun Medoruma, and others, I've gained a deep understanding of Okinawan people and their painful history. Unfortunately, much of this literature still hasn't been translated into English.

About Medoruma and his work

Shun Medoruma won the coveted Akutagawa Prize in 1997 for "Suiteki" [Droplets], a short story praised for its use of magic realism and literary sophistication. Since then, he has won many other literary prizes, and his works have been the focus of books of literary criticism and analysis, both in Japanese and in English. Medoruma has also been in the news for his political activism, especially his participation in the protests against construction of the new US military base in Henoko. He was arrested on April 1, 2016, when he paddled his canoe into a restricted area off the coast of Camp Schwab as part of the protest.

Me no oku no mori [In the Woods of Memory] was first published in twelve installments in the quarterly *Zenya* from Fall 2004 through Summer 2007. After being revised and reorganized into ten chapters, it was published in book form by Kage Shobo in 2009. The novel has received high praise from critics, such as Sadatoshi Ōshiro, who lauds Medoruma for "his powerful use of language in confronting the taboos of memory," and Yoshiaki Koshikawa, who writes that the novel brings Medoruma "one more solid step toward becoming a world-renowned literary figure." Personally, I consider this novel to be Medoruma's masterpiece.

The novel describes two related incidents that took place on a small island during the Battle of Okinawa: the rape of a young woman, and a young man's attempt to get revenge. These two main stories are narrated through various points of view, including those of two Americans. Two chapters are set in 1945, while the other eight are set in 2005, the sixtieth anniversary of the end of the war. The focus of the novel, then, is on how past events have impacted the present.

The opening scenes of the novel take place in the middle of May 1945. At this point in the Battle of Okinawa, US forces had occupied the northern parts of the island, even though intense fighting was still raging in the south. The main setting of the novel, though never directly mentioned, is a village on Yagaji, a small island just off the northwest coast of the Okinawan mainland. The port at which the US soldiers are working is certainly the one at Unten, located on the mainland directly across from Yagaji. US forces occupied the port early in the battle, long before fighting ended in the south.

For Americans—and for mainland Japanese, too—it's difficult to see the connections between World War II and the present, but for Okinawans, those connections are a daily fact of life. This is partly because of the great costs of the Battle of Okinawa, which involved heavy bombing, group suicides, and large numbers of civilian casualties, nearly one-third of the population. As a result, nearly everyone who experienced the war suffered some degree of trauma. Not only do most Okinawan families have relatives who died in the war; they have relatives who were traumatized, too. In addition, the US military bases scattered throughout the prefecture are a constant and visual reminder of the lingering effects of the war. The negative effects of the base economy, the threats to public safety and health, and the regular occurrence of crimes and accidents have kept the bases on the front pages of Okinawan newspapers practically every day.

Shun Medoruma often bases his stories on accounts he's heard from relatives. Although the main plot lines of *In the Woods of Memory* are fiction, they are based on various real-life incidents. In a May 2016 interview published in the *Okinawa Times*, Medoruma said that the rape was based on a story he heard from his mother, who lived on Yagaji during the war. He also discusses the incident in one of his collections of essays. There are also parallels to the infamous 1995 Okinawa rape incident, in which three US servicemen raped an elementary school girl.

The revenge plot has similarities to the 1945 Katsuyama killing incident, in which Okinawans from a village near Nago murdered three US Marines in retaliation for raping village women shortly after the Battle of Okinawa. Medoruma's descriptions of prewar education, detention camps, and the role of interpreters during the war are all accurate.

About this translation

In the Woods of Memory poses many challenges for a translator. Medoruma's experimental use of narrative techniques, mixing of voices, avoidance of quotation marks, and use of Okinawan language make the text a difficult one to render into English. Needless to say, I did my best to produce a translation faithful to the original, but I'd like English readers to be aware of some important changes I decided to make. First, I added chapter titles that identify the point of view and setting of each chapter. Since there are no titles in the original text, Japanese readers are likely to be initially confused before figuring these out on their own, but for English readers the burden would be even heavier, especially for those less familiar with Japanese names or Okinawan history. In addition, I'm sure the titles will make it easier for readers to remember the names and to discuss the novel with others. By the way, I divided the first chapter of the original into two chapters, since they're narrated from completely different points of view.

Second, I decided to use quotation dashes to more clearly mark dialogue, except in the final chapter, where their use would have been inappropriate. In the Japanese text, Medoruma usually refrains from using quotation marks, no doubt to create a more stream-of-consciousness feel to the narration. In Japanese, speakers can be indicated through levels of politeness, the use of pronouns, and in other ways unique to the language, so a direct translation without quotation marks would be confusing. Using dashes seemed like a good compromise in the spirit of the original. In addition, I used italics to mark internal dialogue.

Third, I avoided using the asterisks and letters that Medoruma uses in place of names in some of the later chapters. Replacing names with a letter, blank space, or symbol is a Japanese literary convention not often seen in English literature—and one that I've never liked—so I solved the problem by using pronouns, using the implied name, or assigning a name to the character. Concerning names, I followed the Western convention of putting the given name first. Readers will notice, of course, that most Japanese characters are referred to by their given names, with the obvious exceptions of Kayō, the ward chief, and Matsumoto, the Okinawan writer's friend.

There was, however, one difficulty in translating the novel for which I couldn't find a satisfactory solution: how to translate Okinawan language. Translating dialect or a secondary language is always difficult for translators, but the problem is especially daunting for *In the Woods of Memory*. To begin with, the Ryukyuan languages are not dialects but independent languages, which are not mutually intelligible with Japanese. More importantly, Okinawan language reflects Okinawa's complex political relationship with Japan. After the Ryukyu Kingdom was annexed and became Okinawa Prefecture in 1879, the Japanese government implemented an assimilation policy, which included discouraging the use of Okinawan language. Generally speaking, those assimilation policies were successful, so that by the time of the war, most Okinawans viewed themselves as Japanese and spoke the Japanese language. However, the local language continued to be spoken in many homes and communities, though the pressure to use Japanese outside the home was strong. During the Battle of Okinawa, Japanese soldiers viewed those who spoke the local language with suspicion, sometimes even shooting them as spies. Today, the Ryukyuan languages are considered endangered, but the prefectural government and various local groups are making some effort to revive them. Not surprisingly, the Japanese government has not been supportive of such efforts.

In the novel, the characters that most frequently use Okinawan language (Northern Okinawan) are those who lived in the village for a long time, most notably Seiji, Fumi, and Kayō. Seiji, a young fisherman who had to drop out of school at a young age, speaks only the Okinawan language. I'm sure English readers can see the irony in the fact that although Seiji passionately fights to defend Japan and his village, he cannot speak standard Japanese. Fumi and Kayō, on the other hand, are proficient in standard Japanese, though they often use the local language when they're with other villagers.

Medoruma writes for both a Japanese and Okinawan audience, so in order to convey the use of Okinawan language, he adds a gloss to the right of the Japanese text, which allows readers to "hear" the local language—even if they don't understand it. On top of this, the Japanese is usually given an Okinawan feel, which also conveys that the character is not using standard Japanese. In most chapters, such glosses appear only sporadically, and are relatively easy to ignore, but in the two Seiji chapters the pages are crowded with double lines of text, making the use of Okinawan language extremely conspicuous. The political implication of this should be obvious: Medoruma's use of Okinawan language directly challenges Japanese readers to recognize and accept linguistic and cultural differences.

It's impossible to fully recreate the complexity of Medoruma's use of local language in English, so I ask readers to simply keep the issue in mind, especially for the characters I mentioned above. In my translation, I tried to capture the feel of the local language in idiomatic English, while providing hints that a character is using Okinawan language. The best approximation for an American audience might have been to translate the Okinawan language into Hawaiian, since Okinawa and Hawaii share many similarities: both were formerly kingdoms, both were territories before being annexed, both went through periods of assimilation, both have US military bases, and significantly, both have indigenous languages that are endangered. Such an approach, however, would have been impractical. To begin with, the introduction of Hawaiian would be inconsistent with the rest of the text and would distract readers from the situation in Okinawa. Furthermore, crowding the text with a gloss of a language that most English readers wouldn't understand would be unwieldy and confusing. Still, the comparison should give American readers some sense of the radical nature of Medoruma's use of local language.

Acknowledgments

I'd like to acknowledge the assistance I received in producing this translation. To begin with, I'd like to thank those who guided me in my reading of the original Japanese text, especially Professor Ariko Kurosawa, who let me attend her graduate school classes at Okinawa International University. I'd also like to express my thanks to her students, who generously shared their notes and research. Next, I'd like to thank those who provided advice on the early drafts of my translation, most especially Jonathan Rankine and the anonymous reviewer for University of Hawaii Press. Okinawa International University provided me financial support so that I could spend a year at the University of Vermont doing research and revising my manuscript. During that time, I received invaluable support and encouragement from Professor Kyle Ikeda and the students in his classes. Professor Ikeda has been generous with sharing his insights into Medoruma's work, has provided invaluable feedback on my translations, and has always encouraged me in my research on Okinawan literature. I deeply appreciate his assistance. My translation would never have been published, however, without Stone Bridge Press. I'd like to express my appreciation to head editor Peter Goodman and others at Stone Bridge for their hard work in making this valuable novel available in English. Most of all, I'd like to thank my wife, Yoko, for all of her love, encouragement, and assistance. Her firsthand knowledge of Okinawan culture, history, and language was quite helpful, and without her encouragement, this translation would never have been completed.

Takuma Sminkey
Okinawa, May 2017

IN THE WOODS OF MEMORY

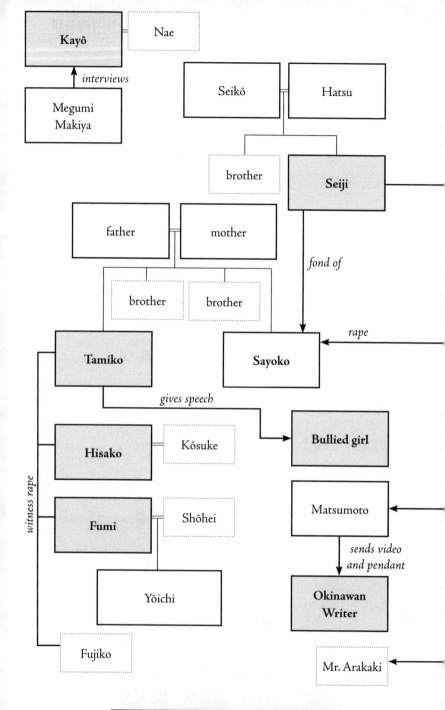

CHARACTER MAP

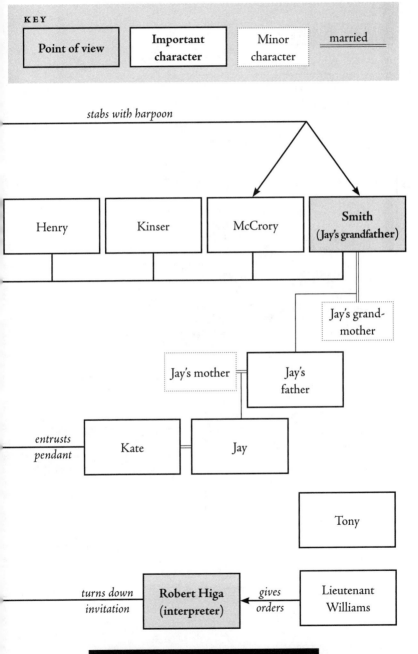

KEY

| Point of view | Important character | Minor character | married |

stabs with harpoon

Henry

Kinser

McCrory

Smith (Jay's grandfather)

Jay's grand-mother

Jay's mother

Jay's father

entrusts pendant

Kate

Jay

Tony

turns down invitation

Robert Higa (interpreter)

gives orders

Lieutenant Williams

AMERICANS

JAPAN AND OKINAWA

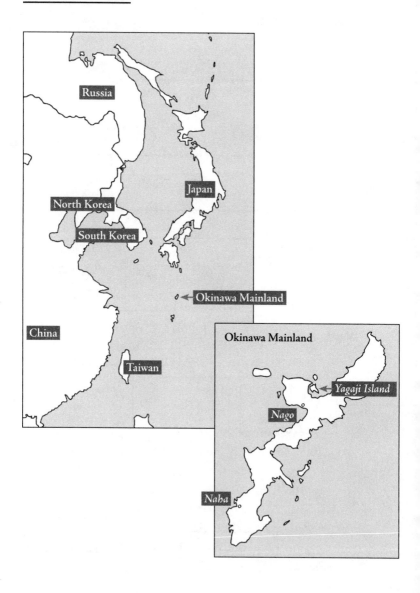

FUMI (1945)

—The Americans are coming! Hisako called out in alarm.

Fumi was searching for shellfish on the seabed and could feel the waves swirling between her legs. She raised her head and looked where Hisako was pointing. At the recently constructed port on the opposite shore, a dozen American soldiers were working. Perhaps because their jobs were done, several had tossed off their clothes and were diving into the ocean. One soldier was already swimming toward Fumi and her friends. He had a considerable lead by the time the other three stopped shouting and started diving in after him.

It was only about two hundred meters from the opposite side, and since the small northern island running parallel to the main Okinawan island formed a narrow passageway, the sea was peaceful. Local fishermen called the inner passage "the bosom," and whenever typhoons threatened, they fled here from the high seas for safe haven. During spring tides, the current was dangerous, but at other times, even children could swim to the other side.

Along with Hisako and Fumi, three other girls were searching for shellfish in the shallows: Tamiko and Fujiko, their fourth-grade classmates, and Sayoko, Tamiko's seventeen-year-old sister. Only Sayoko seemed worried about the approaching soldiers and uncertain whether to flee to the village. She called to Tamiko and the others, but the girls merely edged closer to shore and went on with their work.

Fumi wasn't scared of American soldiers anymore.

Before the war, her teacher had told them horrifying stories about how after catching you, the Americans would gouge out your eyes, slit open your belly, and butcher you like a goat—even if you were a child. Never let yourself be captured, they were told; better to commit suicide than be taken prisoner. One boy had asked how they should kill themselves, but the teacher avoided specifics and said that when the time came, the adults would tell them how to die.

Fumi couldn't imagine herself dying, so being told to take her own life didn't scare her. However, an intense fear of American soldiers had been planted in her heart. Some of the boys had enjoyed scaring the girls by describing how American soldiers ate children's livers or kidnapped women and carried them off to America. As a result, when the war started and some American soldiers found Fumi and her family hiding in a cave in the woods, she felt weak in the knees and couldn't move. A dozen other families from the same village were also in the cave. Fumi was with her grandparents, her mother, and her two younger brothers, aged seven and four. Her father and older brother weren't with them because they'd been conscripted into the Defense Corps, the local militia.

As Fumi rode piggyback on her grandfather down the hill through the woods, she covered her face with her hands, so she wouldn't see the American soldier walking beside them. When he tapped her on the shoulder and tried to hand her something, she flinched, turned away, and clung to her grandfather. The villagers were rounded up in the open space used for festivals. Fumi thought that that's where they'd all be killed.

After her grandfather set her down, she and her terrified younger brothers clung to the hem of her mother's kimono and watched what was happening. A soldier who could speak Japanese was going around and writing down the names of everyone in each family. The soldiers on the perimeter had rifles slung over their shoulders, but they didn't point them at the villagers; they just stood around smoking and chatting in groups of twos or threes. Some of the soldiers offered cigarettes to the older villagers, but nobody accepted. Others tried to hand something that looked like candy to the children, but all of them refused—and hid behind their mothers.

When a truck arrived about an hour later, Fumi and her family were loaded on the back and taken to an internment camp set up in another village on the island. Over the several weeks they spent there, Fumi's fear of American soldiers turned to familiarity.

Far from harming the camp residents, as her teacher had warned, the soldiers gave them food and cared for the sick and wounded. Residents from all six villages on the island were put in the same camp, and by the time Fumi and her family arrived, about four hundred people were already living there in large tents or the houses that hadn't burned down. Some villagers were returned émigrés from Hawaii who could speak English; together with the American interpreter, they explained the rules and routines of the camp to the newcomers.

After Fumi and her family were given simple medical exams and dusted with a disinfectant powder, two American soldiers and a male returnee brought them to the tent where other families from their village were living. Here, for the first time in her life, Fumi tasted chocolate, which was handed to her by a Caucasian soldier about twice as big as her father. She never imagined anything could taste so delicious. Most of the American soldiers were fond of passing out sweets. Within a few days, Fumi was continually pestering them—just like all the other children.

A soldier named Tony often showed up at Fumi's tent, perhaps as one of his duties. He was fond of Fumi and always brought chocolate and canned food. When Fumi sang for him, Tony sat on the ground and listened with great pleasure. One of the village men who could speak some English explained that Tony was twenty-one and had a sister about Fumi's age.

Whenever the boys in the camp saw Tony, they would laugh and jeer:

—Tani, Tani! Magi Tani!

Tony, who couldn't possibly have known that in Okinawan *tani* meant "penis" and *magi* meant "big," always turned to the boys with a friendly smile. Fumi was furious, but too embarrassed to say anything.

The Japanese forces on the island had abandoned their positions along the coast even before the Americans had intensified their bombing. Retreating to higher ground, they entrenched themselves in the caves scattered throughout the woods of the island, only ten kilometers in circumference. Ten days after the American landing, they lost the will to fight and surrendered.

The islanders had diverse views of the Japanese soldiers, who were confined in a separate part of the camp. Some looked upon the emaciated, unshaven figures with sympathy; others scorned them for having spoken with such bravado, only to have been so easily defeated and taken prisoner. Fumi couldn't have cared less; she was just happy to be alive.

The one thing that weighed on Fumi's mind was the fate of her older brother. Her father was reunited with the family in the camp, but they had no idea what had become of her brother, who had moved to the main Okinawan island with the Japanese army. The war in the northern half was over, but in the south, a fierce battle raged on, day after day.

After about a month in the camp, Fumi and her family returned to their village. Forbidden to leave the island and relying on supplies provided by the Americans, the villagers struggled to rebuild their lives. School hadn't resumed yet, but Fumi worked busily all day long: helping in the fields, taking care of her younger brothers, gathering firewood, collecting shellfish, and assisting her family as best she could.

On her first trip to the beach after returning to the village, Fumi was shocked to see how greatly things had changed on the opposite bank. A pier had been built on a reclaimed rocky stretch, and several large warehouses stood where once there'd been a thicket of screwpine trees. Small American military transport ships moved in and out frequently, and trucks spitting black smoke carried off the unloaded supplies. Many soldiers tossed off their drab green shirts and worked stripped to the waist. Their red, white, black, and brown bodies were starkly visible, even from a distance. At night, lights burned brightly, making it seem that a mysterious world had appeared magically across the water.

Since Fumi watched the port while collecting shellfish every day, she had grown accustomed to the Americans and their actions. It wasn't unusual for soldiers to jump into the ocean and go swimming. And today probably wasn't any different. Fumi figured that they were just seeking relief from the heat. So she ignored them and focused her gaze below the surface. In the shallows close to shore were mostly small cone snails. If she moved further out, she could find large horned turbans or giant clams wedged into rocks. But she wasn't allowed to go there unless accompanied by an adult.

Completely absorbed in her work, Fumi raised her head in surprise when she heard the voices of American soldiers nearby. They had already swum across and were now talking loudly as they came walking toward her. At the water's edge, about thirty meters away, Tamiko, Hisako, and Fujiko were gathered around Sayoko and beckoning Fumi to return. Apparently, they had been calling for some time, but Fumi had been absorbed in her search and hadn't noticed. She looked into the bamboo basket hanging from her shoulder. It wasn't full yet, but she knew she'd better join Sayoko and the others.

As she hurried to shore, Fumi was careful not to step on any coral or rocks. Though flustered at not being able to move faster, she soon reached the shallow water where the waves lapped against her calves. The American soldiers were right behind her.

Sayoko hugged the girls close, her eyes darting back and forth between Fumi and the soldiers. Fumi could tell that Sayoko was terrified. The sense of panic had infected her three classmates, and she could feel her own heartbeat quickening as she splashed through the water.

One of the American soldiers passed Fumi just before she came ashore. Sayoko tried to move up the beach to the path leading to the village, but the soldier got ahead of her, blocking her way. Fumi gazed past Sayoko to get a better look. She had never seen him before. He was white and had tattoos on both arms. His sunburned chest was covered with blond hair, and he wore nothing but a pair of trunks. His frenzied mood and expression, so different from Tony's friendly demeanor, was deeply unsettling.

The soldier grinned and said something to Sayoko, who didn't understand English. Sayoko pushed the other girls ahead of her and tried to slip past, but the soldier suddenly grabbed her arm. Sayoko's scream rang out across the beach. The soldier pulled Sayoko close and put a hand over her mouth. She struggled to break free, but then another soldier ran up and grabbed her legs. As the two soldiers carried Sayoko off into the thicket of screwpine trees, Fumi and her classmates screamed and gave chase.

Crying, Tamiko was reaching out toward her sister when a soldier grabbed her by the arm and flung her to the ground. Spitting out sand, she coughed twice and moaned. Fumi clutched at still another soldier. At first, he just held her back, a look of dismay on his face. But when she sunk her teeth into his hand, he yelled and shoved her away. As Fumi fell backward, she saw another soldier slap Fujiko and Hisako and send them flying. The four girls ended up sitting on the beach, unable to do anything.

The soldier that Fumi had bitten stood in silence and looked back and forth between the girls and the screwpine thicket. The other soldier moved around restlessly, punching his open palm with his fist, and muttering to himself. When Tamiko started sobbing, he yelled angrily in her ear and punched her in the face. The other soldier rushed in to stop him. After that, there was no more violence. Even so, the girls huddled together and were too terrified to speak or cry. Screams, groans, and the sounds of punches could be heard from the thicket. With each noise, the girls flinched, hugged each other, and prayed that Sayoko wouldn't be killed. What their teacher had told them before the war turned out to be true, Fumi thought. Today, the soldiers would kill them.

When the two soldiers returned from the thicket, they traded places with the two soldiers on the beach. One headed toward the thicket slowly; the other shouted with glee and dashed over. The two that had returned lay down in the sand, propped up on their elbows, and shouted comments toward the thicket.

Before long, the second group of two soldiers returned to the beach. The four exchanged some words, entered the ocean, and began swimming back toward the port. The sun had already sunk behind the warehouses on the opposite bank, and night-fall was approaching. When the soldiers had got about twenty meters from shore, Tamiko was the first to get up and run toward the thicket. Fumi and the other two girls followed.

—Stay away! a voice called out from within the thicket.

Fumi and the other girls stopped and looked into the shadows of the thorny-leaved screwpine trees. In the dim light, they could see Sayoko squatting and hugging her naked body. Fumi still didn't understand what went on between men and women. But she knew in her bones that Sayoko had not only been kicked and beaten but had suffered a profound violation of her body and soul.

—They didn't hurt you, did they? Sayoko asked the four girls, who were standing transfixed.

Then she told Tamiko to call their mother, adding that she shouldn't forget to bring some clothes. While Tamiko ran to the village and returned with her mother, Fumi and her classmates could only stand there in silence.

That night, the account of the attack on Sayoko spread through the whole village. After supper, Fumi was told to take her brothers to the back room. Meanwhile, her parents and grandparents spoke in whispers in the front room. Then, her father and grandfather went out together and didn't return until late at night. Before they returned, Fumi's mother warned Fumi that she should never go to the beach or the woods alone, and that if she ever saw an American soldier, she should run home right away.

From the next day, the entire village was under a heavy strain. Young women hid in the back rooms of their homes, and men took turns standing at the beach and on the roads leading into the village. A bell, made by removing the gunpowder from an unexploded shell, was hung from the giant banyan tree in the open space where the priestesses prayed to the guardian gods of the village. As the villagers worked in the fields or in their homes, they were constantly on edge, thinking the bell would ring at any moment.

In the afternoon, Fumi asked Fujiko and Hisako to go to the woods to gather firewood. She couldn't ask Tamiko because she had been confined to her house since morning. After being joined by three other girls about their age and some boys who were going to gather grass for the goats, they headed to the woods, located about two hundred meters from the village. Fumi and her friends were picking up dead branches under a large pine tree, not too far into the woods, when suddenly the bell rang out. Struck by the sound of the fiercely ringing bell, the children dropped what they were doing and prepared to run to the village. As they were hurriedly picking up their firewood and grass, one boy yelled:

—Forget that stuff! You can get it later!

It was Chikashi, a boy one grade ahead of Fumi. Everyone threw down what they were holding and dashed off to their homes at full speed.

When they got back to the village, Fumi saw a US military jeep parked near the giant banyan tree. Four of the five soldiers standing around the jeep were the men from the day before. As the children arrived, their parents came running up and hugged them. Hurrying home with her mother, Fumi noticed her father and about twenty other men from the village standing in a circle in the clearing.

The heavy front door to their home was locked from inside, so they went around to the kitchen door in the back. As soon as they entered, Fumi's mother locked the door and led Fumi to the front room to join her grandparents and younger brothers. Fumi's grandmother was fervently praying in front of the family's Buddhist altar. When their mother sat down behind their grandmother, Fumi's younger brothers clung to her. Fumi went up to her grandfather, who was looking outside through a crack in the door. Fumi peered through a knothole and watched, too.

The men from the village were staring in wary silence at the American soldiers. Two of the five soldiers had rifles slung over their shoulders, so the men couldn't move. Standing next to the jeep, the soldiers were smoking and passing around a bottle as they watched the men. Before long, the soldiers started to move. The armed soldiers pointed their rifles at the men from the village, and the other three soldiers disappeared. After a couple minutes, Fumi could hear the sound of a door to a house being kicked down. Then she heard the screams of the residents. Even then, the village men dared not move.

Her mother called, so Fumi had to stop watching. She hugged her younger brothers and cringed. Would their door be kicked down next? The soldiers terrorized the village for about an hour, but Fumi's house was spared. When her father called from outside, her mother hurriedly slid the door open.

—What happened? Fumi's grandfather asked.

In silence, her father pushed the door open the rest of the way. Standing at the entrance, he drank the tea Fumi's mother brought him. Then he picked up the hoe and straw basket sitting outside the door and headed back to the fields. The tormented look on his face as he put down his teacup was something Fumi had never seen before.

Fumi's father wasn't the only one with such a look. The next day, every man in the village, young and old alike, had the same tormented expression. The day before, right before their very eyes, the American soldiers had raped two young women. When Fumi overheard the adults whispering about this, she thought that her house would surely be next. Even with their doors closed at night, she couldn't sleep. Other than her two brothers, no one else in her family could sleep either.

After the second incident, the American soldiers didn't show up for a while. But the strain on the villagers didn't lessen in the least. Everyone looked exhausted, conversation decreased, and laughter ceased entirely. The men were kept busy patrolling the area, so fieldwork and repairs of the damage from the war fell behind. Fumi and her friends had to limit their movement to areas where they could quickly run back to the village. They could no longer go to the ocean to collect shellfish, but they could still cut grass for the goats or collect firewood.

Four days later, Fumi was working along the western edge of the woods. Though the boys and girls usually went their separate ways, Fumi stayed with the boys to pick up firewood. She was nervous about being so far from the village, but since they could clearly see the American port from the cliff facing the ocean, they figured they'd be okay. To be safe, they took turns keeping lookout.

About five minutes into her shift, Fumi spotted a dozen soldiers lounging in the shade of a warehouse. Apparently, they'd finished unloading the freight and were taking a rest. Suddenly, four of them stood up and began taking off their work clothes. Fumi strained her eyes to see what they'd do next. When she saw them walking along the pier in their trunks, she called to Chikashi, who was nearby. Just as he came to her side, they saw the four soldiers diving into the ocean, one after another.

—The Americans are coming! Chikashi yelled to the others.

The other children frantically dashed off toward the village, but Fumi and Chikashi stayed where they were, entranced by the sight before them. Immediately after the soldiers dove off the pier, they spotted a young man on the rocks at the bottom of the cliff running toward the ocean with a harpoon. He wore nothing but a loincloth. As soon as he stepped into the water, he tied the cord attached to the harpoon to his waist and began swimming out to sea. Fumi and Chikashi knew they should return home, but their eyes were riveted on the young man.

—It's Seiji, Chikashi muttered.

Seiji was the boy who lived next door to Sayoko. Due to the glare of the setting sun reflecting off the water, they could only see the heads of the Americans, but Seiji was still close, so they could clearly see him moving through the water, with his harpoon dragging behind. Using a smooth breaststroke, Seiji circled around the soldiers until they were about halfway across the passageway. Then he changed course, moved into the ocean's current, and closed in at a speed about twice as fast as before.

The soldiers noticed Seiji when he was about thirty meters away. They treaded water and stared at him for a while, but then resumed their crawl strokes and continued heading toward the island. Seiji switched to a crawl stroke, too. When he was within four or five meters of the soldier taking up the rear, he dove beneath the surface.

From the top of the cliff, Fumi and Chikashi watched with bated breath as Seiji glided through the clear water. As he passed beneath the soldier, he reeled in the cord tied to his waist and took the harpoon in hand. Then he thrust upward and shoved the harpoon into the man's stomach. The man screamed and frantically tried to swim away. A second later, Seiji popped up out of the water and hurled the harpoon at the man's back. But this time, he missed.

One of the other soldiers swam over to help their wounded friend, and the other two swam at Seiji, who raised his harpoon to confront them. When one of them lunged at him, Seiji stabbed him in the shoulder. Fumi could hear the man's scream even from the distance. The soldier latched onto the harpoon, and even though he was bleeding, refused to let go. Then the other soldier swam toward Seiji. A sudden flash of light revealed a knife in Seiji's hand. As the weapon swung down, the soldier dodged and dove into the water. Next, Seiji waved the knife at the soldier bleeding from the shoulder. When the soldier let go of the harpoon, Seiji turned around and began swimming toward the island. The soldier that had been fended off with the knife resurfaced and started to give chase, but after swimming twenty meters or so, he apparently realized he'd never catch up and returned to his friends.

The soldier who'd been stabbed in the stomach floated on his back with the help of one of his friends. Then the man who'd been stabbed in the shoulder joined them and helped, too. Meanwhile, the man who had chased Seiji swam toward the port and began waving and yelling for help. The soldiers at the port noticed that something was wrong and sprang into action. Seiji swam as fast as he could toward the island. He reached the rocks below the cliff before a rescue boat had even been launched from the port. After coming ashore, Seiji cut the cord tied to the harpoon and picked up his clothes, hidden near a rock. Then he dashed off along the rocks with his harpoon and clothes and disappeared into a thicket of trees.

Transfixed, Fumi and Chikashi had watched the whole scene from beginning to end. When they could no longer see Seiji from the top of the cliff, they became frantic about getting to safety. The bell in the village had been ringing for quite some time.

—Let's get going, Chikashi said.

Then he grabbed Fumi's hand and started running. Too panicked to feel embarrassed, Fumi squeezed the older boy's sweaty hand and ran as fast as she could. When they entered the village, they let go of each other's hands and ran off to their respective homes. As Fumi dashed past the banyan tree, she saw about a dozen men from the village with sticks and hoes.

—You're late! scolded Fumi's mother when Fumi entered their yard.

From outside, Fumi could see her grandmother praying before the family altar. Fumi's brothers were kneeling behind, giggling and mimicking her. Fumi's grandfather, who'd been waiting in the yard, closed the front door behind Fumi as they entered the house. Fumi told her mother about what she'd witnessed. After hearing Fumi's account, Fumi's grandfather immediately dashed off to notify the other men. Fumi's grandmother intensified her chanting, and the two boys stopped smiling. When Fumi saw the terrified look in their eyes, she went over and hugged them and patted them on their backs.

The Americans showed up about half an hour later. Arriving in several jeeps and small trucks, the group of about twenty soldiers disembarked and readied their rifles.

—Throw down your weapons! the interpreter screamed at the thirty men gathered near the banyan tree.

The men hesitated, but then did as they were told. The interpreter was a man of Japanese descent in his mid-twenties.

He ranted on about something, but Fumi couldn't understand what he was saying. They've come to get Seiji, she thought. She could tell that the men were growing more and more upset as they listened.

The soldier in charge said something to the interpreter, who then screamed at the village men. The men exchanged glances and started talking, but the interpreter yelled at them to be quiet. The squad leader gave an order, and the soldiers started moving. At the interpreter's command, the village men followed.

The Americans started searching the houses in the village. When Fumi saw five soldiers coming toward her house, she ran to her mother and clung to her. There was a violent knocking at the front door, and Fumi's grandfather hurried to open it. The soldiers entered their house without even taking off their boots and spoke loudly as they searched every room. After they'd finished searching the pigsty outside and every nook and cranny of the small yard, they moved on to the next house. Terrified by the intrusion, Fumi's grandfather knelt in the middle of the front room with his head hanging down. Fumi trembled in fear and buried her face in her grandmother's bosom.

Nobody left the house until Fumi's father returned after dark. Fumi listened in on his conversation with her grandfather and found out what the Americans were doing. The soldiers had been divided into two groups: a group of about ten was searching the houses, one by one, while the other group was searching the surrounding woods. In the meantime, the leader and the interpreter were at the banyan tree questioning Seiji's parents, the ward chief, and the head of civil defense. They were determined to find out whether Seiji had acted on his own or as part of a group.

The village men had been forced to help the soldiers search the woods. Of course, they just pretended to cooperate, while secretly hoping that Seiji would escape. However, there were a limited number of places to hide, so if the Americans called in more men, they'd be sure to catch Seiji within two or three days.

Everyone felt that his only way to escape was to swim across to the main island. But small US warships were constantly patrolling the area, so it wouldn't be easy to get across undetected. Besides, as Fumi's grandfather pointed out, they'd probably stationed troops along the shorelines.

Fumi's father mentioned that Seiji's parents were completely terrified. Seiji's mother had been crying and saying that the Americans would kill her son if they caught him. Seiji's father had seemed to doubt whether their son could've done what he'd been accused of. The other men were surprised, too. Seiji was only seventeen, and even though he'd been toughened up from his work at sea, he still had a boyish face. Compared to his violent father, Seiji was meek and mild. No one could believe that the weak boy who'd been bullied to tears as a child had stabbed an American soldier with a harpoon. But according to his parents, Seiji had been away from home since early afternoon, and his prized harpoon was missing.

As for the American soldiers, the one stabbed in the shoulder appeared to be fine, but the one stabbed in the stomach was in critical condition. One of the four had remembered Seiji from the internment camp, and the Japanese-American interpreter knew that Seiji had been in the Defense Corps and worked with the Japanese army.

—He's still just a child, isn't he? said Fumi's father.

Fumi couldn't tell if he spoke in admiration or in annoyance.

—Well, I didn't see the adults do anything, said Fumi's grandfather.

The comment caused Fumi's father to fall silent.

That night, the Americans set up a large tent near the banyan tree. A searchlight powered by a generator was trained onto the houses. The soldiers patrolled the village in pairs, while a soldier with a rifle stood at the tent on night duty. With the droning sound of the generator echoing through the village, and the intermittent footsteps and voices of soldiers, Fumi couldn't sleep.

A full-scale search started early the next morning. Just like the day before, the men of the village were forced to cooperate. The women and children felt uneasy about the presence of the Americans, but they couldn't stay locked up inside all day. If they didn't tend to the crops, draw water, and cut grass for the goats, they'd have no way to live.

During her many trips to the spring to fill her family's water jar, Fumi wondered whether the American stabbed in the stomach would survive. She pictured the red blood spreading through the clear greenish-blue water and the wounded soldier holding his stomach. She assumed that Seiji would be executed if the soldier died. She also pictured Seiji coming ashore and dashing across the rocks with his harpoon. Where was he hiding? And did Sayoko hear about what he'd done?

Since the attack at the beach, Sayoko and Tamiko had stayed confined in their home and hadn't shown their faces. Their parents worked in the fields, but no one dared ask about Sayoko. Fumi quickened her steps whenever she passed Tamiko's house. When she pictured Sayoko and Tamiko in the back room, her throat tightened, her breathing became labored, and her eyes filled with tears. During the search the day before, the Americans must've entered Sayoko and Tamiko's house, too. How did the two girls react when the soldiers threw open the door, entered the house in their boots, and started yelling?

When her mother called, Fumi realized that she'd been daydreaming. She picked up the water jar and started to head home. For some reason, the villagers were filing out of their homes and heading toward the woods.

—The Americans, explained Fumi's mother, threw poisonous gas into the cave where Seiji's hiding.

Then she stared into the distance with a terrified look. Fumi's knees shook and she grew restless. Taking her mother's hand, Fumi headed to the woods with the other villagers to witness what was happening.

SEIJI (1945)

The moonlight filtering down into the cave began to flicker, and the shadows on the wall changed into crouching beasts. Then the figures quivered and turned into American soldiers, slouched over their guns. When they started to move forward, Seiji got down on one knee, readied his harpoon, and yelled in a threatening voice:

—You think I'm gonna let you damn Americans take me prisoner? Well, come and get me! I'll rip the guts out of every last one of you!

He lunged out at the soldier in the lead and felt his harpoon plunging into a mud-like substance. Then he heard a moan and felt a weight on the end of the shaft. The form collapsed to the ground, and the figures in the rear retreated. As Seiji plunged his harpoon into the writhing body a second and a third time, he could hear the screams of the American who'd been swimming in the ocean. He could once more see the long-limbed body cutting through the glittering light, which filtered down from the surface. Seiji pictured himself thrusting upward with his harpoon. He had missed the heart, but he knew he'd done some serious damage to the stomach. The iron head, which he'd sharpened with all his hatred, penetrated the flesh and ripped into the internal organs. But a single thrust hadn't been enough. *Suffer and die, you bastard!* Seiji had wanted to thrust a second and third time, tear the stomach into shreds, and scatter the guts into the sea, but he'd been prevented from finishing the job. *Do you bastards think we'll let you do whatever the hell you want on our*

island? I'll feed your damn American blood and guts to the sharks.
He had failed at sea, and now, all that frustration went into the
harpoon thrusting into the rocky floor of the cave. Suddenly, the
sparks shooting up from each blow startled him, and Seiji stood
still, confused. The Americans were nowhere to be seen.

Breathing heavily, Seiji sat down and gave his body to
the embrace of the chilly air of the cave. Though he had goose
bumps, sweat rose on his forehead and dribbled down his neck.
The sweat felt like blood, so he wiped it away with the back of
his hand and sniffed. The sticky substance had a putrid smell,
so he moved toward the opening of the cave to check his sinewy
hand under the blue-tinged light. As he did so, he noticed a mass
of crabs jostling against one another at the bottom of the cave.
Scared that they'd claw at his flesh and start gnawing their way
up from his toes, he scurried to a nearby rock. Just then, he heard
a voice inside his head.

*What're you afraid of? Compared to those blown up during the
American bombing, you're lucky to be alive!* Blood churned inside
Seiji's skull. In agony, he dropped the harpoon, fell to his knees,
and clutched his head. *Mom! Please help me! Please protect me!*
he repeated again and again. He pressed his hands together and
prayed to his mother, who gazed back at him with eyes on the
verge of tears. *I'm fighting all by myself, Mom! Sorry for being such
a lousy son!* Rubbing his palms together, Seiji lifted his head. The
dull blue light cascading down into the cave fell on his face. He
looked outside. The wind carried the warm scents of the woods
and the ocean. Such air could eliminate his pain and calm his
emotions. Seiji opened his mouth wide, sucked in a deep breath
of the night air, and listened attentively to the sound of the
rhythmical rushing beyond the hum of the woods.

It was the sound of the waves, which he knew came from
the ocean, glimmering in the shadow of the trees. Ever since he
was a kid, the ocean was where he'd always gone fishing with
his father, who was an *uminchu*, a man of the ocean. Normally,

the sensations of the waves never left Seiji's body, even when he returned to land. But now the ocean seemed so far away. *You have defiled the pure ocean with the American's blood!* said an accusing voice from above. Instinctively, Seiji dropped to his knees and put his hands together. *God of the Sea! God of the Land! God of the Village! Please forgive me! What I did was for the village. I couldn't let the Americans destroy everything. I had to protect our women. Please forgive me!* He bowed again and again and again. The voice laughed. *You? Protect the village?*

Kiyokazu and Munenori were saying goodbye to their families, just before heading off to join the Blood and Iron Student Corps. Few students from the island had been able to get into junior high school, and these two talented young men, who'd succeeded in everything since they were little, had always made fun of the dummy, who'd often missed school to help his father. However, Seiji never bore a grudge and even looked upon them with awe. As they headed off to the harbor, he said to them:

—You guys can, uh, go and fight with the army for the Emperor, okay? I'll stay here and, uh, protect the village.

They sneered at his words, and then spit out:

—You? Protect the village? Don't make us laugh!

—Yeah! And what a hick! When are you going to learn to speak standard Japanese? You're Japanese, aren't you?

Seiji felt overwhelmed with shame. But the more he'd tried to use the standard dialect, the more tongue-tied and flustered he'd become. Over the years, the problem had only grown worse. As the two headed off, Seiji could do nothing but hang his head.

But even if he couldn't speak the standard dialect the way he wished, he would've done anything for Japan, the Emperor, and the war effort. As a member of the defense forces on the island, he had planned to die alongside the Japanese forces fighting the Americans. During the day, he worked building encampments and digging ditches. At night, he went to sea whenever he could get permission and caught fish and octopuses for the men, who were quite pleased to receive the extra food. When Second Lieutenant Sakaguchi, a young man in his mid-twenties, expressed his thanks, Seiji snapped to attention and stood as straight as an arrow—in complete silence. Instead, he whispered to himself, *It's the least I can do.*

Seiji had sworn to himself that when the Americans landed, he'd kill as many of them as possible, and that when all hope was lost, he'd grab a grenade and throw himself into a tank. Some of the Japanese soldiers laughed at Seiji for standing at attention, saluting, and saying *yes, sir!* to every single order. But others praised him for proving himself through his actions—in spite of his awkwardness and inarticulateness. Seiji had always been scolded at home and at school, so he was happy to hear this praise, and he resolved to completely devote himself to the Japanese army. He was thrilled that a mere fisherman like himself could fight on behalf of the Emperor alongside Japanese soldiers. After his death, he wanted to be remembered as a true Japanese—as a man of action, not of words. And yet . . .

Seiji heard some rocks falling behind him and quickly readied his harpoon.

—Who's there!

His voice echoed through the cave. It occurred to him that the figures lurking in the darkness with their rifles were searching for him. He hid behind a nearby rock and held his breath. *This time*, he thought, *I won't miss*. He strained his bloodshot eyes.

—Stay low and thrust into the solar plexus with all your strength!

Again and again, his teacher had shouted this at him as they practiced spearing the effigy of Roosevelt with their wooden guns during military training. Conscious that his classmates were stifling their laughter, Seiji tried to give a spirited yell, but his voice convulsed into a high-pitched squeak. The teacher clicked his tongue and struck Seiji on the back with his bamboo sword. The blow didn't hurt at all compared to his father's punches, but tears of vexation welled up in his eyes. He couldn't bear the thought that he was a failure not only in his studies but also in repulsing the enemy. Pretending to wipe away his sweat, he dried his eyes with the back of his hand and then thrust into the straw-stuffed effigy with the full weight of his body.

No one's gonna make a fool of me again! I'll fight against the Americans, even if it's all by myself! I'm not afraid to die! he told himself as he stared into the darkness. *Don't talk crazy! The war is over!* said his mother's scolding voice. *The war's not over, Mom! Japan couldn't lose to America!* At these words, Seiji's mother stared aghast. *You still don't understand? All the Japanese soldiers were put in the internment camp. You saw them there yourself, didn't you?* she said. Then she added, *And didn't you hear? The Emperor surrendered, too. And they cut off his head!* She lifted up a white object for him to see. The severed head she clutched by the hair had a blank, expressionless face. Seiji recoiled from the sight in fear. *Mom! What're you doing?!* he screamed. *The Japanese army'll arrest you as a spy!* But his mother laughed and walked toward him, the Emperor's head dangling from her hand. *Oh, I get it!* thought Seiji. *This isn't my real mother. She'd never do something like this. These damned Americans are trying to trick me.*

He gripped his harpoon again. Through her gap-filled teeth, his mother spewed a foul odor that smelled like a decaying rat. When she closed in on him, he thrust at her with his harpoon. *How dare you point a harpoon at your own mother!* She grabbed the shaft and pulled back with a force one wouldn't expect from a woman. As Seiji clung to the harpoon with all his strength, he bowed his head and implored, *Mom! Please forgive me! Please forgive me!* Suddenly, a pole crashed down upon his back. With a groan, he lifted his head.

Seiji's father, sitting in a small *sabani* boat, raised the pole again and was about to bring it down on his drowning son, who was clawing at the air. Seiji paddled frantically, thrashing with his arms and legs, and finally managed to grab the edge of the *sabani*. Smack! When the pole struck his fingers, he screamed and jerked back his hand. A second later, he was dodging a blow coming toward his head. The swimming skill crammed into Seiji—along with many mouthfuls of seawater—was the one thing he had over his classmates.

All of a sudden, the pale blue light at the cave entrance turned into water, gushing down the slope. Seiji tried to swim, but was carried away by the current and sank like a stone. As he was swallowed up into the depths, all light and sound disappeared.

—I'm not gonna die! he screamed in terror. Not like this. I'm not afraid to die, but I wanna kill some Americans first.

Seiji kicked off the darkness pulling him down and propelled himself through the water toward the opening. When he reached the surface, he ravenously inhaled the night air streaming in from outside. Moving his mouth like a parched fish, he sucked the cool night air into his lungs. But this time, it only filled him with anxiety. To calm himself, he groped along the rock face in search of the flat stone he'd placed there earlier. When he found the stone, he lifted if from the hole it covered, reached into the opening, and pulled out the lump of metal. Then he slowly and carefully opened his hand. Under the moonlight, the grenade gleamed dully. The unmistakable heaviness brought him a sense of peace. When the end came, he planned to hurl the grenade at the Americans and rush at them with his harpoon.

Seiji thought of the Japanese soldiers who'd spoken with such bravado before the American landing, only to surrender in an instant once the moment of truth arrived. Then he thought of the village men who didn't resist even when their own women were being raped. *They're like dogs without balls. Well, not me! I'll blow up these damn Americans with this grenade, and then kill some more with my harpoon. Sayoko! I swear I'll get revenge!*

Seiji peeked through the Garcinia trees in Sayoko's yard

and listened to the screams coming through the shuttered windows. He could also hear the cries of Sayoko's younger sister and grandmother. Earlier, when Sayoko had returned home with her mother and the other girls, he could sense from her disheveled hair and lifeless expression that something horrible had happened, but he couldn't bring himself to ask directly. So he had circled around to the back of her house and found a gap in the row of trees. Sayoko's sobs pierced Seiji's heart, the pain cutting into him like the thorns of a citrus *tankan* tree. His wounded heart, pumping with warm blood, cried, *What happened? Why's she crying like that?* Unable to bear it any longer, he ran away. Under the banyan tree, by the house of worship, he saw a group of five or six men staring at Sayoko's house in silence.

Seiji didn't find out what had happened until that evening. The village men were repeating in hushed tones what they'd heard from Sayoko's father. Standing outside the circle, Seiji strained his ears. As he listened, he pictured the Americans holding Sayoko down in the thicket with their brawny arms and covering her mouth with their filthy hands. Then he saw Sayoko, crying and struggling and suffering. Sweat broke out over his body, and he had to restrain himself from screaming. He swore to himself that he'd kill the four Americans that had swum across the passageway. Assuming the other village men felt the same way, he scrutinized their expressions. However, even though some spoke words of anger, no one made a call to action. All they could come up with was to station pairs of men at key points as lookouts and to forbid the women from going to the beach. Seiji could see that the men weren't so much angry as emasculated by fear.

The villagers had relied on the Americans for canned goods, sweets, liquor, cigarettes, and the treatment of their wounds, and that's why they'd started to grovel. Even those who'd been ranting about running the Americans through with their bamboo spears were now happy to talk to them. *Was there any shame they wouldn't endure in silence?* Seiji began to boil over with rage. His face turned red, and he struggled to breathe. Turning his back on the men, he hurried down a deserted village road heading to the ocean.

At the beach, Seiji watched dark clouds move across the sky, block the moonlight, and cast shadows that ravaged the white waves and pure sand, only to then vanish into the night. The light, the shadows, and the waves seemed to be living things with wills of their own. Seiji was greatly disturbed. Glaring at the lights of the port, he again heard Sayoko's heartbreaking cries. Grieving, he ran up the beach and plunged into a screwpine thicket. He heard the thorny leaves rustling overhead, and hermit crabs scurrying through the piles of dead leaves at his feet.

Then he heard the laughter of some Americans and footsteps coming up the beach. He picked up a piece of driftwood, hid among some nearby trees, and stared at the screwpine thicket. When an American approached, Seiji jumped out and brought the dry, white wood crashing down onto the man's head. The force of the blow against the skull caused the driftwood to break in two. Seiji shifted the remaining piece in his hands and plunged the sharp point into the back of the soldier cowering at his feet. When the wood rebounded from the man's ribs, Seiji swung down again and again, until finally, the American's moaning grew faint. *Scum like you can never be allowed to live!* Seiji kept pounding until the wood was as small as his hand. Then he heard Sayoko whisper in his ear. *That's enough. You don't need to suffer any more.*

The moonlight filtering down into the darkness flickered with the rustling leaves of the trees and the roaring waves of the sea. Seiji struck the bottom of the cave with his fists and broke down sobbing at his own powerlessness.

—I'd do anything for her.

Sayoko was always so kind, his mother had said. *Ever since she was a child, she was quiet and had a pure heart. And then she grew up into such a beauty.* True to Seiji's mother's words, Sayoko had kindly protected Seiji when other children had bullied him. They entered school together, but as they moved up in grades, they had fewer opportunities to interact. Yet just like before, they exchanged smiles whenever they met. But everything changed when they were in the fifth grade. One day, Seiji was cutting grass for the goats. Nearby, several girls were collecting firewood, Sayoko among them. Her presence weighed on Seiji's mind, so he averted his eyes. Suddenly, someone knocked him down from behind. Before he realized what had happened, three boys jumped on top of him, held down his arms, and plucked his sickle from his hand. *Oh, no!* he thought, *another practical joke!* From experience, he knew that if he resisted, he'd get the worst of it, so he let them have their way. First, the boy on his back moved down onto his legs. Next, the other two twisted his arms so he couldn't move. Then the first boy got off and yanked down Seiji's tattered pants. After that, they flipped him over onto his back and exposed his genitals.

—Hey, check it out! they yelled.

Then they turned Seiji toward the girls, who screamed and turned away. But when the three boys taunted them, the girls cast glances in their direction, and one of the girls laughed. Seiji struggled to escape, but the boys punched him in the face until he relented. As blood dripped from his nose and tears ran down his face, Seiji saw Sayoko staring at him with pity. The additional excitement caused his penis to stiffen against his own will. The three bullies laughed. The girls pretended to be disgusted, but they couldn't avert their eyes.

—Look! Even a dimwit can get a hard on! yelled one of the bullies. I guess he's a real man!

As the coup de grace, they lifted Seiji up and tossed him into the bushes. Humiliated, Seiji pulled up his pants and ran off into the woods, leaving behind his sickle and the cut grass.

From the next day, Sayoko turned and ran away whenever she saw Seiji. As for Seiji, he couldn't even bear to look at her. Even if he saw her in the distance, he immediately ran off and hid. He felt ashamed that his body always reacted at the mere thought of her, not to mention the sight of her. When he recalled the look on her face as she stared at him—with his legs spread and his genitals exposed like a dog—he became overwhelmed less with anger toward the bullies than toward his own repulsiveness. He wished that she'd never lay eyes on him again. Since they lived next door to each other, however, there was no way to avoid her.

As the months passed, though, Sayoko started smiling and talking to him again as if nothing had ever happened. But Seiji couldn't speak to her like before, and could only drop his head and stammer. After that, they celebrated their Coming of Age ceremonies, graduated from school, turned fourteen, and then fifteen. From then on, Seiji spent all his time helping his father with fishing. After big catches, Seiji helped distribute fish and shellfish to the families in the neighborhood. Handing fish to Sayoko and hearing her words of appreciation were the happiest moments of his life.

That all seemed so long ago. Seiji pictured Sayoko smiling and saying, *Thank you*, as he stood at her door with some fish. *I'll never hear that voice again*, he thought. *Never again.* He leaned back against the wall of the cave and pressed the harpoon to his forehead.

—I'm the only one left! The only one left!

Seiji's words rippled through the cave. *You can do it! You can do it!* replied the echo from the cave's depths. *Yes, I'll kill every American that hurt Sayoko.* He picked up his canteen, took a swig of the tepid water, and closed his eyes. The rage heating his body caused him to sweat even more. Suddenly, he felt an insect in the back of his right eye. No bigger than his smallest fingernail, the insect started to move, then multiply. Before long, more were in his ears and nostrils, and under his skin, scratching their way toward his back, hands, and feet. They even worked their way into his head and started squirming inside his brain. At the internment camp hospital, he'd thought the insects implanted in his body by the Americans were trying to kill him. He jumped up screaming and scratched wildly at his head.

Suddenly, a shell from a warship landed next to the cave, and the blast rushing through the entrance shook Seiji's body. The smell of burning trees sent him into a panic. Outside, bombs rained down on the sandy beach shimmering in the sun. With each explosion, sand flew up and heaps of screwpine trees leapt into the air. Seiji dropped to the bottom of the trench and covered his ears.

The night before, he had received two grenades from a Japanese soldier in anticipation of an American landing. He was ordered to throw the first one, and then while the enemy was recoiling from the blast, charge into them while holding the second. Seiji was hiding with the other Defense Corps members in a trench they'd dug along the woods near the beach. As the sky began to lighten, they stared at the enemy ships lined up off the coast. The Americans seemed to have read the minds of the Japanese, however, and instead intensified their bombing along the coast. From the blurry space between the dawn sky and the gray sea, red lights shot up in rapid succession. A moment later, Seiji heard something ripping through the air, followed by a deafening roar and a blast that blew across the trench. Leaves, branches, and trunks of mowed-down screwpine trees rained down with the sand. In a daze, he raised his head. Ōshiro, a man from the neighboring village, grabbed him by the scruff of the neck and yelled at him:

—If you don't get out of here fast, you're dead!

The other Defense Corps members jumped out of the trench and chased after Ōshiro, who had started running toward the slightly elevated woods on the western edge of the beach.

Taking up the rear was a man in his fifties named Uehara. He turned around and yelled to Seiji:

—What're you doing?! Hurry up!

Just as he'd finished yelling, Uehara tripped on the root of a tree and fell. Aghast, Seiji again heard something splitting the air. The combined sound, force, and heat of each blast pressed down on his body, which was pinned to the bottom of the trench. In the woods, hidden in a trench at the base of the cliff, they had machine guns ready to open fire from the flank on any American forces that landed. Seiji knew that running there would give away their position, so he wanted to stop the Defense Corps members from fleeing in that direction. However, the bombing was so intense that he couldn't even lift his head. Before long, he was buried under the sand and splintered trees that rained down with each rumbling of the earth. *Am I going to die here?* he wondered. *I don't want to die yet. No, I don't want to die.* He tried to get out of the trench, but he couldn't move. Overwhelmed, he threw his arms over his eyes and ears, and started yelling:

—Mom! Mom! Mom!

When he regained consciousness, Seiji found himself buried up to his waist in sand. All traces of the screwpine thicket had vanished. The larger trees on the western edge of the sandy beach were now half their previous height. Smoke rose up from the charred remains into the clear blue sky. As he stared blankly at the scene, he realized that the ringing in his ears was actually coming from nearby. He looked over and saw innumerable flies swarming around some objects scattered on the ground. When it dawned on him that they were Ōshiro's remains, Seiji collapsed on his back in the sand. As the sky suddenly turned dark, he muttered:

—I guess I'll be dying soon, too.

He pictured Sayoko looking down with tears in her eyes. *You'd cry over someone like me?* Seiji gritted his teeth. His fingers crawled through the sand and picked up a grenade lying on the ground. He took a long time to get up.

—I'm not going to die. I'm not going to die. For Sayoko, I have to live.

His voice echoed through the cave.

Where am I now? he wondered. Wounded soldiers on cots were moaning with pain and resentment, pushing the stiflingly hot tent to the breaking point. Through the jumble of voices, Seiji heard a foreign one moving toward him, and then sensed a presence hovering over his bed. When he opened his eyes, he saw a pale face with colorless eyes, eyebrows, and skin. Seiji couldn't even move the finger that had been on the grenade pin. Nor could he refuse the water held to his lips and then poured down his throat. Against his own will, his feverish body craved more and more. The white face with goat eyes smiled and offered him his fill. *Yes, I was saved by the Americans*, Seiji thought.

He was treated for his wounds for over a month. At first, he had refused to eat, until the Japanese soldier next to him screamed:

—Eat, you fool!

When he finally forced himself to eat something, he was surprised by how good it tasted. The nourishment in the canned meat and beans healed his wounds so quickly that he could practically see his flesh repairing itself. By the time he could stand up and walk, he felt something like gratitude toward the Americans who'd nursed him back to health. Upon his release, he was temporarily sent to the camp area for Japanese soldiers, but he was soon relocated to the area for those from his village. There, he was reunited with his parents and siblings. But mixed with the joy was confusion over having been helped by the Americans. Even after returning to the village, he couldn't resolve the conflicting emotions, the hatred instilled in him earlier and the gratitude he felt later.

Is the war over? What happened to the Emperor? He doubted

that anyone in the village could answer his questions, but when he saw the US military transport ships moving in and out of the port on the opposite bank, and the soldiers busy at work there, he knew the answer. *The war isn't over. It's being fought elsewhere.* However, the Japanese soldiers had just sat on the ground like cowards, begging the American soldiers for cigarettes with obsequious smiles. When their weapons had been taken away, they hadn't shown an inkling of having the guts to fight. *If they'd fight, I'd fight, too*, Seiji thought. But the opportunity never arose, and he had to worry about getting food to live. His *sabani* boat had been commandeered by the Japanese army and destroyed in the bombing, so he worked the shallows along the coral reefs instead. He stayed busy catching shellfish, octopuses, and fish, and also plowing the long-neglected fields.

One day, Seiji went deep into the woods and entered a cave abandoned by the Japanese army. He was hoping to find a tool or anything that might be of use. What he found instead was a hand grenade lying in the shadow of a rock. It was a bit rusty but looked usable, so he wrapped it in a towel, located a dry part of the cave, and put the parcel in an opening in the wall. Then he covered the opening with a flat stone.

Now, after removing the lid, pulling out the lump of cold metal, and holding the object to the light, Seiji understood. *Ah, that's why. This grenade was left for me to avenge the deaths of those killed by the Americans.* The heaviness in his hand gave him confidence. *I will get revenge without fail*, he swore. *Even if I'm the only one, I'll never forgive them.* He heard some Americans laughing at him, while a woman screamed in the background.

How can you just stand there watching as a girl from your village is being raped? How? His words got stuck in his throat and echoed inside his head. The woman's screams sliced through Seiji's flesh like a razor and chipped away at the exposed bone. The two Americans next to the jeep turned their rifles on the men and laughed when they cringed in fear. When the three

Americans came out of the house, they changed places with the men at the jeep. Stripped to the waist, they stood talking and chewing gum. The stench of their sweaty bodies made Seiji want to throw up. Another house was entered. An old man pleaded for mercy on his hands and knees, but his entreaties were dismissed with contempt. A moment later, they heard another woman screaming. The village men stood motionless, their eyes darting back and forth between the house emitting screams and the ground at their feet. Some glared fiercely at the Americans, but as soon as the guns were pointed at them, they hung their heads. *We should steal their guns and kill them all*, Seiji thought. But he couldn't move. Though tears flowed from his stony eyes and dripped from his twitching lips onto his sandy feet, he was powerless to move a single step. Inside the cave, Seiji bit his arm until it bled and scratched at the wounds inside his chest. After the Americans trampled the holy ground near the banyan tree, they sped away in their jeep. The revving of the engine and the screech of the tires echoed inside the cave. The smell of gasoline drifted in the air. After the men had left, Seiji stood there by himself for a while. Then he went home and grabbed his favorite harpoon. Squatting next to the well, he sharpened the head with a whetstone—until the slightest touch made his finger bleed.

Beyond the trees in Sayoko's yard, the sound of sobbing never let up. *Sayoko will never feel true happiness again. From now on, her heart will always be crying.* Seiji was furious at himself for allowing the Americans and their guns to cow him into inaction. *The war's not over. It'll never be over. Not for Sayoko. And not for me. No, it'll never be over.* Staring at the harpoon head shimmering in the moonlight, Seiji swore to keep fighting against the Americans. Over the next couple of days, he carried water and provisions to the cave when no one was watching. From early morning to early afternoon, he went fishing with his father. From early evening, he stood beneath the cliff with his harpoon and watched the Americans working on the opposite shore. *I'll wait here even if the warning bell rings. At sea, they won't be able to use their weapons. At sea, I can beat them.* Day after day, Seiji waited for the Americans to swim to their island again.

And yet, when the time came, he could seriously wound only one of them. *Forgive me, Sayoko! I couldn't avenge you. . . . But it's not over yet.* The grenade in his hand bore the full weight of all their grudges—those of Sayoko, himself, the villagers, and all the dead Japanese soldiers. *This grenade will redeem me,* he thought.

He wasn't sure how many days he'd been awake, but he was so restless and excited that words bounced around in his head and made it impossible to sleep. As he waited with his eyes closed, he suddenly felt something warm on the back of his neck. Before he'd even realized it, the light filtering into the cave had changed to sunlight. He grimaced and squinted at the sparkling rays. Suddenly, a man's voice echoed through the cave:

—Seiji, come out! We know you're hiding in there. If you come out now, you'll be spared. Don't worry. Come on out. Your mom and dad, and everyone from the village, are waiting for you. Don't do anything stupid. The American you stabbed isn't going to die. So even if you're arrested, you'll be able to return home after a while. So come on out!

The person on the megaphone must've been Kayō, the ward chief. During the war, the guy had been the head of the Defense Corps and had spoken of the Americans with loathing. But in the camp, he did an about-face and got himself put in charge of distributing provisions. Before they knew it, Kayō had become the new ward chief. Seiji recalled his father always spitting out, *Dirty rat!* whenever he saw him. *The rat's trying to trick me in order to help the enemy. The bastard only thinks about himself—even though our women are living in desperation. I'll stab him along with the others.* Seiji stared at the entrance and waited for the Americans to enter. *I'm not afraid of dying. But before I'm shot, I'm taking one or two of them with me.* He kept a finger on the grenade pin, so that he'd be ready at any moment. *Just wait, Sayoko! I will have my revenge!* The ward chief's voice cut off, and a silence like that of the bottom of the ocean filled the cave. Seiji hid and waited with bated breath.

Just then, he heard something fall into the cave. White plumes of smoke rose up toward the light streaming through the opening. *Poison gas!* Seiji clicked his tongue and immediately poured water from his canteen over a towel, which he then pressed to his nose and mouth. Then he pushed his face into a crack in the wall and tried to suck in fresh air from outside. The gas filling the cave engulfed him and sank deep into his eyes, nose, and skin. Tears poured from his eyes, which began to hurt so much he couldn't open them. Splashing them with water from his canteen made no difference. Mucus poured from his nose and made his towel sopping wet. *God of the Land!* he prayed. *God of the Woods! God of the Sea! God of the Village! I beseech you to protect me!* But Seiji knew that like a poisoned fish floating with its white belly to the surface, his damaged lungs would soon fail, making it impossible to move. He finished off the water in the canteen and sucked in the last remaining scents of the woods and the sea. Then he wiped his eyes with the towel, turned toward the entrance, and lifted his swollen face to the light. *Sayoko! Mom! Please protect me!* With the grenade in his right hand, and the harpoon in his left, Seiji dashed out of the cave.

KAYŌ (2005)

—Do you remember the name of the Japanese-American soldier who handed you the megaphone?

After changing the cassette tape and pressing the record button of the portable player on the table, the small woman only two years out of college looks at you and gives you a little smile. You drop your eyes and look at the tape turning inside the transparent plastic window. You can't remember her name or the name of that soldier. And that makes you feel uncomfortable.

Was it Henry? Or did you say Smith? You can clearly picture him. He was in his mid-twenties, and his tanned face had a little cut on the left cheek. You can also remember thinking that if you took him out of his military uniform and put him in Okinawan clothes, nobody would know the difference. But you can't for the life of you remember his name. *No, Henry was the name of that black soldier that caused trouble at the comfort station. And Smith was the guy that Seiji stabbed in the stomach with his harpoon.* At a loss, you raise your head and return her gaze.

—I'm pretty sure it was Robert. . . .

You're surprised at the words that pop out of your mouth. But after you say the name aloud, you're pretty sure that that's right. *And didn't you say that his family name, from his Okinawan father, was Higa?*

—Robert Higa. Yeah, I'm pretty sure that was it. . . .

Saying the name reminds you that Robert was also the name of that American politician who was assassinated. You were working on the base when the Americans were watching

TV in the office and making a big fuss. Maybe that's what made you say Robert in the first place. But you don't correct yourself, even after the woman starts scribbling in her notebook.

Who cares about the name of some Japanese-American who could've passed for an Okinawan? Making excuses for yourself causes you to feel a relapse of the anger you felt toward him. The interpreter looked down on you, even though he was young enough to be your son. As you pick up the teacup on the table, you're reminded of the weight of the megaphone he handed you. You could feel the piercing stares of the villagers on your back. When you turned around, you noticed Seiji's father, Seikō, glaring at you with particular intensity. His tanned face was covered with a beard, and his inflamed eyes in their sunken sockets were like white stones burning in a cavern. He should've been pleading with you to help his son, but his eyes were full of undisguised hostility and menace instead. When you reflected that this guy had despised you since childhood, you spit out to yourself, *Seiji can go to hell!* But when you saw Hatsu praying at his side, you were immediately filled with a desire to help.

—So you and the Japanese-American interpreter named Robert Higa tried to talk Seiji out of the cave?

The expression on her face reminds you of how Hatsu looked when she was young. You stare at her, and she nods with an innocent smile. The fact that you can't remember her name, even though you've heard it many times, along with being uncertain about the name of the interpreter, makes you conscious of your age. This causes your confidence to wither. Trying not to get depressed, you do your best to focus your mind on your cloudy and uncertain memories.

—Yes, the interpreter asked me to help, so when he handed me the megaphone, I tried to talk Seiji out. . . .

The huge bishopwood and banyan trees that had hid the cave were blown up during the naval bombardment. Hazy light from the overcast sky shone into the depths of the cave, which slanted downward into darkness from the entrance at the bottom of the limestone cliff. You could see empty bottles, clothes, and pieces of boards scattered around inside, and on the gravel outside. The scene in the woods was vividly seared into your memory. You had also hidden in that cave, along with the nearly hundred other villagers who'd fled there for cover. By becoming the head of civil defense, you had avoided being forced into the Defense Corps. At the cave again, it was as if you could hear the shells from the naval bombardment flying through the air. And that made your hands shake. As the interpreter handed you the megaphone, he noticed your hands shaking, and laughed. Annoyed at his condescending attitude, you took the megaphone in your hands, and ignored his explanation about how to turn it on. Then you called down to Seiji, who you knew was hiding in the depths.

—Seiji, we know you're hiding in there. If you come out now, the Americans will let you live. . . . Don't worry!

You didn't know if that second part was true. The interpreter had told you that the stabbed soldier wasn't going to die, but when you asked what would happen to Seiji, he only shook his head. You bent the truth to soothe not only Seiji but also Hatsu. You added, *Don't worry!* to soothe Hatsu and yourself.

—Come out!

Your words bounced off the cave's walls and echoed back out through the entrance. You wanted to believe that you spoke for the entire village. However, you realized that not everyone there trusted you.

When you handed the megaphone to the interpreter and turned around, you were greeted with the same looks that had been thrown at you earlier. The villagers stared at you and shook their heads as if you were a friend of the Americans. And you felt humiliated just like before. *Those people never understood anything! They never considered how much I did for the village by negotiating with the Americans! They never understood how much trouble I went through to get more food distributed to them! And then when Seiji stabbed an American and put the entire village at risk, they praised him and acted as if I were to blame!*

You stare through the plastic window at the tape still turning and get the feeling that the words racing through your mind have been recorded. Flustered, you hold back the words about to gush out of your mouth and reach out for your cup of tea.

The woman waits for you to put down your cup and then pours you some more.

—Are you tired? she asks.

—No, not at all. As they say, old folks living on their own go senile faster if they don't have anyone to talk to. So I appreciate your coming.

—Is that right? Well, I appreciate being able to listen to you. Since you say it's okay, let's continue. But let me know if you start to feel tired.

You nod and smile, and wonder how long it's been since you've been able to smile like this. Ever since Nae, your wife of over fifty years, passed away, you've been living alone. Recently, you haven't been playing croquet or going to other events for seniors. You've been spending all your time locked up in the house without anyone to talk to. If your only son hadn't died of malaria after the war, you'd probably have grandchildren about this woman's age. As you look at her, tears begin to well up in your eyes. Pretending to blow your nose, you surreptitiously wipe away the tears.

—Maybe you're the one that's tired. You must be tired of hearing war stories from an old guy like me.

—No, not at all. I enjoy your stories. And your accounts of the war are quite valuable.

From her words and expression, she seems to be telling the truth. She wrote her graduation thesis about the Battle of Okinawa. Since last year, she's been working at the Board of Education in a temporary position. She visited you for the first time about two months ago. Initially, you were a bit suspicious and acted rather unsociably. But after a while—partly because she reminded you of Hatsu, and partly because you were happy to have someone sincerely interested in what you had to say—you invited her inside to talk. After living alone and sometimes going a week or longer without exchanging a single word with anyone, you started looking forward to her visits. *So what did she say her name was again?* You feel sorry for having forgotten, but you can't very well ask again. You just hope that by some chance she'll mention it once more.

—Did you think the Americans wanted to capture Seiji alive?

—I'm sure they did. If they didn't, they would've thrown in a grenade. But they threw in a tear-gas canister instead.

—Oh? It was tear gas? Not poison gas?

—I might've said poison before, but I remembered later it was tear gas. Their aim was to smoke him out. Even though he might've suffocated if he'd stayed in too long.

She gives a little nod and scribbles something in her notebook.

When one of the Americans threw in the gas canister, shrieks rose up from the crowd of villagers, who were watching from about thirty meters away. The interpreter told you it was tear gas and that Seiji wouldn't die right away.

—It's not poison gas, so don't worry, you told the villagers.

But the wailing of the women didn't let up. You got nervous thinking that if something happened to Seiji, you'd be accused of treachery after the Americans left. To avoid the glaring stares of Seikō and the other men, you moved away from the interpreter. Everyone watched the gas rising up from the cave, which seemed connected to the very heart of the island. When you shrank back from the gas irritating your nose and eyes, the interpreter and several soldiers with guns also edged back a few steps. A dozen or so soldiers were positioned in a semicircle surrounding the cave. Behind them, there must've been over a hundred villagers.

The partly cloudy sky made it difficult to determine whether it would clear up or rain. The sunlight wasn't particularly bright, but the villagers, gathered in the woods with its lingering stench of burnt trees, were drenched with sweat. The interpreter talked with the commander. Once your role was finished, you were ignored. But your fate was far from sealed. *Goddammit! Come out, you idiot!* Cursing to yourself, you began to worry that Seiji might not actually be in there.

You found out where Seiji was hiding from Buntoku Ōshiro. After returning home from the search and washing off, you were enjoying the whiskey you'd traded with an American acquaintance for a Japanese sword. Just then, you heard someone calling from outside. You opened the door, and Buntoku was standing there. He was the one who'd brought you the sword, which cost you more canned goods than usual. But you could see by the moonlight that this time he was empty-handed. When you told him you weren't giving away anything for free, he whispered that he knew where Seiji was hiding. You signaled for Nae to hide the whiskey, checked outside to make sure no one was watching, and invited him inside.

Buntoku explained that earlier in the day he'd been searching for mushrooms while collecting firewood. All of a sudden, Seiji came running naked through the woods carrying his harpoon and clothes. It didn't seem wise to call out, so Buntoku hid and watched—and saw Seiji enter the cave. He suspected that something unusual had happened, and sure enough, when he returned to the village, everyone was in an uproar. If he'd spoken carelessly, the Americans would've suspected him, so he remained silent.

—But you've got Americans you can trust, he said with a smile. You can keep it secret that I told you, and pass on the information yourself. In exchange, I'd appreciate if you'd give me some of those spoils of war of yours. You know what I mean: those food supplies you somehow got from the Americans.

—Are you telling the truth? you asked to make sure. Because if you're lying, the Americans will arrest you, too.

After threatening him, you went to the back storeroom, picked out some canned beef and cookies, and put them in a sack. When you handed them over, Buntoku looked dissatisfied.

—I'll give you more later if what you said is true and Seiji is captured, you explained, having him step outside. Let's keep this between ourselves.

You nodded to each other, and Buntoku disappeared into the darkness. Then you closed the door and went back to drinking your whiskey.

—But how did the Americans find out that Seiji was hiding in that cave? the woman asks.

—It's a small island, so it was impossible to hide without being discovered.

—I heard that Seiji was a pretty good swimmer. Couldn't he have swum off the island?

—Yes, he probably could have. But the war was still going on, so even if he got off, he'd have had nowhere to go.

—I guess that's true.

—Besides, Seiji wanted . . .

You hold off saying what you were thinking and avert your eyes. As you look at the purple lilacs blooming in the garden, you think to yourself, *Seiji wanted to die and take some Americans with him.*

The next morning, you went up to the Japanese-American interpreter, who was with the soldiers gathered at the banyan tree in preparation for the search. You explained that someone told you where Seiji was hiding, but the interpreter stared at you with suspicion.

—Who is this *someone?* he asked.

—He has nothing to do with it, so please don't ask, you answered with an obsequious smile. Just by chance, he saw where Seiji was hiding.

The interpreter still seemed doubtful, but he took you to see the commander, a thin Caucasian man of about thirty with razor cuts on his chin. The commander stared at you as he listened to the interpreter's explanation. When the interpreter was finished, the commander spread a map out on the hood of a jeep and said something. You guessed he wanted to know the location, so you went to the map before the interpreter had a chance to explain. However, you couldn't connect the thin lines on the map to the island's topography. You suggested leading them to the cave yourself. After getting the translation, the commander nodded and signaled for you to get in the jeep. Villagers had been curiously watching you from the moment you went up to the interpreter, and now they saw you get in the back seat.

As you sat there in the jeep, you felt both proud and guilty. When the interpreter, who was sitting next to you, asked if you were absolutely certain about where you were taking them, you suddenly felt uneasy. You nodded, and glanced over at the group of men to find Buntoku, but he wasn't there. At the commander's order, the soldiers standing around smoking and chatting jumped into their jeeps, and you told the interpreter to head toward the woods.

About three hundred meters from the village, the road became too narrow for the jeeps to pass. Everyone got out, and you and the interpreter led the way up the slope. You went deeper into the woods than anyone had during the previous searches. When you reached the small hill in the center of the island, you halted. Through the bishopwood and chinquapin trees, you could see the mouth of the cave at the bottom of the cliff, about fifty meters away. You pointed it out to the interpreter. He nodded, looked at the cave, and said something to the commander, who stepped forward and peered through a small pair of binoculars. He had a young soldier spread out a map to confirm their position. Then he sent two scouts with rifles ahead to investigate.

As you watched the backs of the two soldiers, you prayed that Seiji was in the cave. The two soldiers, apparently assuming that Seiji didn't have a gun, showed no signs of caution. They went right up to the cave and peered inside. Up until several months ago, the woods had been dense with trees, but the repeated naval bombardments aimed at Japanese soldiers in hiding left only burnt trees and piles of broken branches. Around the cliff, tree stumps were visible under the dim light of the cloudy sky. The two men peering into the cave with their rifles readied gave a signal, and the commander ordered the other soldiers to join them. The interpreter had you follow diagonally and to the rear of the commander. The soldiers were all positioned about thirty meters from the cliff in a tight semicircle facing the cave. You thought their formations were vastly superior to those of the Japanese army, and felt it only natural that the Japanese had been powerless against the Americans. For a moment, you felt in awe of Seiji for facing down such a powerful military on his own, but you immediately nipped those feelings in the bud. *Why'd he have to do that? And what the hell was the lunatic thinking?* you spit out to yourself. *I have no idea*, you replied. *Oh, don't pretend! You know exactly why!* another voice told you. In confusion, you lift your head.

—Are you all right? the woman asks, with an anxious look.

—Yes, why do you ask?

—Because I've been calling you for a while, but you've just been sitting there with your head down.

—Sorry, I had something on my mind.

—If you're tired, why don't we call it a day?

—No, I'm not tired at all.

—You're not?

—I really appreciate having someone record my war experiences. I've often thought about doing it myself, but it's really hard to write. I just haven't been able to do it.

The woman nods at what you say, with an expression

of kindness and joy. At least, that's what you feel and want to believe. You feel sorry about getting special treatment, but you're happy to get it, all the same.

—Did Seiji come out right after the tear gas was thrown in?

—No, not immediately. I think it took a minute or two.

No, it must've been longer. As you watched the bluish white smoke rise up from the mouth of the cave, you kept repeating in your mind, *Hurry up! Come out!* Suddenly, you heard a woman scream behind you and then soldiers yelling. You turned around, and saw that Hatsu had rushed forward and that some soldiers were holding her back with their rifles. Seikō grabbed her arms from behind, forcing her to the ground. Hatsu's cries were so intense that the trees shook. The villagers were getting restless.

Over a hundred voices, which up until then had been silent, hurled words of anger, one after another. With their veins popping out of their arms and legs, the crowd pushed forward like an uncontrolled beast. The Americans showed a fear that caused you to shrink back in terror. At the commander's signal, the soldiers trained their guns on the crowd. When the villagers saw this, their faces went rigid. Though you were frozen, you felt a sense of relief that the Americans must've shared.

—How did Seiji look when he came out?

—He was staggering and looked like he'd collapse any minute. He used his harpoon to support himself.

—His harpoon?

—Yes, he apparently planned to use that to fight the Americans. And in his other hand, he held a grenade.

—Were grenades available at that time?

—He probably found one left behind by the Japanese forces. Back then, there were even people who emptied out the gunpowder and used unexploded shells to catch fish.

—Did he throw it?

—Huh? What?

—I mean, did Seiji throw the grenade?

—If he did, he would've been shot dead immediately. He tried to throw it, but he collapsed before he could. Besides, the grenade was a dud.

Hatsu suddenly stopped crying, and Seikō and the villagers turned their attention to the cave. You turned back around. Seiji had staggered out of the smoke and now stood supporting himself with the harpoon in his left hand. His unrecognizable face was covered with mud, and tears flowed from his eyes, which were swollen shut. As if trying to locate the Americans with his ears, he moved his head back and forth. The commander yelled something, and the five soldiers near the cave leveled their rifles at him. When you noticed that he was holding a grenade, you wanted to run, but your feet wouldn't move. In response to the commander's voice, Seiji started to pull the pin of the grenade.

If he hadn't collapsed, he would've been shot dead. At least that's what you thought later. Several shots rang out in rapid succession. Seiji fell forward but never let go of the grenade. With a shaky hand, he pulled the pin and pounded the fuse into the ground. Then he lifted his upper body and tried to throw the grenade, but it only tumbled from his hand and rolled beside his face, which was buried in the dirt. When you saw the interpreter and the commander dive for cover, you instinctively threw yourself to the ground in a panic, too. You covered your ears, pressed your face into the ground so hard that the stones burrowed into your forehead, and waited for the grenade to explode. You heard the shrill buzzing of the cicadas. A considerable amount of time passed, but that was all you could hear. When you lifted your head, two soldiers were standing next to Seiji. One pointed his rifle at Seiji's head while the other squatted down and slowly reached for the grenade. After cautiously picking it up, he threw it into the cave and immediately crouched down. You pressed your face into the ground again, but the grenade didn't explode.

Damn Seiji! Scaring the shit out of everybody! you muttered so that no one could hear. Then you got up and scurried to catch up to the commander and the interpreter, who were walking toward Seiji. Covered with sweat and mud, Seiji's tattered, faded jacket clung to his back, which slowly moved up and down. One of the soldiers stuck his boot under Seiji's chest and flipped him over onto his back. Seiji's pale face was covered with tears, sweat, and mud. Saliva mixed with blood dripped from his purple lips. His swollen eyelids had turned dark red, and shimmering tears flowed from the corners of his eyes. Blood streamed from his right shoulder and soaked his jacket. Another soldier pried Seiji's fingers open, grabbed the harpoon, and laid it on the ground. Then he frisked Seiji to make sure he didn't have any other weapons.

The interpreter asked if you were absolutely certain that this was Seiji. When you nodded, he explained to the commander. You took two or three steps back, but you didn't have the courage to turn around and confront the villagers. Not knowing what to do with yourself, you tried to be more inconspicuous by moving to the side and watching the commander and his men. Two of the soldiers were given an order and started running toward the road. The interpreter picked up the megaphone and announced to the villagers:

—Don't worry! He's alive!

You imagined that everyone looked greatly relieved, but you didn't actually check to make sure.

Ten minutes later, the two soldiers returned with a stretcher. After placing Seiji on it, they started walking toward the villagers. Seiji's right hand, trembling as it dangled over the side of the stretcher, was curled up as if still grasping the grenade. Some of his toenails had been torn off, and streaks of blood ran down the soles of his bare feet. Apart from Hatsu, who was wailing and trying to rush to her son's side, and Seikō, who held her back, the villagers watched in complete silence as Seiji was carried toward them. The silence terrified you. You couldn't help thinking that when the anger suppressed at gunpoint finally erupted, you'd become the target.

The soldiers grew tenser and tenser as they approached the villagers. With their fingers on the triggers, they tightened their formation on all sides of the stretcher. Overwhelmed, Hatsu's cries gradually died down. You were standing about five meters from the cave as you watched all of this. You had the feeling that if you stayed behind after the Americans left, the village men would beat you to death and toss your body into the cave. So when the last soldier passed by, you scurried after him. Even so, you made a point to leave a couple of meters between you and the soldiers. The thronging crowd of villagers split apart, and the soldiers passed through the center and headed down the hill. Hatsu, Seikō, and Seiji's other relatives chased after them. The path was jammed, and you were forced to wait, so you turned to your childhood friend, Bunsei Shinzato, who happened to be standing nearby.

—So they finally caught him, you said.

Shinzato stared at you with a look of disbelief and then moved away without answering. Just then, you noticed a space about to open up.

—Seiji's the bad one, you said so that others could hear, so I don't think they'll blame the village.

You knew that your words rang false. Your comment was met with the reproachful stares of the women, and you smiled drolly to cover yourself. When you saw Buntoku, who was watching from the shade of a tree, you averted your eyes.

—Hey, Mr. Kayō!

Having your name hurled at you from behind made you shiver in spite of yourself.

—How did you know Seiji was hiding in this cave?

Kazuaki Tamashiro, a young man nearly two dozen years your junior, stood facing you. His defiant stare and words made you nervous, but you knew it'd be a mistake to turn this ringleader into your enemy. His words had drawn five or six other young men to his side. Your face hardened as you sensed that one wrong step would land you in a kangaroo court.

—You don't need to worry. The Americans said they wouldn't execute him.

Tamashiro laughed derisively and scowled.

—I asked how you knew Seiji was hiding here.

—The American he stabbed isn't going to die, so it's probably just as well they caught him before this developed into something bigger.

—Answer the damn question!

The one who screamed this at the top of his lungs was Yūko Kuda, who always fell in line with Tamashiro. He was small but one of the strongest on the island in Okinawan sumo, and he had learned karate from his uncle, Yūsei. You wiped away the sweat breaking out on your brow and pointed toward the cave. The group's gaze was diverted in that direction.

—Where else would he have hidden? You never thought he'd hide there?

As if anticipating your tactic, Tamashiro immediately countered:

—Even if we did, we wouldn't have told the Americans.

—You talk like it's bad to cooperate with them, but you all participated in the search, too, didn't you?

—Who said we cooperated?

—*He* just did, didn't he?

Kuda's quick reply to Tamashiro's question caused the other young men to break out laughing. But they weren't the only ones. Among the fifty or so people still there, women, the elderly, children, and even people of your generation were smirking, some even scowling when your eyes met theirs.

—I'm just thinking of what's best for the village.

—You mean what's best for yourself! a woman screamed.

But you didn't know whose voice it was. You'd already

turned around and started heading down the slope. As you hurried along, a rock fell at your feet and tumbled down the hill ahead of you. Then came a second and a third, falling to your left and your right. You figured they were just trying to scare you, but then the next stone hit you square in the back. You moaned in pain and stopped walking. *Don't turn around*, you told yourself. Then you raised your head and proceeded on your way. Other stones came flying after that, but none of them hit you. But the pain, humiliation, and anger remained.

—What happened to Seiji after he was carried away on the stretcher?

—I don't know the details of what happened next. At the time, there still weren't any courts or prisons. Since he wasn't a soldier, he couldn't have been tried in a military court. I wonder what happened to him. . . .

—So he wasn't executed, right?

—That's what the interpreter told me, so I'm sure he wasn't.

—So there's a possibility he returned to the village, right?

—I left the island a year after the war ended, so I don't know.

That wasn't true, but you don't feel like going into that with her. After Seiji was taken away, the villagers continued to harass you. Not having people say hello to you on the street and being ignored even when you spoke to people wasn't such a big deal. You also endured having your fields torn up during the night and having excrement scattered in your yard. You assumed that Tamashiro and his friends were doing it, but if you said anything, things would've only gotten worse, so you put up with it. Thinking your effort as ward chief would be appreciated eventually, you did your best to increase the food rations from the Americans, to acquire more construction materials for rebuilding homes, and to reopen the schools. Your hard work did in fact bear fruit, and the harassment decreased. But just when you thought your struggles were over, malaria broke out on the island, and you lost both of your parents, one after another. Many people noticed and appreciated the hard work you did as ward chief, even while your own family was suffering.

But then your children started getting beat up and ostracized instead of you. Compared to when you yourself were getting harassed, you felt much more bitterness toward the villagers than before. Unwilling to suffer any more hardships for such people, you resigned your post as ward chief. Originally, your grandparents were ruined aristocrats who had come to the island in search of land after the fall of the Ryukyu Kingdom. The family gave up their aristocratic traditions, spoke the local language, and did their best to get accustomed to the island. Among those who had moved here, many remained proud of their aristocratic lineage and refused to associate with the islanders, but your father was different. Your family had lived on the island for over fifty years, but behind your back, you were considered only a temporary resident. At the beginning of the new year, after getting permission to move off the island, you relied on relatives to help you and your family relocate to Naha, the capital city on the main island in the south.

At first, you helped with the family business, but after about a year, you got involved in military operations. Working on a US military base, you brought up three children. The concerns of everyday life kept your mind occupied, and you tried to forget about the island. When the island was mentioned in newspapers or on television, you couldn't even bother to look. After the children grew up and moved away, and you and Nae were living on your own, you never even talked about the island, to say nothing of going there. You lived alone with Nae for over ten years, and she didn't want to have anything to do with the island either. She was probably angrier about the violence inflicted on the children than you were.

Recalling Nae, you glance over at the family's Buddhist altar. You're not wearing your glasses, so the writing on the mortuary tablet appears blurry. But in your mind, you can see Nae's name clearly, for you wrote it yourself.

—After that, you never returned to the island?

—No, I never did. We're not originally from there.

—Haven't you ever thought of visiting?

—No, I haven't. Not at my age.

—Is that so?

The tone of her voice suddenly makes you feel uneasy. You stop watching the tape recorder and lift your head.

—Are you planning to go to the island to check on everything I've said?

—Huh?

—Because if you are, you should forget it. Some people don't want to remember the past.

After staring at you for a while, she mutters that you're probably right, and stops the tape. She thanks you repeatedly as you accompany her to the front door. After she's gone, you recall that her name was Megumi Makiya. But you immediately lose your confidence and wonder if you remembered correctly.

You return to the room and put away the cushion she was sitting on. Glancing down at the table, you picture the tape that was turning inside the transparent plastic window. *Even if I die,* you think, *my voice will remain, and my memories will be passed down to the next generation.* This thought causes you to feel overwhelmed with the sensation that you're no longer in this world. At the same time, a mutter slips from your lips:

—I couldn't communicate anything, and my memories will die with me.

Loneliness suddenly creeps upon you. You light an incense stick and place it upright in the burner before the altar. You face the mortuary tablet, fold your hands, and bow deeply.

You raise your head and look at the mortuary tablet. The apparition appears again! Drawing back in terror, you lose your footing and fall backward onto the table. You tumble off the mahogany tabletop and stagger toward the veranda. As you try to crawl away, your right hand goes numb. Unable to support yourself, you fall forward and hit your chin. You want to call out for help, but you can't speak. Saliva dribbles from the corners of your mouth, like the apparition of Seiji you just saw. A foul odor makes you notice that you've wet your pants. After you lift yourself up with your left hand and lower yourself onto the paralyzed right side of your body, you hear a woman shrieking. Is it Hatsu? The screams come closer and closer. Over the hedge outside the window, you see a young woman with long disheveled hair running past. The name of this woman, screaming as if fleeing from some unspeakable horror, is on the tip of your tongue. But you just can't remember it.

Nae! Nae!

The name you try to call gets caught in your throat. The shrill buzzing of the cicadas echoes in your head, and an intense pain cuts into your back. You try to turn around but fall down again. Pummeled by the stones that fly at you one after another, you scream. But both your screams and groans are drowned out by the intense droning of the swarm of cicadas.

HISAKO (2005)

She could hear footsteps running toward her in the dark. Then the woman's feet and calves appeared, dashing across the village road covered with white sand. Blood dripped down, forming a speckled pattern on the woman's sand-covered feet. Her disheveled black hair repelled the sunlight, and her exposed breasts swayed, while sweat and tears splashed onto the road from her transparent skin, through which the veins were visible. The woman's screams cut through the sounds of the crashing waves and buzzing cicadas, and pierced the hearts of all who heard them. As the woman ran past, a group of spectators stared at her glazed eyes and gaping mouth. Even after she'd disappeared into the woods, her final scream lingered in their ears as their eyes filled with tears.

—Are you okay?

Hisako awoke to someone shaking her, the tears flowing from her eyes. The pillow under her head was wet.

—You have the same dream again?

Her husband's voice was husky but soft and gentle. Consoled by his voice, she reached up and touched the hand resting on her shoulder. Just as when they were young, he entwined his fingers in hers and caressed her palm with his thumb. Behind the white lace curtains drawn across the window, the day was dawning.

—It's still early, so you can sleep in late.

In the dim light, the outline of her husband's shadow was indistinct, and she knew he'd fade away soon. Refusing to let go, she tightly squeezed his hand. The sensation passed away like gentle water flowing through her fingers. Fresh tears fell from her eyes before the previous ones had even dried. Lying on her back with her eyes closed, Hisako desperately tried to hold on to his fading presence. But her efforts were in vain.

—Come again, she whispered.

Once the loneliness had settled in her heart, she took a deep breath and climbed out of bed. She washed her face, changed her clothes, and glanced over at the clock. It was only six twenty. Breakfast started at seven. She wasn't hungry, but considering the day's schedule, she knew she should at least have something light.

She couldn't recall how many decades had passed since her last trip alone. Kōsuke, her late husband, had loved to travel, so for the ten or so years after his retirement, they had gone on trips together twice a year. Thanks to him, she was used to traveling, but it was completely different now, on her own. The stress of trying not to forget the keys when leaving the house made her realize how much she'd depended on him.

At the restaurant on the first floor, she had a simple breakfast of rice porridge, pickled plums, and miso soup. When she'd finished eating, she returned to her room and packed her bag. Then she sat in the chair in front of the veranda and looked out the glass door. Puffy white clouds appeared in the deep blue sky. Looked like it was going to be a hot day. Through the aluminum railings, she could see fishing boats and ferries moving in and out of the harbor. Her room was on the eighth floor of a hotel near Naha Airport. She wondered if the white ferry loaded with freight was heading to the Kerama Islands.

If Kōsuke were here, she could've asked him. Her eyes moved to the bed, and she was again reminded that the comforting voice she'd heard upon waking from the dream was also just a dream. Her nightmares about the woman had started only three months ago, more than a year after Kōsuke's death. He couldn't possibly have ever consoled her about them. The realization deeply saddened her. She had another two hours until checkout, but she picked up her bag and left the room.

❖ ❖ ❖

It was a short walk to the bus stop from the hotel. Within five minutes, a bus bound for northern Okinawa arrived. Hisako stared in disbelief as four chattering high school girls cut in front of her and climbed the steps. Then she boarded the bus behind them. The facial features of the passengers and the general atmosphere made her keenly aware that she was now in Okinawa. But making the distinction pricked her conscience.

After sitting in one of the second-row seats reserved for the elderly, she placed her bag on her lap and looked out the window. It was her first trip to Okinawa in three years. The last one was with Kōsuke to visit her parents' grave. The memory depressed her, so she tried to focus on all the new buildings and other surprising changes in scenery. However, she didn't succeed.

She was filled with regret that on their last trip to Okinawa together, she hadn't taken her husband to the island. But that had been utterly impossible. This would be Hisako's first trip there since returning as a child with her family to Naha sixty years ago, shortly after the war ended. After moving to Tokyo as an adult, she had rarely even visited her hometown on the main Okinawan island. If she hadn't started having these bad dreams, she probably wouldn't have considered visiting at all. That was how alienated from the island she'd become.

Sixty years ago, her father had sent her and her brother to the island before the Battle of Okinawa started. At first, he'd considered sending them to Kyushu, but after hearing that the Americans had torpedoed a ship loaded with evacuating civilians, he quickly changed his mind. Instead, he sent them with Hisako's mother and grandmother to stay with relatives on the remote island in the north. During the war, the four of them ended up spending many days huddled together in dark air-raid shelters, which caused her to resent having been sent away. But a few years after the war, once Hisako fully understood all that had happened, she appreciated what her father had done. Many of her classmates had gotten caught up in the war with their families, and many had lost their lives.

When the bus entered Urasoe, Hisako saw a US military base beside the road. She lowered her eyes and stopped looking out the window. She didn't want to see any American soldiers in their camouflage-colored military uniforms. After she started having the dreams about the screaming woman, other fragmentary memories started bubbling up out of her subconscious, too. She saw several American soldiers swimming toward her from across the ocean. And who was the girl that took her hand as she frantically rushed to shore, tripping over the waves and choking on the salty seawater? She recalled that it was still light out, and that the sand clinging to her wet feet was still hot. When the soldiers closed in, they became huge black shadows blocking the light. Laughing, they grabbed the girl hugging Hisako and carried her away. Hisako also vividly recalled the thorny green leaves of the screwpine trees. When she saw the soldiers heading under them, she could hardly breathe and had to struggle not to scream. She couldn't think about what happened next.

Hisako raised her head and glanced out the window. Behind a wire fence topped with three rows of barbed wire, green grass stretched off into the distance beneath the blue sky. She didn't want to think the lawn was beautiful. Considering such a possibility risked being drawn into the agenda of those who had built the base. Ammunition wasn't the only thing hidden beneath that well-kept grass; also buried there were the multi-layered history of the people and the sad and painful memories of the land.

The bus passed the base entrance. Two American soldiers in camouflage fatigues stood beside the guard box, next to a large sign on which was written the name of the base. Hisako dropped her head again, closed her eyes, and struggled to control her breathing. Though she felt chilly from the air conditioning, she began to sweat. She reminded herself that she was no longer that ten-year-old child of long ago. Nowadays, American soldiers could no longer do whatever they wanted—as they could back then. But telling herself this didn't stop the sweating.

She recalled what had happened ten years ago up in northern Okinawa. An elementary school girl had been raped by three American soldiers. The incident made the front pages of every newspaper in the country and led to intense protests throughout Okinawa. When Hisako read about it in the newspaper, she suddenly had difficulty breathing, causing her husband and children to worry. *How much had things really changed since then?* The question made her feel guilty for having so long avoided her memories of Okinawa and for not knowing what was happening in her own hometown.

But what else could I have done? How else could I have gotten through all these years? That was what she told herself ten years ago in order to keep going. But after she started having these dreams, she could no longer shake off the feelings of guilt. She decided to go to Okinawa in order to resolve those feelings. A year had passed since Kōsuke's unexpected death, so she wanted to tie up all the loose ends of her life.

Kōsuke had collapsed suddenly at the go club he'd been devotedly attending since retirement. Apparently, he was in the middle of a game when he fell across the board, causing the black and white stones to scatter across the floor. He was rushed to the hospital in an ambulance, and Hisako hurried to his side as soon as she'd heard what had happened. He was already unconscious when she arrived. After an emergency operation for a brain hemorrhage and a mere two days in the intensive care unit, he passed away.

Hisako had struggled through the hectic period from her husband's death up until the important memorial service commemorating the forty-ninth day after his death. She wasn't able to consider her situation calmly until another six months had passed. She became obsessed with the idea that she herself could collapse any day now, just like her husband. Her three children took turns visiting with her grandchildren, so that she wouldn't feel alone. Thanks to their attentiveness, she never suffered any serious bouts of depression.

Even so, the daily words she'd shared with Kōsuke for decades now had nowhere to go. They withered, crumbled, and piled up inside her heart. The burden slowly robbed her of energy. To compensate, she tried to get out and talk with people as much as possible, but she felt distant from others. And the feeling grew worse with each passing day. Sometimes a fragment from the pile of words would whirl up like dust and float inside her without meaning, causing her considerable unease.

Gradually, she stopped going out. Talking to people who weren't members of the family began to feel like a nuisance. That was when she started having the dreams about the running woman. The sound of footsteps in the dark closed in on her from behind. Hisako shuddered when the young woman with long disheveled hair ran past. The woman was practically a girl. Her obi sash had come undone, and the front of her kimono was open. Her breasts swayed, and blood flowed down between her legs to her ankles. The woman stopped in the middle of an open space and screamed something incomprehensible. Then she began to flail her arms as if fighting some invisible enemy. Somebody held Hisako's hand. The woman repeatedly stamped on her own shadow, which the strong sunlight cast on the ground. Beating her breasts with her fists, she shrieked with a ferocity that made Hisako's hair stand on end. When the woman dashed off toward the woods in the northern part of the village, a woman of about forty and a girl of about ten, both in tears, chased after her.

The first time Hisako had the dream, she couldn't stop crying for a while after she woke up. She knew immediately that the dream was connected to the island she'd been evacuated to. But why would scenes that she'd witnessed sixty years ago revive in her now? She didn't know. Even so, the conviction that she should go to the island to find out grew stronger day by day. The young woman with glazed eyes and a gaping mouth made a lasting impression on her. Everything else in the dream was a blur. She had even forgotten the woman's name, though that was something she wanted to find out.

After she'd started having the dreams about the woman, other memories also started to return. American soldiers with guns were standing around a cave in the woods. Behind them, the villagers watched, too. Hisako was among them. Clinging to her mother, she stared at the cave under the cliff. Several scorched tree trunks stood nearby, and the sloped ground was covered with rocks and stones that had rained down from sections of the cliff pulverized by the bombing. In the dull sunlight, the combat uniforms of the soldiers looked faded, compared to the shiny green of the trees, which glistened as if wet. Before long, a young man emerged from the cave. He screamed like a wild beast, and the moment he raised his right hand, a gunshot rang out. The man's body jerked back in reaction, and then his knees buckled, and he fell forward. The American soldiers screamed, and Hisako's mother covered Hisako with her body.

The next thing she remembered was the man being carried away on a stretcher. His swollen and distorted face was covered with splotches of gray, purple, and red. His slimy skin glittered in the light. Tears flowed from his eyes, which were swollen shut. At this point, the memory jumped ahead again, and Hisako saw her mother yelling something as she threw a stone. This was the only memory she had of her mild-mannered mother showing such rage. The stone struck the back of a man who was heading down the hill through the woods. One after another, the other women started throwing stones, too. Copying them, Hisako threw a jagged stone of her own.

As with the young woman, Hisako couldn't remember the name of the man who'd been shot or of the man at whom they'd thrown stones. But she felt certain they were both from the village. However, she couldn't understand how these memories were connected to the screaming woman. Or maybe she just wasn't letting herself understand. The thought made her realize that the memories were alive inside her, but that she was afraid of letting them come to the surface.

But, then, there must've been a good reason why she'd forgotten. As soon as she graduated from high school, she'd moved to Tokyo and started working there. Her parents had pleaded with her to come home, but she'd refused and ended up settling in Tokyo. In those days, Okinawans needed a passport to travel to Japan, and typical Okinawan surnames, such as Shimabukuro, were still considered unusual and led to people talking behind your back. Maybe that was why she'd left Okinawa and avoided going to the island during her rare visits; she had wanted to completely cut off all those memories.

That was probably the case, but after sixty years everything had grown hazy. On the one hand, she wanted to confront the past and piece together the fragments that were floating up out of her fading memory. On the other hand, she was terrified about knowing the past. Up until now, she'd lived without remembering, so surely there was no need to dredge up what she'd forgotten. But at the same time, she knew that if she left everything in its current vague state, she'd end up regretting it later. If her health took a turn for the worse, she wouldn't be able to travel to the island anymore, and then it would be too late.

About a month ago, Hisako contacted her cousin Masao in Naha and asked him to find out if someone named Fumi Matsuda was living on the island. Fumi was a grade-school classmate who'd often taken her to pick up firewood or search for shellfish. She was the one who'd treated Hisako with the most kindness. If Fumi had gotten married, her last name would've changed, but Hisako remembered that Fumi had lived in a house facing a large open space near a huge banyan tree.

About a week later, Masao called with some information. He explained that he'd gone to the island over the weekend and asked around. He found out that Fumi had gotten married, and that her family name was now Toyama. She'd left the island and was now living in Nago, just to the south. After his explanation, Masao gave her Fumi's current address and phone number.

Instead of calling right away, Hisako wrote a long letter first. It wasn't just a matter of etiquette. If she'd phoned, and Fumi didn't remember her, it would've been awkward. So she wanted to be cautious. In the letter, she wrote about some of the things they did together, and asked Fumi to reply if she remembered her. She ended with an apology for her rudeness in sending a letter so suddenly, after neglecting to write for nearly sixty years. After putting the letter in an envelope, she hesitated for another two days before finally mailing it. Hisako had lived on the island for only about a year, so she'd forgotten the names of almost all her classmates. She wouldn't have been surprised if Fumi didn't remember her. Hisako mailed the letter without expecting a reply, but she received a phone call from Fumi three nights later.

Fumi spoke as amiably as if they'd been in constant contact. Her voice sounded like that of an elderly woman, but her tone and use of the island language reminded Hisako of the girl from her childhood. After exchanging several letters and phone calls, Hisako wrote about her dream and asked Fumi if she knew what it might mean. She added that since she'd be visiting the island in a few days, Fumi could tell her what she knew then. An answer came in a letter. This was unusual because Fumi hated to write and usually phoned. In her letter, Fumi wrote that she knew the place of Hisako's dream and would guide her there when she arrived in Okinawa. She added that she would also explain everything about the woman in her dream and the man in the cave.

Flights and hotels for Okinawa were mobbed during the summer, so Hisako's children were nervous about her traveling alone and wanted her to wait until it got a little cooler. However, Hisako felt she was ready, so she went ahead and booked her flight anyway.

The bus arrived at the terminal at nine forty. They had agreed to meet at ten, but Fumi was already sitting on the bench at the station, waiting. When the bus stopped and their eyes met through the window, they recognized each other immediately. It was uncanny how Hisako could detect the remnants of childhood in Fumi's face, even though she was over seventy years old. When Fumi smiled, her stern expression turned kind and gentle. *Oh! It's Fumi-chan!* she thought when she saw her old friend's smiling face. Sixty years had dissolved in an instant.

When she got off the bus, she saw that Fumi was with a man of about forty.

—Long time, no see, said Fumi.

Fumi beamed with delight as she grasped Hisako's arms. Hisako had been chatty on the phone, but she was speechless at seeing her old friend's face. For a few moments, they tugged each other's arms and gazed into each other's eyes.

—This is my eldest son, Yōichi.

When Fumi finally introduced the man at her side, he lowered his head as if attempting to make his huge body smaller.

—Let me take this to the car, he said, picking up Hisako's bag.

They walked past the concrete block wall of the terminal to the car. Once everyone got in, they headed for the island. The plan was to explore until evening, and then have dinner and spend the night at Fumi's house. Hisako normally wouldn't have been so imposing, but since this was probably her last visit, she decided to accept Fumi's kind offer.

On the way to the island, Hisako and Fumi filled each

other in on their lives. Fumi had graduated from the University of the Ryukyus. She spent the next thirty plus years working as an elementary school teacher. Talking on the phone, Hisako had heard that Fumi's last years before retirement had been spent at their old school, that she had married Shōei, who was also an elementary school teacher, and that they were now living with their son, Yōichi, and his family. When Hisako asked about Yōichi's family, Fumi answered that Yōichi had three children and that the seven of them were living in a duplex.

—Every day is a lot of fun, she said.

But then, she suddenly fell silent, perhaps out of consideration for Hisako, who was living on her own. Yōichi, who was driving, picked up where his mother had left off. He was also a teacher, he said, and taught social studies at a junior high school. He explained that even though they were on summer break, he was busy with teacher training and supervising club activities. After Hisako thanked him for taking the time to be with them, he answered that he'd really wanted to hear about his mother's wartime experiences, too. He added that up until now, he'd never heard anything. Fumi, who was looking over at him, seemed mildly annoyed. Hisako pictured the screaming woman with disheveled hair and became nervous. She reminded herself that she hadn't come merely for a vacation but to confirm the truth with her own eyes and ears.

The concrete bridge crossing over to the island was approximately two hundred meters long.

—It's so beautiful, said Hisako, commenting on the ocean.

—Not like it used to be, Fumi muttered.

Hisako couldn't remember how the ocean looked, but she recalled crossing in a small boat with her family when they were moving back to Naha. As the boat pitched and rolled in the strong winds, she had clung to her mother and tried not to cry. The memory reminded her that her parents were now gone, and she felt overwhelmed with loneliness. She looked out the window to hide her tears.

After crossing the bridge and going a short distance, they stopped at a store and bought some bottled water and a bag of Okinawan brown sugar. Then they got back in the car and headed toward the woods on the hill in the central part of the island. Fumi explained that that was where the man Hisako remembered had hidden. On the way, Hisako was surprised at how much the scenery had changed. The narrow farm roads had been paved, and plots of farmland stretched into the distance. Everything was so different from the densely wooded island in her memory. As she stared at the sugarcane and pineapples planted in the reddish soil, she searched for signs of the scenery she remembered. But she could find nothing.

—It's really changed, hasn't it? said Fumi.

—If I'd come here on my own, I wouldn't have known this was the right island.

—It confuses me sometimes, too, said Fumi in a sad voice.

When they reached the woods, they got out of the car. The path heading into the trees was covered with overhanging branches. If Yōichi hadn't cut through the brush the day before, it would've been too dense for them to pass.

Yōichi broke off a branch and pulled off the leaves to make a whip.

—To keep the *habu* snakes away, he laughed.

Swatting to the right and the left, he headed down the path into the cool shade of the woods. Fumi followed behind him, and Hisako took up the rear. Poisonous *habu* snakes tend to shy away from the first person and aim for the second, Hisako recalled her father telling her as a child. *That's why Fumi's in front of me*, she thought, thanking her old friend in her heart. Hisako didn't know the name of a single plant or tree, but the colors and smells of the subtropical varieties were much more intense than the cedar, zelkova, and ginkgo with which she was familiar. The density and vigor of the vegetation overpowered her, and the intense buzzing of cicadas echoing through the woods seemed to be right on top of them.

Sixty years ago, she and her mother had raced up this path with the other villagers. By the time they'd reached the top, everyone was completely out of breath. Now, she couldn't climb at even half that speed. *Why on earth had we been in such a hurry?* As Hisako was pondering this, Fumi turned around and asked if she was all right. Hisako nodded with a smile and looked down at her feet. Her shoes were wet from the dew. She wondered what shoes she'd been wearing back then, but couldn't remember.

After walking for nearly ten minutes, they still couldn't see the cave. In her memory, they had arrived right away, so she was surprised they had to go so deep into the woods. Yōichi must've spent a long time cutting through the brush for them.

—Sorry for having caused so much trouble, Hisako called out from behind.

—Huh? asked Fumi, turning around.

Apparently she hadn't heard.

—I didn't know it was so far. I feel bad that Yōichi had to cut through so much brush.

—I had a grass cutter, so it wasn't so bad, Yōichi replied before his mother could say anything.

He had overheard their exchange.

—But you must be tired, he added. Would you like to take a break?

—I'm fine. Before the end of the war, I used to pick up firewood here all the time.

—It's a bit different now, put in Fumi. You were a child then.

The three laughed and stopped to wipe the sweat from

their brows. Then they drank some of the bottled water and popped pieces of sugar into their mouths. With his branch, Yōichi pointed into the depths of the woods.

—You can see the cave over there. Just hang in there a little bit longer.

Hisako looked to where he was pointing. Through the woods full of trees so large you could barely get your arms around them, she could see a cave beneath a cliff. The scene of sixty years ago revived within her. Back then, so many trees had been blown up during the US naval bombardment that you could see the sky through the openings. Now, the cave's entrance was half hidden by the dense growth of brush and the outstretched branches of trees clinging to the cliff. The entrance was a dark gaping hole. In spite of the chirping birds and unceasing buzz of cicadas, the area around the cave seemed to be engulfed in silence. Hisako was struck by how much the trees had grown in sixty years.

When they started walking again, Hisako had to grab branches to pull herself up the steepening path. She was glad she hadn't waited to come to the island. If she had, she'd have been too old to make it up this hill. After going down into a hollow, they started up the final slope to the cliff. The hollow was overgrown with plants with big leaves that looked like those of the taro potato. She had seen them displayed as houseplants, but never in the wild. The leaves were a darker green and had so much vigor that they looked like they'd start moving.

—They're *kuwazu-imo* potato plants, said Fumi, noticing Hisako looking at them. They're poisonous, so you can't eat them.

Hisako nodded and continued climbing. When she reached the top of the hill, Yōichi pulled her up to the rocky area in front of the cave. The entrance was flanked by two human-sized stones, covered with moss and fern. Several daddy longlegs scurried across the stones and ran off in various directions. The bugs looked creepy, but the green moss was beautiful. Hisako peeped into the cave. The tunnel sloped downward for several meters and then opened into a cavernous space.

—I took a look inside yesterday, said Yōichi. But after going about ten meters, some bats came flying at me, so I got surprised and turned back.

He laughed with embarrassment. The chilly air from the cave smelled like mud mixed with vegetable matter. Beer cans and candy wrappers were strewn along the walls. Since they were new, Hisako could tell that people still visited.

—This is the cave you remembered, isn't it? said Fumi.

Hisako was at a loss.

—I guess so. But with all the trees, it's hard to tell.

—During the war, everything was blown up from the bombing. The trees around here were burnt up, so there was more open space.

Fumi looked around at the area and then up at the trees.

—This *is* the cave you were talking about.

Surprised at the change in her friend's tone of voice, Hisako stared at Fumi as she turned her gaze to the cave. Fumi's furrowed brow and pursed lips revealed determination and tension, as if she were simultaneously digging up and burying the memories that welled up from the cave's depths.

—That day, I got here before you did. Like you, I was with my mother. I remember seeing you coming up the path, and thinking, Oh! Hisa-*chan*'s come, too! I didn't wave because I was worried about what was happening. So I don't know if you noticed me.

—I noticed you, Fumi-*chan*.

Getting used to Fumi's childlike tone of voice, Hisako started talking like a child, too. But that was okay.

—You mentioned Seiji, right?

—Who?

—The man you mentioned. The man hiding in the cave.

Hisako stared into the dark cave and pictured the man's

bloated face and swollen eyes. Imagining that the grotesque figure might emerge at any moment, she felt the hair on the top of
her head tingle to the roots.

—Why was Seiji hiding here?

Fumi stared at Hisako in disbelief.

—You remember that the Americans surrounded the
entrance, right?

—Yes.

—But you don't remember why?

—No, I don't.

—It was because he stabbed one of them. He stabbed an
American with his harpoon and hid in the cave to get away.

—But why did he do that?

Fumi looked over at Yōichi, who stood to the side listening.
He stared back at her with a calm expression. After brushing
away a mosquito, Fumi turned her eyes back to the bottom of
the cave. Hisako could hear the wind swirling around inside. It
was as if the whole woods was a huge living thing, taking deep
breaths.

—He did it for Sayoko.

—Sayoko?

—The woman in your dreams.

Though hazy and unclear, Hisako thought she could
remember the name.

—Sayoko had shiny black hair that went down to her
waist. She was very pretty. Seiji lived next door to her. We lived
nearby, too, so my mom knew that Seiji liked her. But she also
thought Sayoko was too good for him. She used to laugh at the
idea of someone like Seiji getting married. But you know what?
Seiji was braver than any other man in the village. He fought the
Americans with just one harpoon.

Now Hisako could remember Seiji in front of the cave.
There he was: leaning on his harpoon, on the verge of collapse.

HISAKO AND FUMI (2005)

Fumi stared into the cave and spoke to Yōichi and Hisako without looking at them:

—When Sayoko was raped, the men didn't do anything. Some of them talked about getting revenge, but when the Americans actually showed up, nobody said a word. And then, when the Americans ordered them to help with the search, they joined in without protest and even swore to capture Seiji themselves. In those days you could be shot for resisting, so I guess they didn't have much choice. Still, I really despised my father when I saw him grab a stick and head off to the woods with the other men. And not just my father. I despised all the men in the village. I wonder how those men felt about Seiji standing up to the Americans all by himself. He exposed them as cowards, so they probably felt angry and humiliated. But I was angry at *them*. When I heard that Seiji had stabbed an American with his harpoon, I was happy. Really, really happy. Anyone who could've done such terrible things to Sayoko deserved to die. I was disappointed to hear later that that American had survived....

Fumi had started speaking more rapidly and with more of the island language, so Hisako could barely follow what she was saying. At the mention of rape, a vision of the glittering white beach and screwpine thicket appeared before Hisako's eyes, and her skin started to burn, even though she was standing in the shade of a huge bishopwood tree. Just then, a piercing cry from a brown-eared bulbul rang out, and Hisako's heart skipped a beat. Throwing her head back to find the source of the cry threw her breathing off, too. The thick layers of leaves turned into the murmuring waves of the ocean. Who had explained to Hisako about what had happened in the thicket? Had she overheard the adults talking? Even though she hadn't fully comprehended the precise nature of the event, she knew that she'd witnessed something horrible. She remembered that for a short time afterward, they had been forbidden to go to the beach.

Staring at Fumi as she continued talking, Hisako felt uneasy at seeing how stern her friend's expression had become. The voice emanating from Fumi's unceasingly moving lips echoed back from the cave. Hisako suddenly had the feeling that invisible beings had crawled out from deep inside and were listening on the rocks and at Fumi's feet. She wanted to hold Fumi's hand to protect her but felt unable to do so.

—When the gas canister was thrown into the cave, everyone thought it was poison gas and started to panic. I thought Seiji would die. But after a while, he came out, staggering and leaning on his harpoon, just like you wrote in your letter. And then he tried to throw the grenade. My mother covered me and pushed me to the ground, so I couldn't see what happened next, but I definitely heard gunshots. When I pushed away my mother's hands and looked at the cave, Seiji was lying on his back, with blood covering his shoulder, stomach, and feet. Even then, he wouldn't let go of his harpoon. He raised his head and tried to find the Americans, but his eyes were too swollen. My dad told me later it was from the gas. Anyway, I don't think Seiji could've seen anything. I wanted to scream and tell him that the Americans were right in front of him, but I couldn't. I just stared as he struggled to get up. If the grenade hadn't been a dud and had exploded, dozens of Americans would've died. And Seiji would've been happy, even if that meant dying himself. But that's just like Japan, isn't it? Whether it's soldiers or grenades, when push comes to shove, it's completely useless. . . .

Yōichi was visibly anxious about his mother, who was

practically foaming at the mouth as she spoke. Hisako didn't think they should try to stop her. If they interrupted her now, Fumi might lose control of the words coming out of her mouth, and go completely crazy.

The wind caused the light filtering through the trees to flicker, which in turn caused the green moss to glisten and speckles of light to dance over Fumi, Yōichi, and Hisako. The light also reflected off something inside the cave and flickered against the walls. Hisako's feeling that so me unseen beings were with them grew stronger, and she imagined their contours beginning to take shape. She turned and looked at Fumi's profile. It occurred to Hisako that she'd always depended on her. Suddenly, Fumi turned toward her. Hisako flinched, but the reaction confused her.

Fumi pointed at Hisako's feet and continued:

—There. Right there. Seiji fell down right where you're standing. As he was trying to get up, one of the Americans pointed his rifle at him and pressed his boot down on his hand, the one holding the harpoon. Another soldier picked up the grenade and tossed it into the cave, and the soldier standing on Seiji's hand took the harpoon, and passed it back to one of the others. Then he started kicking Seiji in the head. Seiji's head was jerking back so hard that the American who'd tossed away the grenade had to step in and stop him. So then that damn American gave Seiji one last kick in the stomach, as hard as he could. And then he stooped down, just so he could spit in Seiji's face. When I saw that, I knew he must've been one of the soldiers who'd raped Sayoko on the beach. After that, Seiji was lying there unconscious for I don't know how long. Two Americans ran off to get a stretcher, and while we were waiting, the other soldiers kept their guns pointed at us. The villagers couldn't move, so they just stared in silence. At first, I could only hear the ward chief, the interpreter, and the tall American commander. Later, I could only hear the buzz of the cicadas. I assumed that Seiji would be shot, so I couldn't bear to watch as he was being put on the stretcher and carried away. I just hid behind my mother and cried. That's why I never knew what happened next, until I read your letter. But when I read what you wrote, I knew that that's how it must've been. I could picture Seiji's face as if I'd seen it myself: his swollen eyelids, his pale face covered with purple bruises, and his body wet with sweat and blood. That's how he looked when he was carried off, right? You also wrote that we'd thrown stones at someone, didn't you? And you wanted to know who it was. Well, I think it was probably the ward chief, the one at the time. I don't remember anyone throwing stones, but I was crying, so I probably just didn't notice. But if what you wrote was true, judging from the situation at the time, it must've been him. Cooperating with the Americans helped us in some ways, but it also caused a lot of resentment. My father, for example, talked about it for years after. But I wonder how qualified the other villagers were to throw stones? They also received things from the Americans and cooperated in various ways. And when Sayoko was suffering, they didn't do anything to help. I really don't think they were any different.

Fumi stopped speaking. A moment later, her knees started to buckle, and she tried to sit down. Yōichi ran over to support her.

—I'm okay, she said.

When Hisako took her hand, Fumi smiled weakly and explained:

—It's nothing. When I realized I was finished, I suddenly felt drained. I'm okay now, so you can let go.

Fumi pushed their hands away and stood up. Hisako handed her the bottle of water, and Fumi thanked her and took a few sips. Then she screwed on the lid and handed it back.

—That's all I remember about the cave. Did that help?

—Yes, it did. Thank you.

As soon as she said this, Hisako realized that she still had many unanswered questions, so many that she didn't know where to start. But she was worried about Fumi's physical condition and didn't want to take any more of her time. Fumi nodded as if she'd read Hisako's mind and looked back at the cave.

—How many years has it been since I've come here, I wonder? As I was talking, I was looking down into the cave, and I had the strange feeling that some invisible beings were sitting there listening to me. I wasn't born with spiritual powers or anything, but they say some people died here during the war. The cave wasn't hit during the bombing, but people hid here for weeks, and there wasn't enough food. Some of the sick and elderly grew weaker, and some of them died. Right here in this cave. My heart breaks when I think that their souls have been left behind here.

With these words, Fumi took some black incense sticks out of the paper bag Yōichi was carrying. Then she had him light the sticks with his lighter. Yōichi also had a bottle of *awamori* liquor and a plastic cup. Fumi filled the cup with the strong liquor and placed it at the entrance of the cave. Then she leaned the incense sticks against a fist-sized stone and knelt down to pray. Hisako and Yōichi knelt behind her, and all three of them folded their hands. Fumi murmured some words of prayer, but Hisako couldn't understand their meaning. During the war, Hisako had hidden in another cave, closer to the village. She couldn't remember whether people had died there. When she considered that for sixty years the spirits of the dead were still wandering inside this cave in the woods, she felt her skin turn cold with the thought of how terrifying it was to be so utterly forgotten. She prayed that their souls would soon be able to go to the afterworld and rest in peace.

✧ ✧ ✧

On the way back to the car, Yōichi took the lead and Hisako the rear, just as when they'd come. As they headed down the wooded path, the two kept an eye on Fumi in the middle, so they could offer a helping hand in case she collapsed again.

As they drove off, Fumi leaned back in her seat and closed her eyes. She looked extremely exhausted. Hisako thought they should change their plans. They had planned to listen to Fumi's explanation as they walked around the community center, and then drive to the beach. The sunlight was so intense that even with sunshades it would be exhausting to walk in the noon heat.

—Yōichi, Hisako called.

Yōichi looked back at her in the rearview mirror and slowed down. They were driving along a farm road surrounded by sugarcane fields.

—Yes?

—Your mom looks really tired, so why don't we just see the rest of the island from the car, and then head home early?

—What're you talking about? I'm fine, said Fumi, patting Hisako's hand. You went to so much trouble coming down from the mainland. And it's not easy getting over to the island either. If we don't see everything today, who knows when you'll be able to?

—But this is really tough on you, isn't it?

—I don't know what happened back there, but the words just came pouring out of me. I got really worked up and lost in the story. I'm just a little tired. Now that I've taken a breather, I'm perfectly fine. I walk every day, so my legs are strong. Besides, I really wanted to tell you about this. And you, too, Yōichi. If I don't get this out of my system, I'm sure I'll regret it later on. So, you see, you're the one doing *me* the favor. I hope you'll stay with me.

As Fumi spoke, she grew increasingly more animated. But that only made Hisako more worried. Getting so worked up would only further drain Fumi of her strength and spirit. And the repercussions wouldn't hit her until later.

—But there's no need to overdo it. . . .

—I'm not overdoing anything! interrupted Fumi with a smile. Like I just said, if I don't take you around and talk about this, I'll regret it later. It's a small island, so we don't have to walk all that much. And it won't take long either.

After saying this, Fumi pointed out Hisako's window.

—Look, over there. That's our old school. Do you remember it?

Hisako turned and looked out the window. They were about to enter the village. A small school was on the road parallel to theirs, separated by an irrigation canal. Rows of beefwood trees encircled the grounds. It was summer vacation, so there weren't any students, but you could tell it was an elementary school from the jungle gym and horizontal bar. The white paint of the concrete building stood out against the blue sky, and the three silver flagpoles at the back of the playground glittered in the sunlight.

—It was here?

—You don't remember, do you? That's because the school was made of wood and nearly burned down during the war. Afterward, we had our classes under those tents that the Americans gave us. Oh, look! Do you remember that banyan tree over there? That's been there since before the war.

—I guess so.

Now that Fumi mentioned it, Hisako vaguely remembered playing beneath a large banyan tree. And that brought back other memories: how the rain pelted the roof of the tents; how she loved her young teacher, Miss Kiku; and how before the war, they trained in the yard with bamboo spears, with the male teachers spurring them on. But the memories were like blurry black and white photographs, which she couldn't connect to the colorful bright scenery before her.

—Why don't we head over? asked Yōichi, glancing back at Hisako.

—No, that's all right.

Hisako felt uncomfortable after she'd answered. Her lack of emotional attachment to the school reminded her that she'd only spent a year here, as an evacuee and outsider.

When they entered the village, Hisako remembered the Garcinia trees with thick foliage, which had cast shadows on the white sandy roads and the concrete block walls that surrounded the houses. The walls and sandy roads were now gone. In their place were asphalt roads, burning under the scorching sun.

Yōichi pulled into the community center parking lot, and Fumi jumped out immediately, as if to prevent Hisako from helping her. The community center was a one-story reinforced-concrete building, which looked relatively new. Hisako thought it looked impressive. Fumi walked across the gravel parking lot and headed toward a banyan tree off to the side. Hisako clearly remembered the tree.

She and Yōichi hurried to catch up with Fumi, who waited for them in the shade of the tree, with its branches spread wide.

—Do you remember the bell made from an unexploded shell? Fumi asked. It was hanging from this tree.

A memory stirred in Hisako: she was cutting grass in the woods when the bell started ringing to notify them that American soldiers were coming.

—Oh, that's right! I remember.

Fumi looked pleased.

—So what happened to it?

—The bell? It was donated to the city museum and is now on display. Though by *display*, I only mean it's just sitting there with other household items used after the war, without any explanation.

—Right, said Hisako, laughing at her friend's dissatisfied look.

Fumi joined in the laughter and slapped the trunk of the tree with her palm.

—When you get older, the one thing that never changes

and that best helps you remember the past . . . is trees. People die, one after another; buildings and roads change; and there's hardly anything in town that stays the same. But trees like this stay rooted to the same spot for hundreds of years. Standing under this banyan tree has helped me to remember the past more than anything else.

—That's so true. . . .

Hisako nodded at Fumi's words and looked up at the tree. The branches were the same as when she had climbed them as a child. She could practically hear the cheerful shouts of children playing beneath them.

—See that house over there?

Hisako looked to where Fumi was pointing. In the distance, facing an open space and hidden behind the Garcinia trees that seemed to be the only unchanged remnants of the past, were the red tiles of a roof.

—That's Seiji's house.

—Oh! He's still alive? asked Hisako in surprise.

Her memories of Seiji's being shot and carried off on a stretcher, together with what Fumi had said at the cave, had led her to assume he was dead.

—That's right; I didn't tell you about that. Well, Seiji returned. How long was it after the Americans shot him and took him away? Everybody was saying he'd be executed, so I don't know how he was saved. One day, I saw a man sitting under this banyan tree. I thought I recognized him, so I moved closer to get a better look. When I did, I practically had a heart attack! His face had changed so much you wouldn't have recognized him. Even though he had the same close-cropped hair, I didn't think it was him at first. But it was! He looked angry and was muttering to himself, so I got scared and ran home. Later, I heard from my father that a US military jeep had dropped Seiji off at his house four or five days earlier. After that, I saw him all the time. After the second time, I realized he was blind. Everybody said it must've been due to the tear gas. He's been living in that house ever since. Seiji's younger brother inherited the family home. He graduated from university with good grades and got a job working for the government. That's why he could afford to rebuild the house like this, and have a separate little house on the grounds for his brother. . . .

Hisako couldn't see the smaller house, but the dark green leaves and red roof tiles beneath the bright blue sky looked like the placid scene of a picture postcard. However, she knew that what Fumi had explained in only a few minutes had covered dozens of years. No doubt, much of that time had been far from peaceful. How much of a burden had it been to take care of a blind older brother? And how much discord had it sown between Seiji's brother and his wife? For Seiji, too, being supported by his brother must've been humiliating. But perhaps Hisako's assumption was the result of having lived in the city. Perhaps family relations were warmer on the island? But she realized that this was only wishful thinking. At the same time, she was puzzled that she didn't have any memories of Seiji returning to the village. If what Fumi had said was true, she must've seen Seiji many times before her family moved away.

—So even though I said it's Seiji's house, actually it's his brother's. And see that area over there? Off to the side and overgrown with weeds? That's where Sayoko used to live.

The weed-filled yard, partially surrounded with tall Garcinia trees, had what looked like two orange trees, each about as tall as a human being.

—Sayoko was always confined to the house, so Seiji never met her again, even after he returned. Even if he had, he wouldn't have been able to see her. But that was probably for the best. Sayoko's younger brother inherited the family home. He's held on to the land up to now and planted a couple of citrus *tankan* trees in the yard, but he lives in Naha and hasn't looked after them, so I don't know if they'll ever bear fruit. Though it's just as well they don't.

Hisako could understand the desire to hold on to land even

after leaving the island. Her uncle's house, where she had lived as an evacuee, was now vacant, owned by her cousin living in Naha. There were many offers to buy the property, but her cousin never considered selling.

The three stared at the abandoned premises in silence for a while, and when Fumi started speaking again, it was in a more subdued tone of voice.

—In your letter, you wrote about a woman that came running toward you, right? And that she was screaming, and that blood was dripping down her legs. You know that was Sayoko, right?

Hisako had assumed that that was the case, so she nodded. Fumi looked into Hisako's eyes and nodded in return. Then she looked back at the abandoned property again.

—Even now, when you walk on the gravel here, your shoes get covered with white powder. But back then, the whole area was covered with limestone, so your feet got really white. Do you remember being here with me when Sayoko came running? She bolted out of her house and came running through this lot. Her bare feet were white, her breasts were exposed, and she was screaming. I was right next to you. She was waving her arms as if fighting with some invisible force. Her eyes were wide open and bloodshot. She muttered something and then ran off toward the woods. We saw Sayoko's mother run after her, and then I suddenly felt scared, and you looked like you were going to cry. Even after you left the island, I sometimes saw Sayoko running past the banyan tree like that. Sometimes laughing, sometimes crying. The adults said that after she was raped, Sayoko spent all her time locked up in the house, refusing to eat, never sleeping—until she went crazy. She was locked up in the back room, but sometimes she broke out of the house and sent the family into an uproar. I felt sad to see that because I gradually understood. You only saw the beginning, but things got much, much worse. Sometimes she came out completely naked, and the men would laugh and jeer and whistle. That made Sayoko's parents angry, but the teenage boys only thought that was funny and whistled more. I can still hear their catcalls. Sayoko's mother would chase after Sayoko with clothes in her hands, but she couldn't catch her, so the teenage boys would pretend to help, and then fondle Sayoko when they caught her. Then she'd start screaming and punching and kicking. It was so painful to watch! Those teenagers were no different than the Americans. And when an uproar started, Seiji would come running out of his house with a stick. He'd start screaming and cursing at those teenage boys and try to hit them. But he was blind, so of course he never could. They'd always trick him, take his stick away, and knock him down. After a while, there were rumors that Sayoko was pregnant, and that one of the men in the village was the father. One time, she had run off and hadn't returned until the next morning, so people figured that someone had taken advantage of her. After that, Sayoko disappeared for a while, and the rumors were that she was placed in a hospital in the south. I was just a kid, so I only overheard my parents talking, but it was painful for me to hear. Why did someone like Sayoko have to suffer like that? It broke my heart. And just like that, Sayoko disappeared from the island. Her family left, too. Do you remember our classmate Tamiko? She was Sayoko's younger sister, and we went to the new elementary school together. I still can remember her telling the class that she was transferring to another school. I haven't seen her since. I can't believe sixty years have passed since then. . . .

There was no wind, but the grass and the two citrus trees standing in the sunlight seemed to be swaying, perhaps due to the tears in Hisako's eyes.

—Sayoko came out of her house, which used to be over there, ran through this open space here, and then headed down that road.

Fumi pointed to a road, now paved and lined with houses. The road used to lead to the woods, but Hisako had no idea where it led now. For a split second, she imagined she saw a naked girl running down it.

—Let's go take a look.

At Fumi's prompting, they left the shade of the banyan tree and walked over to the area where Sayoko's house used to be. As the bright sunlight poured over them, Hisako's exposed upper arms and neck began to burn. She opened her sunshade and held it over Fumi as they stood next to the tall grass. The citrus trees, with their worm-eaten leaves, looked quite forlorn. Tall weeds pushed against them, and they looked like they would just wither away. The property covered an area of about 330 square meters. In the corner was an old well, covered with a concrete lid. Hisako remembered a young girl washing something there, but couldn't get a clear picture of the girl's face. But she had a dim memory of someone calling her, *Hisa-chan*! Imagining a terrified young girl and her sister locked up in the dark back room of the now absent house, Hisako wanted to run away from there immediately.

—Actually, I'd completely forgotten, too.

Fumi's voice sounded weak, so Hisako worried that her friend had reached her limit. But she knew she needed to listen until the end.

—Maybe I didn't so much forget as just couldn't bring myself to remember. During high school, I lived in a dorm, so I had to leave the island. At the time, I felt relieved. When I went to university, I had to move even further away, but even though I was the only woman from our class leaving, I hardly missed anyone and mostly felt glad. And then, when I became an elementary school teacher, I avoided working at schools on the island. I only transferred to our old school just before retiring. When I was young, I worked hard for Okinawa's reversion to Japan, but I always avoided peace education, and only went through the motions on Memorial Day. You see, if I spoke about the war, I would've had to remember Sayoko. So that's how I made it to retirement. But shortly after I retired, there was that incident where three American soldiers raped an elementary school girl. I was immediately reminded of Sayoko. Reading about the incident in the newspaper or seeing reports on TV always reminded me of her. I couldn't help thinking that in Okinawa, nothing's changed, not even after fifty years. But at the same time, even though I tried to pretend that I'd forgotten Sayoko, I started to feel guilty about trying to forget the war. As a teacher, I should've spoken with my students about the Battle of Okinawa and the US military bases. Now that I'm retired, there's nothing I can do about that, but I've spent the past ten years regretting my silence. . . .

Fumi took a deep breath, turned around, and asked Yōichi to get the car. As Hisako watched him walk off, it occurred to her that Fumi's last words were meant for him.

—Thanks for talking about your painful experiences.

—What painful experiences? Sayoko's the one who's had it rough. I didn't do anything. I've been no better than the adults back then.

Hisako felt ashamed of her lighthearted words of thanks.

During the five-minute drive to the next location, the three were lost in their own reflections. Hisako watched the scenery outside the window while sometimes glancing over at Fumi, who was leaning back in her seat with her eyes closed. Compared to the black and white scenery of her memories, the green trees and colorful bougainvillea and hibiscus flowers seemed to be overflowing with vitality. Even so, she felt seized with the sensation that the island in her memory was now nothing more than an empty shell. She was glad to have heard Fumi's account, but how would she be able to live with her memories of Sayoko? The question disconcerted her.

They drove along the coast, with the port visible on the opposite shore. Yōichi stopped the car in a vacant lot with several old abandoned cars. Fumi opened her eyes, nodded to Hisako, and jumped out of the car. Hisako ended up having to chase after her again. After walking four or five meters through tall grass, they soon reached the shore. Narrow concrete stairs led down a small slope and opened up to a gentle arc of steps about a hundred meters wide at the water's edge. The sandy beach was gone.

—Is this it?

Fumi smiled wryly at Hisako's question.

—Whenever I come here, I really feel disgusted at Okinawans. Even though it was small, this was a beautiful beach. As payback for accepting the US bases, they've been destroying the environment with public construction projects, and calling it stimulus for the local community. This beach was destroyed ten years ago. Some people opposed the construction and pointed out that the sea turtles would lose their spawning ground, but the campaign never got off the ground. I knew about the construction from the beginning. But that's about the extent of my awareness. Besides the beach, we've also lost the screwpine thicket. The whole area's changed beyond all recognition. I really can't understand why we didn't stop such a stupid project. But standing here like this, I can still picture what happened sixty years ago: how the Americans swam across from that port over there, came running up the beach here, and then carried Sayoko off to, uh . . . I guess the screwpine thicket was over there, but it's changed so much that I'm not sure. . . . You can remember, can't you?

Following Fumi's gaze, Hisako looked over and tried to picture a thicket of screwpine trees in the area covered with the terraced embankment. She then tried to picture several American soldiers carrying off a girl. But the concrete scenery seemed to plaster over what had happened here, leaving Hisako to fumble through her dim memories.

An old man with short gray hair was sitting on the steps watching the sea. His face, upper arms, and neck showed the dark complexion of one who'd spent many years in the sun. Hisako had been aware of the man as soon as they arrived.

Fumi whispered in Hisako's ear from behind:

—That's Seiji. He comes here when the weather's fine. Even though the beach is gone, he sits and stares at the ocean. He's been doing this for decades. Of course, he can't actually see anything. I guess he just listens to the waves and imagines the ocean he knew so long ago. Back then, those who knew how Seiji had stood up to the Americans treated him with great respect, even though they must've had guilty feelings, too. But after twenty, and then thirty years, there've been more and more teenagers and children ignorant of the past. Some of them have made fun of him. But Seiji has never gotten angry or said anything in return. He just sits beneath the banyan tree at the community center and plays his *sanshin* banjo or listens to his radio. Then he comes here and sits facing the ocean. He's been doing this for years. The sandy beach is gone, and has been replaced by these concrete steps, but he comes every day. Unless there's a typhoon or heavy rain. . . .

Fumi's voice faded away into the sound of the wind and the waves. Hisako walked across the steps toward Seiji. When he sensed someone approaching, his face lit up. Startled at his reaction, Hisako stopped in her tracks. She noticed him furrowing his bushy eyebrows and twitching his nostrils. He must've been trying to determine her identity through his senses of smell and hearing. His swollen face revealed that he was in poor health. Then his chapped lips moved, revealing several brown teeth.

—Sayoko, is that you?

Hisako shuddered at the passion in his hoarse voice, but she couldn't move any closer.

SEIJI (2005)

Can you hear my voice, Sayoko? . . . Can you hear it riding on the wind and on the waves in search of you? The sun sinks in the west, the wind blows gently, and the air grows cool. How is it where you are? Are you facing the ocean? Do you feel the wind in your hair? Do you hear the sound of the waves? . . . I hear the wind rustling through the screwpine leaves, crabs scurrying across the sand, and small fish splashing out of the water as they flee a mackerel. But what I most wish to hear, Sayoko, is your voice. . . . I can't see the physical world, but I see you clearly. . . . You're walking on the white sand of the village road, a basket on your head, as you come toward me. . . . When you leave the shade of the Garcinia trees to cross the road, you squint your eyes. *It's so sunny today*, you say with a smile. . . . I can't say anything and drop my head. . . . *Did you catch any fish today, Seiji?* you ask. But I can only nod. . . . Even I know I'm pathetic. In front of you, I get so embarrassed. . . . I'm awkward with everyone, but with you it's so much worse. . . . But you never get mad and you're always so nice. . . . That's why I . . . That's why *what?* . . . What do you mean? . . . I asked, *Why what?* . . . Who the hell are you? . . . Sayoko's not here. She left the island long ago. . . . Who the hell are you? . . . She doesn't remember you, and she's forgotten the island. . . . What're you talking about? Sayoko wouldn't forget me. You're trying to trick me. Who the hell are you? . . . Sayoko left the island decades ago. There's no way she remembers you. . . . What the hell do you know? Do you know what happened here? Or how much I've done for her? You don't know anything. . . . Forget about what you've done. Sayoko's living happily. You gonna complain about that? . . . No, I'm not gonna complain, but . . . Well, then be happy for her! Sayoko's better off forgetting what happened, and forgetting you. . . . Who the hell are you? . . . What do you mean, *Who am I?* I'm your friend. . . . My friend? . . . Your *best* friend . . . Hey, Seiji, look out! That American's right beside you. . . . Where?! . . . Be careful not to get shot! . . . Ah, ha! You're that Japanese-looking guy. You can't trick me. . . . Why would I wanna trick you? You'll hurt me if I don't watch my step. . . . I know your ways. . . . I can't understand this lunatic. . . . Your father was Okinawan, wasn't he? Aren't you ashamed to be fighting with the Americans? . . . **Answer the question!** . . . You don't need to answer, Seiji. Don't let them trick you. . . . Shut up, you! And you, too! Shut up! . . . **You attacked four American soldiers in the ocean and stabbed one of them with your harpoon. Isn't that correct?** . . . Seiji, you should tell them the truth. Not all Americans are bad. If you tell the truth, they'll forgive you. . . . Who the hell are you? How do you know my name? . . . Don't, Seiji, don't let them trick you. . . . That's right! Just be quiet! If you let these fast-talking Americans trick you, you'll be executed! . . . And who the hell are you? Be quiet! Be quiet! You people don't know anything about me. . . . **Tell the truth! The soldier you stabbed was seriously wounded, but he didn't die.** . . . He didn't die! Oh, Sayoko! When I heard that, I felt so frustrated! . . . **If you tell the truth and apologize, we'll reduce your sentence.** . . . What do you mean *apologize?!* You apologize to Sayoko! . . . **Answer the question honestly.** . . . I knew as soon as the harpoon went in that I didn't get him in the vitals. . . . **You stabbed him with a harpoon, right?** . . . It's tough to get the heart, so I aimed for the liver. If only I'd swum further and gotten closer. . . . **How did you stab him?** . . . Things didn't go as planned. I couldn't destroy the enemy. . . . **What're you waiting for? Don't you understand the situation?** . . . If I get another chance, I definitely won't miss. . . . **We're at war. We**

could shoot you and say you were killed in action. That would be just fine with me. . . . They're only saying this because they feel sorry for you, Seiji. You should tell the truth. . . . If you believe what this Japanese-looking guy is telling you, you'll be killed, Seiji. . . . That's right! He only looks Japanese! . . . **But I don't want to do that. That's why I want you to talk.** . . . I'm not afraid to die, Sayoko! Compared to your suffering, it'd be no big deal if I were killed. . . . **If you talk, you'll get a reduced sentence. That'd be much better for you.** . . . I don't care if I die. . . . You coward, Seiji! Don't make me laugh. You're just too scared to talk. . . . Who the hell are you? What do you know? . . . I know a lot. I saw you get shot, carried off on a stretcher, treated by the army's doctors, and interrogated by that officer and his interpreter. I've seen everything. . . . You're lying! Who the hell are you? You couldn't possibly have seen all that. . . . **You have nothing to gain by staying quiet.** . . . I've got nothing to gain by talking. . . . This is no time for joking. . . . **America is a democracy. If you tell the truth, even though you'll be punished appropriately, no further injury will be inflicted on you.** . . . A dummy like you who's never gone to school wouldn't know about democracy, would you? When I heard them say that, Seiji, I had to laugh. . . . Shut up! You're always making fun of people. . . . **You're a fisherman, right? You're a good swimmer, so you planned to attack them in the ocean, right?** . . . Come on, Seiji, answer the question! Just tell them you're a fisherman. If you don't answer this time, you really might get shot. . . . Why the hell should I tell you! I'm not afraid to die! . . . If you die, Seiji, you'll never see Sayoko again. . . . They said if you answer, they won't shoot you. . . . You're pretty stubborn for an idiot. . . . **You figured that in the ocean you'd have a chance, didn't you?** . . . Sayoko, the idea of never seeing you again was depressing, but I didn't want the Americans to win. . . . Did you really think a guy like you could beat them? Don't be so stupid! . . . Everyone was so scared that they couldn't do a thing. But I took action! . . . Listen to this! Seiji's starting to brag again. . . . **You're the one that did it, right?** . . . I wanted to see them die. . . . **Why did you attack those four men?** . . . Sayoko, I'll never forgive those men who made you suffer. . . . **Were you acting on an order from the Japanese army?** . . . The Japanese army can't do anything. They're all talk. . . . What do you mean you won't forgive them? They've survived and gone back to America. What? Are you gonna go to America to get revenge? . . . For Sayoko, who you love, huh? . . . I'm laughing so hard, it hurts. . . . **Did the Japanese army tell you to do this?** . . . Who'd take orders from them? I acted on my own. . . . Could Seiji really have done this by himself? . . . He might be an idiot on land, but he knows what he's doing at sea. . . . Because his father trained him. . . . When I saw his father's methods, I thought if that were me, I'd rather be sold into bondage, like they used to do in Itoman. . . . **Is this your harpoon?** . . . I did what no one else could do. . . . **You knew what would happen if you stabbed someone with this, didn't you?** . . . Die! You damn Americans! . . . **You wanted to kill them, didn't you?** . . . Yes, I wanted to kill them! I tried to kill them! . . . Do you really have the guts to kill someone? . . . Yes, I do. What do you know? I dove under him as he was swimming and stabbed him in the stomach. . . . **Did anyone help you?** . . . If you really wanted to kill him, why didn't you get him in the vitals? . . . The light on the ocean surface was flickering, and the American's arms and legs were creepy and long. . . . **Start talking! Answer the question!** . . . The light made it difficult to estimate the distance. . . . Don't answer, Seiji! If you admit that you did it, you'll be executed. . . . You can't answer because you didn't do it, right, Seiji? . . . What're you talking about? Everyone on the island knows he did it. . . . And that caused trouble for everyone. . . . What trouble? You coward! Just because you couldn't do anything. . . . Are you trying to protect him? . . . Every woman in the village has changed her opinion of him. They say Seiji's the only one with courage. . . . That's right. I think so, too. You were wonderful, Seiji. . . . **You're hiding something, aren't you?** . . . You helped with the search just because the Americans told you to. Aren't you ashamed of yourself? . . . If we didn't, well, who knows what would've happened. . . . **Answer the question! If you don't talk, your family's going to be in trouble, too.** . . . Don't worry about us, Seiji. We'll be fine. . . . I'll take care of Mom, Seiji. . . . The men on this island are cowards. . . . You complain about Japanese soldiers not committing suicide and becoming prisoners, but you're no different. . . . What could we have done? Even our army couldn't do anything. . . . So no matter what happens to the women, you just pretend not to notice, huh? . . . Hey! We're pretty angry, too. . . . Well, then, fight like Seiji has! . . . You're in no position to criticize. . . . Seiji, don't worry about your family. We'll take care of them. . . . **You won't talk, so we have no choice. Take him away!** . . . They should just execute him. . . . Don't say such a thing! . . . Dad, forgive me! . . . Now the Americans suspect me because of him. They took my boat and all my fishing gear. How am I supposed to live? . . . Some people have praised Seiji. . . . **I guess we'll have to beat you to death.** . . . They're pretty strong, so if they do start beating you, you'll be dead soon. . . . Japanese soldiers were no match for them, so he must be pretty crazy to fight them on his own. . . . **Give him the barest minimum for meals.** . . . We should just let him eat dog shit. . . . What did Seiji do, Mom? . . . Your brother is a brave man. You should be proud of him. . . . **Make sure he doesn't bite off his tongue.** . . . I'll put a gag in his mouth. . . . Mom, forgive me! . . . I'm always worried about you, Seiji. . . . You're shaking violently. Are you cold? Hurry up and confess! Then you can get out of here. . . . What happened to Sayoko? . . . The Americans did something bad to her. . . . Something *bad?* . . . You're no match for the Americans, so don't be so proud. Apologize, and let's go home. . . . She spends every day crying in the back room. . . . She doesn't eat and sometimes goes crazy. . . . **You're a fool.** . . . I heard her making strange noises like a dog in heat. . . . Why would you say something like that? . . . **We've provided food for everyone in the village, and we treated the wounded**. . . . She was assaulted by some Americans, wasn't she? . . . What do you mean *assaulted?* . . . American men are well endowed, so I'm surprised they could get it into her. . . . Aren't you ashamed to be talking like that? You're classmates from the same village! . . . **Cooperate and follow our instructions**. . . . Oh, lighten up! We're just kidding. . . . That's right. Everybody knows all about it. . . . You're just saying that because you're jealous of her. . . . I'm not jealous. What're you talking about? . . . **If you cooperate, we'll do our best for all of you**. . . . Because she was so pretty. . . . Ever since she was little, all the boys liked her. . . . Even Seiji, huh? . . . I wonder if he really thought she'd have anything to do with him. . . . Sayoko was kind, especially to people like him. . . . So he must've misunderstood. . . . **Let's work together to rebuild this beautiful island**. . . . I know he's stupid, but couldn't he even figure out that a girl would never fall for someone like him? . . . That's precisely why he couldn't figure it out. Because he's so stupid. . . . Stop it! I don't want to hear anymore! . . . Maybe that's why he stabbed that American with his harpoon. Because he's stupid. . . . No sane person would've been able to do anything like that. . . . Maybe that's why the American army didn't execute him, because they thought he was crazy. . . . **America is a democratic country**. . . . How can you say such horrible things? Can't you consider how Sayoko and Seiji feel? . . . Can *you?* . . . Acting morally superior, and pretending like you know something. . . . **America will bring freedom and peace to Okinawa**. . . . Did you suffer, Sayoko? . . . So when she was running, her face was contorted, her mouth was open, and tears were running down her cheeks? . . . Were you in pain, Sayoko? . . . And blood was dripping down between her legs. . . . I heard she got naked and ran down the road in front of the banyan tree. . . . Why was she running to the woods? . . . Come and hide in this cave, Sayoko! . . . You could see her tits, and down there, too. . . .

Come! Come and be with me, Sayoko! . . . Crazy people can run fast, so her parents couldn't catch her. . . . Don't cry! Are you afraid? The Americans will never come again, Sayoko. . . . Where was she going, I wonder? . . . You never know. Maybe she was running to those American guys. . . . Yeah, because you never forget your first man. . . . You guys are the lowest. How can you talk about Sayoko like that? . . . I'll protect you from now on, Sayoko. . . . The lowest? Are you talking to us? . . . You think you can get away with comments like that? . . . You women should stop fighting. It's unbecoming. . . . Maybe we should make *you* go running naked. . . . You're awful! Come on! Knock it off! . . . Apologize! . . . What's with that look! You must really wanna go running naked? . . . I'm sorry. . . . Who is this Sayoko you're talking about? . . . Some woman who lived on the island a long time ago. . . . She was raped by some Americans and went crazy. . . . Too bad! If you'd moved here sooner, you could've seen her running naked, too. . . . She's not on the island anymore? . . . The entire family moved away. . . . Some guy from a nearby village impregnated her, so they left. . . . Because she used to run around naked. . . . Nearby village? It was one of you guys, wasn't it? . . . You gotta be kidding! We wouldn't touch a woman like that. . . . Keep talking garbage, and I'm gonna beat the shit out of you. . . . Go ahead, Seiji, say that again. . . . Were you eavesdropping on us? . . . They say blind people have great hearing. I guess it's true. . . . You think just because you're blind we won't hit you, huh? . . . If you bastards make fun of Sayoko, I'm gonna make you pay. . . . Listen to this! Seiji says he's gonna make us pay. . . . So how are you gonna do that? Let's see what you got. . . . Hey, Seiji, what are you swinging at? . . . We're over here, Seiji. . . . Sayoko! If I could've seen those guys, I would've stabbed them with my harpoon! . . . Check it out! The dimwit's crying! . . . I was so frustrated. . . . Disgusting! Stay away from us! You stink! . . . Seiji, you don't wanna make us angry! . . . Boy, you're easy to knock down. Remember, you're the one that started it. . . . Knock it off! You might kill him. And then what'll we do? . . . A guy like this? Who cares? His family will be glad to be rid of him. . . . If you make fun of Sayoko, I'm gonna make you pay. . . . He still talks like a man. . . . If he's got the energy to talk, he's not gonna die. . . . Don't kick him in the stomach! No, not in the head, either! . . . Seiji, you fought against the Americans, didn't you? . . . Try to stab us like you stabbed them. . . . If I weren't blind, I'd kick your asses. . . . Come on, that's enough! Let's get out of here. If we don't knock it off, there's gonna be trouble. . . . Seiji, if you try to act tough next time, we'll beat you to death and dump you in the ocean. . . . Oh, forget it! Leave the guy alone. Let's get going. . . . They knocked me down, and I couldn't get up. The ground was so cold against my back, Sayoko. . . . Check it out! He looks like a frog run over in the street. . . . My face was swollen, and I couldn't open my mouth. . . . His lips are twitching. . . . I tried to spit out the blood, but there was too much of it. . . . Ugh, red slobber is dribbling from his mouth! Disgusting! . . . Don't go near him. Pretend you don't notice. . . . I tried to get up, but I couldn't move my arms or legs. Just like when the Americans shot me. . . . You're an idiot for fighting with kids who are just goofing off. . . . Sayoko, I'm so tired. I just want to sleep. . . . You can't sleep here! You're causing a nuisance. . . . Who are you? . . . It doesn't matter who I am. Get up. I guess playing the *sanshin* and drinking are your only pleasures in life, huh? . . . Thank you. . . . Don't misunderstand. I'm only helping because you're in the way. . . . Sayoko, I can play the *sanshin*, even though I'm blind. If we meet again, let me play you a song. . . . Hey, mister, what're you doing? . . . I'm playing the *sanshin*. . . . Wow, you're pretty good. . . . Kids are so cute, Sayoko. They're happy to talk to anyone, even me. . . . Mister, are you blind? . . . Mister, why do you have those cuts on your face? . . . If only I had kids like this. . . . Mister, you smell! Have you been drinking? . . . Mister, don't those cuts hurt? . . . Sayoko, do you have any children? . . . Mister, what are these bugs called? . . . Mister, why are you barefoot? . . . Kids are soft and smell nice, Sayoko. . . . Mister, is it true that sprites live in this banyan tree? . . . Yes, it's true. . . . What're sprites? . . . Little creatures about your size, but with red hair. . . . So they have hair like our friend Sāchi? . . . But you're blind, so you wouldn't know. . . . Do sprites eat people? . . . No, but they eat fish eyes. . . . That's weird. . . . Why do you say that? Fish eyes are delicious. . . . I heard eating them makes you smart. . . . Really? . . . Is it true that sprites kidnap kids and throw them in the ocean? . . . Are sprites scary? . . . They run away if you fart, so if you're scared, just let one go. . . . I can't fart on command! . . . Well, then, if you see a sprite, call me. I'll show you how it's done. . . . Mister, that stinks! . . . That made me laugh, Sayoko. The only time I ever laugh is when I'm with kids. . . . Mister, were you really shot by the Americans? . . . Yeah, the bullet went in right here. . . . Wow! It's all lumpy. . . . Let me touch it, too. . . . Does it hurt, mister? . . . Not anymore. . . . Are those cuts on your face from the Americans, too? . . . Yeah, they also hit me. . . . Why'd they hit you? . . . Why did they shoot you? . . . I don't know. I can't remember. . . . Did you do something wrong? . . . No, I didn't. . . . They hit you even though you didn't do anything wrong? . . . And shot you? . . . That's right. I didn't do anything wrong. . . . You're lying! You must've done something really bad. Otherwise, they wouldn't have hit you. . . . Or shot you. . . . I didn't do anything wrong! . . . Seiji, stop talking to the kids. . . . What did that guy do to you? Tell us. . . . There've been a lot of complaints, and the ward chief warned me. . . . He did something strange to you, didn't he? Tell us what he did. . . . He didn't do anything. . . . Stop lying and tell the truth! . . . I *am* telling the truth! . . . The villagers are watching you, Seiji. . . . We can't understand when you're crying. Settle down, and tell us what he did to you. . . . You're blind, so you can't tell, but everyone's watching. . . . Scary, isn't it? I always thought he might do something. . . . I heard he touched Kinjō's kid, too. . . . He's your brother, isn't he? Can't you take care of this? . . . If he does it again, I'm calling the police. . . . Seiji, is it true that you touched a girl? . . . If I don't touch them, I can't tell what they look like, or how tall they are. . . . Is it true that you wouldn't let go, even though she was crying? . . . She wasn't crying. . . . So you admit that you touched her? . . . Where did he touch her? . . . She's a kid, so she was crying and couldn't say. . . . I heard he put his finger in her, and that she was bleeding. . . . Unbelievable! That's horrible! . . . The girls are scared and can't go outside. . . . I haven't done anything wrong. . . . Seiji, if you do it again, the police are going to arrest you. . . . I haven't done anything wrong. . . . The open area near the banyan tree is a place for kids to play. As ward chief, can't you drive him away? . . . That's been his reserved spot for years and years now. . . . He blasts his radio from the crack of dawn. . . . I'll ask him to turn it down. . . . We feel bad that he's handicapped, and we don't really want to complain, but there were those incidents with the kids. . . . Don't let him off just because he's blind. . . . Ward chief, don't let these women say whatever they want. . . . We're not gonna sit here and listen to these groundless accusations. . . . Would Seiji really do such things? . . . We're just protecting our children. . . . If we wait until something horrible happens, it'll be too late. . . . Seiji, go ahead and play your *sanshin* as much as you like. And listen to your radio, too. . . . Hey, Seiji! You molest another girl, and we're gonna break your arms! . . . I haven't done anything. . . . A scumbag like you? Those Americans should've shot you. . . . Where'd you insert your finger, Seiji? . . . Not just your arms. We'll break your fingers, too. . . . You'll never play the *sanshin* again. . . . Seiji, we brought some rope, so you can hang yourself from this tree. . . . I never did anything wrong. That's the truth, Sayoko. . . . What're you grinning about? . . . You screwing with us? You're gonna get yourself killed. . . . He always was kind of weird. . . . He thinks he's a big shit 'cause he got in a magazine, and everyone's making a big deal about it. . . . He also got a big photo spread. . . . That damn Japanese reporter's article was half lies! . . . It called him

"the old man who sings the tragedy of the Battle of Okinawa."...
What a joke!...I heard he was a spy for the Japanese army....
Really?...Yeah, that's what my grandfather said. He said Seiji
was in the Defense Corps and on great terms with the Japanese....Is that right?...But I heard he was a spy for the Americans....If that were the case, why'd they shoot him?...Yeah,
that doesn't make any sense....Spies are usually eliminated in
the end....Some people say the Japanese army shot him....
You're both wrong. He wasn't shot at all....That's what I heard,
too. He's senile, so he doesn't know what he's talking about....
My grandmother saw him get shot. She said he was shot in the
shoulder, and that he was covered in blood when they carried
him off on a stretcher....In the middle of the woods, right?
Hiding in a cave....Why was he shot?...He stabbed an American soldier to get revenge for his girlfriend....That old man?
Don't make me laugh....Seiji, can you hear everyone laughing?...
In other words, we want you to get the hell off the island!...
People are scared of you....You're an eyesore....They've built a
new bridge, so tourists will be coming....How about going into
an old folk's home?...What're you saying? You guys have no
idea what great things this old man's done....I'll be happy if I
can just sit here....Mister, aren't you cold? Here, have a steamed
bun with meat....Thank you....It's beautiful when the cherry
blossoms come into bloom....*Airuyan na* (Is that right?)....I'm
sorry, mister, I don't understand Okinawan dialect....The
white-eyes are singing....White-eyes? You mean those tiny
green birds, right? My grandfather told me about them....
Sayoko, can you hear the white-eyes singing?...Seiji always had
birds when he was a kid....They were always singing....When
I went to catch white-eyes in the woods, the leopard plant flowers were in bloom....Ah! I can see the yellow flowers before my
eyes....Mister, it's a shame you can't see all these flowers. They're
in full bloom....There were red azaleas in the woods, too....
One time, he climbed a cliff to pick some azaleas for Sayoko....

I tried to give them to you, but my hands were shaking so bad. . . .
Mister, I heard you fought with the Americans over a girl. . . .
That's right. I fought all by myself. . . . That's so cool. . . . I dived
under the water and stabbed one of them with my harpoon. . . .
Did he die? . . . No, but there was a lot of blood in the water as he
struggled to survive. . . . But why'd you stab him? . . . Sayoko,
when I heard you crying behind your shutters, I almost went
crazy. . . . Did the American do something? . . . The Americans
weren't the only evil ones. . . . Hold down her arms. . . . Stop
struggling! You let the Americans have their way with you, so
why not us? . . . I've been crazy ever since I heard what
happened. . . . Ever since? Don't make me laugh, Seiji. You were
crazy from birth. . . . Spread your legs! No matter how much you
scream, no one's gonna save you! . . . Crazy! I'm going crazy!
What the hell is happening to me? . . . Hurry up! It's my turn! . . .
I'll kill them! I'll kill them! I'll kill them! Anyone who hurts
Sayoko is gonna die! . . . This old man was crazy to begin with,
and now he's going senile. Nothing he says makes any sense. . . .
That's not true, is it, mister? . . . I'll kill them! I'll kill them! I'll
kill them! . . . Ow! That hurts! You bite me again, and I'm gonna
knock out your teeth! . . . Mister, what's your girlfriend doing
now? . . . Sayoko, what're you doing now? . . . Jeez, you really stink
for a girl! Take a bath once in a while! . . . I'll kill them! I'll kill
them! I'll kill them! . . . Haven't you seen her? . . . I want to see
you. . . . 'Cause we wanna spend more time with you. . . . Don't
you know where she is? . . . Sayoko, where are you? . . . I'll kill
them! I'm going crazy! I'll kill them! My head aches! I'll kill
them! Words are buzzing inside my head like little bugs! I'll
kill them! Everything's so mixed up! I'll kill them! Voices are
swarming all around me! I'll kill them! . . . Sayoko, look at your
belly! . . . I'll kill them! Sayoko, what are you doing now? I'll kill
them! . . . She was crying in the woods. Crying and crying and
crying. . . . It's too late. An abortion would be dangerous. . . . In
the darkness of the woods, the red fruit of the screwpine looked

like a setting sun. . . . Still, we'd like you to go ahead with it. . . . I'll kill them! Sayoko, I'll kill those that made you suffer! I won't allow it! I'll kill them! . . . She was just sitting on the crushed grass staring at that red fruit. . . . You can't kill them. Sayoko wouldn't be pleased. . . . That's right, Seiji. Sayoko doesn't want you to suffer any more. . . . Tell me where she is. I'll go to her. . . . I'm sorry, Seiji. I don't know either. . . . Are you gonna spend the rest of your life thinking about Sayoko? Look, there's a woman standing next to you. . . . I already knew that. Two women and a man. . . . She's been staring at you for a long time. . . . But it's not Sayoko. . . . She's looking at you and crying. . . . It isn't Sayoko. . . . A woman crying for a man like you? How unusual. . . . Sayoko, when will you return to the island? . . . It doesn't have to be Sayoko. She wants to talk to you. . . . I only want to talk to Sayoko. . . . Don't glare at her with those unseeing eyes of yours. You're scaring her. . . . The sound of the waves has faded. . . . She's given up because you look like that. . . . The wind has grown heavy. . . . She wiped away her tears with her handkerchief and bowed to you, Seiji. . . . The scent of the sea has grown stronger. . . . The other woman bowed, too. They're standing side by side looking at you. . . . It's gonna rain tomorrow, Sayoko. . . . They're leaving with the man. Say something, Seiji. . . . But I'll come even if it rains, Sayoko. . . . You'll never see them again. Say something! . . . Are you staring at this ocean and listening to the waves? . . . They're gone. . . . Are you listening to the sound of this wind? . . . The lunatic is hopeless. . . . Riding on the waves, riding on the wind, has my voice reached you? . . . Could it possibly have reached her? . . . It will reach her, Seiji, without a doubt. . . . Even now, I'm still thinking of you! . . . Will it rain tomorrow? . . . Can you hear my voice, Sayoko?

OKINAWAN WRITER (2005)

—Surprised to hear from me, aren't you? Getting a video like this out of the blue. As you can see, I've changed quite a bit from ten years ago. That's because I've got a pretty serious illness, and, uh . . . well, I'll tell you about that later. For now, I've got a really important favor to ask of you. You're the only one I know living in Okinawa, so please watch to the end. I'll explain everything. . . .

I had to admit I was a bit surprised when I saw the name of the sender on the parcel. I had stayed in touch with Matsumoto for only about two or three years after graduating from college. Back then, we spoke on the phone occasionally, and got together for drinks whenever I was in Tokyo. But as time passed, we saw less and less of each other. Our last meeting was during the summer about ten years ago. I was in Tokyo on business, so I gave him a call, and we got together in a coffee shop near Shinjuku Station. But after about half an hour, Matsumoto seemed to be in a hurry and said he had another appointment. As I watched him leaving the shop, I couldn't help thinking that I'd been a nuisance. After that, I never called him again. He never contacted me either, so I figured our relationship had simply run its course. I didn't even feel disappointed.

—To tell the truth, I feel kind of embarrassed talking into a camera like this. Guess I should've written instead, huh? But, you know, it's a real strain for me anymore, staring at the computer. So, uh, I hope you don't mind if I just make a video. Because even like this, I know I won't finish in one go. Just let me divide it up into a few days, okay? Anyway, thanks for your understanding. . . .

Matsumoto nodded with a weak smile, and then the video cut off. A second later, he reappeared on screen in the same clothes. Obviously, he'd resumed after a short break. Behind the sofa on which he was sitting was a bookcase filled with books and CDs. Though I had no way to know for sure, I assumed he was at home. Matsumoto had loved to read when we were in college. I was curious about what he'd been reading lately, so I hit the pause button and tried to read the titles. But they were too blurry.

I was born and raised in Okinawa. After graduating from high school, I entered a private university in Tokyo. The change of environment was so overwhelming that I wondered if I'd survive the four years required to graduate. The first train ride of my life was when I went to Tokyo for the entrance exam, and other than the Yamanote Line, I struggled to figure out the trains on my own. I was a country bumpkin, and my keen awareness of that fact made me even more withdrawn. So when Matsumoto, a student in my department, spoke to me, I considered it a favor.

Yes, a favor. Matsumoto made such a big difference in my life, that even now I see it that way. At the time, world music was all the rage. You could hear Shōkichi Kina, Rinken Band, and other Okinawan bands, even on the Japanese mainland. Matsumoto was really into Okinawan music, and that's why he spoke to me. I answered all his questions about the music, and other questions about the military bases and life in Okinawa. Before long, we were sharing meals and exploring Tokyo together. Gradually, we became friends. Matsumoto was born and raised in Tokyo, so he was a great guide for me. For his part, he seemed to enjoy my surprised reactions to whatever he showed me.

At Matsumoto's invitation, I joined the literary arts circle. Matsumoto had watched a considerable number of movies and plays, and the breadth of his reading was incredible. So when I submitted my first short story for the group to critique, I couldn't help feeling embarrassed. Matsumoto had written a quasi-autobiographical novel describing a relationship with an older woman, a work that struck me as being rather sophisticated.

My submission was a forty-page piece about a young island girl raped by American soldiers after the Battle of Okinawa, based on a story I'd heard from my grandmother. The mainland Japanese seemed confused about how to evaluate my work, and few of them expressed an opinion. But Matsumoto complimented me for writing a story that none of them could've produced.

Now that I'm older, I'd be embarrassed to read the stories we wrote back then. But when I was young, receiving unexpected praise gave me the strength to continue writing. If I hadn't been praised during that first critique, and instead had been criticized about contradictions in the details as others had been, I might never have written another story. Matsumoto referred to that shared past in the video:

—You might be surprised to know, I've read every story you've written. To tell the truth, they're not my cup of tea. But, uh, I still enjoyed reading them. Guess there really are stories that can only be written by an Okinawan. Only someone like you, who was born there, can really capture the, uh, atmosphere, I guess you'd call it, and the language. Reminds me of that first critique after you joined the literary arts circle. You remember? Back then, I gotta tell you, I secretly resented you for having a world of your own. You know, something that only *you* could write about. Sure, my story might've looked impressive. But, really, it was just a rehash of the same old stuff. But yours! The writing might've been a little stilted, but your stories were unique. Nobody else could've written them. But enough about that. Once I start talking about the past, I can go on forever. . . . So anyway, you noticed the contents of the envelope, didn't you?

I mean the one enclosed with this video. If you haven't, take a look now. . . .

After a long pause, Matsumoto continued:

—So about that pendant. It was made from the head of a harpoon. Would you call it an arrowhead? Hmm. I guess not. I mean, it's not from an arrow. But, uh, there's no such word as *harpoonhead*, is there? Well, whatever it's called, it couldn't have rusted in the mail, so I'm sure it's still black, and shiny, and smooth, just like when I sent it. It's pretty old, I guess. Made into a pendant about sixty years ago, apparently. An American guy had it. But originally, it was from Okinawa, like you. It was part of a harpoon used by a guy living on an island there. Actually, my favor has to do with this pendant. And that's why I'm sending you this video. Sorry for beating around the bush and all. . . . First, let me tell you about the guy with the pendant. After I graduated from college, I started working for a publishing company, as you know. But about ten years ago, which would've been about, uh, six months after I saw you last, I quit. Even before I was out of college, I knew I didn't have much talent for writing fiction. But I figured that by supporting writers as an editor, I could help get some good stuff published. Oh, I guess now I'm just making excuses. And I'm tired of that. Besides, my motive for joining the company hardly matters now. The truth is, I just couldn't stand it any more. All the boring manuscripts, all the boring writers, all the boring work. Yeah, some of my colleagues tried to get me to reconsider. Said that pretty soon I'd be able to pursue the projects I wanted. But I didn't want to hear it. Well, sorry for all the, uh, all the complaining. . . .

At that point, Matsumoto had an intense coughing fit and couldn't continue. The video cut off, and then immediately resumed. Of course, the recording had been stopped and restarted. In reality, a considerable amount of time must've passed. Matsumoto was still sitting on the sofa and wearing the same clothes, but he now looked completely exhausted. After he cleared his throat and was about to resume talking, I hit the stop button.

I had returned home from work shortly after eleven in the evening. As soon as I entered my apartment, I opened the parcel I'd picked up from my postbox and popped the video into the player. I still hadn't showered or eaten. Now that I could see it was going to be a long explanation, I figured I'd have dinner first, and then sit down to watch the rest. I live alone, so I can be pretty flexible with my time.

After graduating from university, I returned to Okinawa and started working as a part-time instructor at various vocational and cram schools, while working on my writing on the side. Four years ago, I won a literary magazine's award for new writers. Since then, I've managed to get two or three new stories published a year, all short ones under a hundred pages in length. Trying to write while holding down several part-time jobs really cuts into my sleep. I've had some ideas for a full-length novel but not the time to finish one. To compensate, I try to make my short stories rich in content. I was thrilled to hear that Matsumoto had read everything I'd written.

I showered and changed, had dinner at a nearby twenty-four-hour coffee shop, and returned to my apartment. Then I settled down on the sofa with one of the beers I'd bought on the way home, and restarted the video.

—Sorry about that. I've had a really bad cough lately. Anyway, shortly after resigning from publishing, I spent about a year in New York. No great objective. Just wanted to get out of Japan. Acquaintances there helped me find an apartment, and I relied on friends to show me around, just like when I showed you around Tokyo. But in my case, I wasn't a student anymore, so I was probably a real pain in the ass. Of course, I don't mean to suggest that *you* were, because you weren't. . . .

When Matsumoto smiled, his dried-out-looking face filled

with wrinkles. His bluish yellow complexion, however, might've been due to the poor lighting or video quality.

—Anyway, I guess I need to stop jumping around and get to the point. A guy I'll call Jay lived two floors above me. He was a white guy in his mid-twenties, just a little younger than me. I'd see him all the time at this, uh, bar I used to hang out at. And then one day, he just comes up to me and starts talking. Well, before long, we became pretty good friends. He invited me to his place a few times, and I met his beautiful wife, who I'll call Kate. They didn't have any kids, so the three of us would go out to dinner or to the theater together. Yeah, thanks to my relationship with Jay, I made some fond memories that year. Well, at least for the second half of the year . . . So anyway, the pendant, that was something Jay always wore around his neck. One day, we were drinking at the bar, when he suddenly asks me if I heard of Okinawa. I told him all the stuff I remembered from TV, magazines, and yeah, my discussions with you. He seemed really interested for some reason. Then he asks if I've ever been there. So I told him about my two trips. Said you could still see American military walking around, what with all the US bases and all. . . . All of a sudden, Jay pulls the pendant out of his shirt and says, *This was made from a harpoon that a young Okinawan used against my grandfather during the war.* Then he takes it off and puts it in my hand. It was heavy and kind of crudely made. Come to think of it, the way the chain was attached was kind of crude, too. But hearing it was a memento from the war, well, that just made it seem all the more authentic. So as I was checking out the pendant, Jay explained that his grandfather fought in Okinawa as a Marine, and that he was twenty-two at the time. . . .

Matsumoto looked like he was on the verge of another coughing fit. He picked up the bottle of water on the table and took a few sips. Then he put it down and continued:

—According to Jay, his grandfather's unit took control of a peninsula in the north. After that, they were stationed in some village doing mop-up operations against the Japanese hiding in the mountains. So one day, Jay's grandfather and some of his buddies were swimming to a small island across from the village. And while they're swimming, this young guy from the island comes out of nowhere, and stabs him with his harpoon. It was only like a month after the start of the battle. You know, the Battle of Okinawa. Ironically, Jay's grandfather survived the war as a result. You see, he was hospitalized, and right after that, his unit was relocated. And wouldn't you know it? They suffered heavy casualties during the fighting. . . . Apparently, the guy who made the pendant was from the same unit. Just before leaving for the front, he visited Jay's grandfather in the field hospital. He was joking about it being a good luck charm, and said something like this: *Yeah, lots of guys make charms out of bullets or shrapnel, but you're gonna be the first with one made from a harpoon.* Sad to say, the guy who made it was killed in action. And after Jay's grandfather heard about his buddy's death, he wore the pendant all the time. . . .

I took a swig of beer and looked over at the clock. It was one in the morning, but I felt wide awake.

—The Okinawan who stabbed Jay's grandfather was caught hiding in a cave in the woods. After that, he was interrogated. Nobody knows what happened to him. And nobody knows why he stabbed Jay's grandfather. It couldn't have been a personal grudge, so he must've been one of those crazy kamikaze types. Too bad for Jay's grandfather, he ended up being the unlucky target. That's not my theory, though. It's what Jay heard from his father when he received the pendant. Apparently, Jay never heard anything from his grandfather directly. . . . As for Jay's father, he was given the pendant when he enlisted in the Marines. Unbelievably, he signed up right in the middle of the Vietnam War. I suppose Jay's grandfather thought the pendant saved him, so when his own son was about to head off to war, he gave it to him as a good luck charm. And that's when he talked about his experiences in Okinawa. Apparently, the one thing Jay's father never forgot, was how his father praised the man who stabbed him. Even said he was brave. Can you believe that? . . . Now, I doubt that pendant had magical powers or anything, but Jay's father made it home safely from Vietnam. And shortly after that, Jay was born. Many years later, Jay graduated from college and got a job in New York. Just before he headed off, his father gave him the pendant. By then, Jay's grandfather had been dead for many years. But like I said, Jay's father passed on all the stories, too. . . .

Matsumoto coughed several times, and then continued:

—Well, let me give you a little bit more detail about Jay's grandfather, okay? To begin with, he died when Jay was about seven. Apparently, the guy reeked of alcohol all the time. Really stunk. And all he ever did was sit around watching TV or locked up in his room. And here's the real shock: he died in a car accident, while he was still in his fifties. Supposedly, his car went off a cliff. Well, at least that was the official story. . . . Looking back, Jay suspected that it wasn't really an accident. So one time on a visit home, Jay brings it up with his father. Asks him if something happened in Okinawa. Well, Jay's father gets really annoyed and says something like, *There must've been things that could only be understood by those who fought in combat.* . . . Up until then, Jay's father had never spoken about his experiences in Vietnam. But about a month later, Jay gets a late night phone call. It's from his father, saying he wants to clear some things up. Yeah, about the pendant and his feelings and stuff. So anyway, he starts talking about how he was really torn and, uh . . . No, hold on. Let me try to dramatize it for you. . . .

With that comment, Matsumoto reached over, picked up the water, and took a swig. Then he cleared his throat and continued:

—Okay. So this is Jay's father talking: *You know, son, I was really torn about whether to give you that pendant. When a man's* cornered, he wants to cling to something. And in Vietnam, I clung to that pendant and prayed several times. But such peace is only temporary. Clinging to a pendant provides some relief, but getting out of trouble ultimately depends on two things: luck and your own strength. Well, son, I guess you already know all that. But, uh, the real reason I'm calling is this. I've thought about it, and I can't help thinking that my father's death was somehow connected to that pendant. Like you said, maybe something happened during the fighting in Okinawa. And maybe that's why he was always in a bad mood and always getting drunk. The only thing I ever heard about the war was about that pendant. So I don't want to speculate any more. When he gave it to me, he never said anything about passing it on to my own son. But I sensed that that's what he wanted. And that's why I gave it to you. But before I did, I wondered if I was doing the right thing. And I still have doubts. And then, when you asked about his death, those doubts grew even stronger. And that's why I called. You see, I feel bad about it now. I know I should've kept my doubts to myself and saved you all the unnecessary anxiety. However, I think it's best to return that harpoon head to where my father fought. So, listen, son. If you ever have children of your own, I don't want you to pass it on to them. I want you to go to Okinawa and throw that pendant into the ocean yourself. . . .

I paused the tape, grabbed another beer, and then pressed the play button again.

—So that was the phone call from Jay's father. As he was listening, Jay realized he felt the same way about what to do with the pendant. As he pointed out, there was just no way for them to find out about his grandfather's war experiences in Okinawa. But he knew that his grandfather must've really valued that good luck charm made from a young Okinawan's weapon. Otherwise, he wouldn't have held on to it all those years. Or passed it down to his grandchildren. Yeah, there must've been some really powerful emotions involved. Especially considering that he survived, while his buddies died. . . . But the fact that Jay agreed with his father didn't mean he made any specific plans to take care of it. I mean, he wore the pendant all the time, but he was pretty busy with work, so the idea of going to Okinawa just passed out of his mind. . . . What got him thinking again was that, uh, incident. You remember, don't you? About ten years ago, shortly after I met you, three US soldiers raped an elementary school girl in Okinawa. When you're living in New York, you don't hear too much about Okinawa, you know. But not surprisingly, Jay heard about the rape. He was shocked to learn that there are still huge US bases in Okinawa and over 20,000 troops stationed there. He said he couldn't believe the US military was still there after all this time. . . . After that, Jay was on a mission. He researched about Okinawa in the library, started questioning all his Japanese acquaintances, and, uh, yeah, I was one of them. Don't think we Japanese were too helpful, though. I mean, I couldn't even answer half his questions. I could tell he knew more than I did. Jay also mentioned that he wanted to go to Okinawa some day. Said he wanted to see where his grandfather fought with his own two eyes. And that if that young Okinawan who stabbed his grandfather was still alive, he wanted to meet him. . . .

Matsumoto cleared his throat several times, took some of his medicine, and faced the camera once more.

—Long story, wasn't it? Of course, I didn't hear it all at once. No, I pieced it together from the many discussions Jay and I had at the bar and his apartment. I told him that if he ever had the chance to come to Japan, to let me know before heading down to Okinawa. . . . However, Jay never got that chance. . . . Well, I'll tell you about that next time. Sorry, but I'm too tired for today. . . . Talk to you later.

The smile on Matsumoto's face was a strained one. He waved with his right hand, and the video broke off. He reappeared a moment later. Though sitting in the same place, he now wore a cream-colored polo shirt. Sunlight streamed through the window and fell across his face, making his complexion

look healthier. His expression and voice seemed more energetic, too.

—Well, I watched what I recorded up to this point. But you
know, it's not easy talking into a camera like this. Nothing like
talking face-to-face, which would've been much better. I mean,
I could've gotten your reactions and answered all your questions. Unfortunately, this was the only way. . . . So anyway, about
Jay. After I returned to Tokyo, we lost contact with each other.
Oh, I suppose we could've kept in touch, if we really wanted to.
Long-distance phone calls, mail, whatever. But I guess our relationship wasn't that close. I got busy with everyday life and rarely
thought of him. And just like that, five years passed by. Until one
day, I suddenly got a packet in the mail from Jay's wife, Kate. It
contained a letter and the pendant. Hold on a sec. I'll read you
my translation.

Matsumoto reached over to the side, picked up a notepad,
and started reading:

—*I'm writing to let you know that Jay was in one of the Twin
Towers that collapsed on September 11 four years ago. He was attending a business meeting with a company that had its office on one of
the higher floors. His remains were never found. You already know
about the enclosed pendant. Jay wanted to go to Okinawa some day
and throw it into the ocean near the island where his grandfather
fought in the war. He said that he told you all about it. He usually
wore it, but on that day, for some reason, he left it on the dresser at
home. I cheered myself up by thinking that he'd be coming back home
to pick it up, so I left it in the same spot all this time. But eventually,
I realized I couldn't just leave it on the dresser forever. He greatly
valued that pendant and always kept it close, so it's been an important keepsake for me, too. However, I think it would be best to make
Jay's wish come true. I spoke with Jay's parents and they agree. I'd
like to go to Okinawa myself and do as Jay wished, but I don't know
if that will ever be possible. So I'd like to ask you to do it for me. I
know it's rude to ask after being out of touch for so long, but you're*

the only person I know in Japan, so you're the only one I can turn to. Any time that's convenient for you is fine. If you ever have an opportunity to go to Okinawa, would you please fulfill Jay's wishes? I would greatly appreciate your help.

With the notepad still in his hands, Matsumoto continued:

—Well, that's my own translation, but I'm sure you get the gist. You remember those endlessly repeated images on TV, don't you? You know, the planes plunging into the towers, one after another, and the moment of each building's collapse. Yeah, I'm sure they're burned into your memory, too. Honestly, I can't say the thought never crossed my mind, but I never really imagined that Jay was in there. I mean, really in there. . . . So when I read this letter, I got really, really depressed. Up until then, all my memories of Jay had been fond ones. And I'm sure he felt the same way. Admittedly, we weren't close friends who shared all our darkest secrets or anything. But still, having someone you know in one of the towers, somehow changes how you see it. Of course, I'd always felt bad for the people that died, but a part of me kind of felt that the US had it coming. But when I heard about Jay, that feeling completely vanished. . . . To tell the truth, though, and I know I'm contradicting myself, Jay's death wasn't all that much of a shock to me. And I apologize to Jay and Kate for saying this. What depressed me was my bad health. I guess hearing about Jay's death made my own death really vivid. I couldn't help thinking, In a flash, you're gone. And then gradually you're forgotten. I know, I know. I'm thinking too much. . . . When was it? Oh, about a year and two months ago, I guess. They found a malignant tumor in my lungs. They operated right away, but the results weren't too good. You see, the cancer has spread through my entire body. Now I'm at home taking anti-cancer drugs. Yeah, I'm trying to stay positive. So anyway, about Jay and Kate. I'd like to fulfill their request myself, but I don't think I can get on a plane. Way too exhausting for me. You know I'd love to go on a nice trip to Okinawa, if it were possible. But it's not. And that's why I'm sending you this video, to ask you to do this favor for me. I've got a few other acquaintances in Oki-nawa, but none that I could ask. . . . I know I should've gotten your approval first. I also know that I'm not really giving you much of a choice. Still, I hope you'll accept. . . .

The video stopped and started again. As Matsumoto was sitting down, he put the notepad with his translation on the table.

—I should point out that, uh, when I first heard about the pendant, in that bar in New York, I immediately thought of you. And then when Jay mentioned a peninsula in the north, I remembered your hometown was up there. I also remembered that first story of yours. I mean, nobody from our generation still writes about the war. So I thought maybe you, only you, would understand how Jay feels. I know I'm being extremely pushy. But I really need you to take care of this for me. Take the pendant and throw it in the ocean. You know which island, don't you? One you can swim across to, from a peninsula on the mainland? I guess this final request of mine sounds like a threat. But, uh, it really will be my *final* request, so I hope I can count on you. . . .

At that point, Matsumoto tried to smile but fell into a coughing fit. When he recovered, he nodded and grinned as if he'd accomplished some formidable task. I thought he looked awfully old for his age. But then I felt guilty for thinking so. Matsumoto took another sip from his bottle and put it back on the table. Then he gave a self-deprecating smile and continued:

—I'd also like to ask that you not reply to this video. Not by mail, and not by phone. I know it's rude just sending you this video and Jay's memento, and telling you not to reply. But, uh, that's exactly what I'm asking. This is just too much for me to handle right now. No matter what you say, whether you accept or not, I'll get emotional. And emotion, whether it's happiness or disappointment, just really drains me. I guess I'm putting even more pressure on you, aren't I? But, really, I'd appreciate if you wouldn't reply. I'm sorry, but let me end here for today. . . .

The screen went dark for a second or two, and then Matsumoto reappeared. I stopped the video and got another can of beer from the refrigerator. After returning to the sofa, I picked up the pendant on the table and slowly looked it over. The point that had stabbed Jay's grandfather was so worn down, either from the passing of sixty years or from having been filed down, that it couldn't even pierce the skin. The barbs on the sides, however, were sharp enough to hurt when I pushed them against my finger. From Matsumoto's explanation, I didn't know where Jay's grandfather had been stabbed, but I remembered Matsumoto saying that he was swimming at the time. I pictured a young man hiding in the coral as he waited for the US soldiers.

The man in my imagination was waiting with his harpoon for hours. Suddenly, ripples appeared on the silvery surface, followed by the silhouette of a long-limbed American, crawling through the water. The man pushed off from the coral and sped toward the surface. Like a marlin, he sliced through the water with his harpoon. When he plunged it into the soldier's abdomen, plumes of blood spread out across the glittering surface.

My grandmother once told me that during the war, men and women, young and old alike, trained with bamboo spears. Using a harpoon must've seemed equally futile. And yet, that young man managed to wound one of their soldiers. His action probably didn't have any impact on the war. In fact, his act of defiance might've caused the islanders to suffer some sort of retaliation. Still, I couldn't help feeling deeply moved. With a single harpoon, a solitary islander had struck a blow against the US military. And the wounded American considered him courageous.

The video resumed on what appeared to be a different day. Matsumoto was wearing a dark blue T-shirt, and his face looked brighter. Having watched this far, I'd noticed that Matsumoto had been growing more lethargic as he continued. I'd assumed that would happen again. This time, however, Matsumoto spoke with strength and conviction. There was an urgency in his voice, as if he were saying something that must be said.

—Just one last thing. Jay's death was regrettable, but I can't completely dismiss what happened on 9/11. Sure, indiscriminate terrorism is wrong, and we shouldn't accept the chain of violence. But saying that won't get us anywhere. Those of us in Japan, who enjoy the peace we rely on America to provide, can say whatever we like. But, you know, our words have no meaning to people planning second or third 9/11's all round the world. I don't know, but if there's anyone in Japan who can understand the meaning of 9/11, wouldn't it be that guy who stabbed that American sixty years ago? I mean, if he's still alive. Because you know what? And I know it's just my own wild imagination. But as I was staring at the pendant and thinking about that guy, the shape of the harpoon point began to look like one of those planes that flew into the towers. Yeah, I know. I can hear you laughing at my deluded idea. But I'm telling you, for a split second, that's exactly what it looked like. So not just for Jay and Kate, or for Jay's father and grandfather, but also for that guy from the island. Throw that harpoon head into the ocean. Throw it right where Jay's grandfather and that man fought. I know my request sounds sentimental. And I don't want you to feel unpleasant. But please, please go to the island when it's convenient. I don't have the strength, and I don't have much time left. So I'm asking you, as my one final dying request. Sorry for ending like this, but I'm counting on you....

After a slight nod, Matsumoto stared straight at me from the other side of the screen. And just like that, the video ended. I rewound the tape and finished off my beer. I knew I'd fulfill Matsumoto's request, but I hadn't processed everything yet. I picked up the pendant on the table and draped the chain over my fingers, so that the harpoon head dangled before my eyes. If you viewed the barbs of the V-shaped head as the main wings, you could see a slight resemblance to a plane. Still, I had to admit Matsumoto's comparison was a strained one.

I put the pendant back in the envelope, took the video out of the player, and placed them both on the table. Then I glanced over at the calendar on the wall to consider when I'd be able to go to the island. It'd be June in another week. *At this time sixty years ago*, I muttered to myself, *Okinawa was a battlefield*. My heart stirred. A dark red stain spread out on the envelope. I pulled out the pendant, and a smell of blood wafted up from the shiny, black harpoon tip. I thought I heard the sound of waves in the distance, so I glanced around the room. The furniture and various items under the fluorescent lights were still lifeless objects in their regular places. The harpoon tip smelled and looked like an organ plucked from the body of a living organism. For the first time in a long while, I wanted to return to my hometown. But the ache that filled my heart puzzled me. The sound of waves drew nearer. This time, I was sure that's what I heard.

JAY'S GRANDFATHER (1945)

The red lump floating in the darkness wriggled and divided into cells again. It was the fruit of some kind of palm tree that grows along the beaches of this island. Instead of straight trunks, however, these trees have twisted ones that crawl along the ground with their skinny, thorny leaves. A girl lying on her back in the sand was staring up at the red fruit. Her lower body was sticky and disgusting. Wafting up from her was the stink of crushed plants and bodily fluids, including sweat and blood.

—Shut up and stop crying! one of my buddies yelled from behind.

But the terrified girl's crying only intensified.

The red fruit looked like a huge snake eye glowing in the dark. The first time I saw one was just after we'd landed on the main island. Jumping off the landing craft, I had lost my footing in the surf. As I stumbled forward, I held my gun over my head so it wouldn't get wet. Choking on seawater, I regained my balance and rushed to shore. If I didn't keep moving, I'd get a bullet in the head. Screaming, *Run! Son of a bitch! Run!* I dashed up the sandy beach to a thicket, where those fruit were lying in wait. Just like now, the repulsive objects looked like the eyes of snakes ready to strike.

The girl's face was battered and swollen; her lips, mangled and oozing blood. Her vacant eyes avoided mine and stared blankly at the red fruit dangling behind my head—as if I didn't even exist. I grabbed her jaw, turned her face toward mine, and screamed:

—Look at me, goddamn it!

As I violently moved my hips, a chunk of the fruit separated along the grenade-like notches and came flying toward me. I felt a spear rip into my body, and then saw blood gushing from my side. As I frantically pressed down to stop the bleeding, I woke up. The intense pain in my side, however, wasn't a dream.

I was so drenched in sweat that even my cot was wet. Two other rows of beds were visible by the moonlight coming through the window. Some of the wounded were awake, due to the heat or their own private pain, and I could hear them moaning and cursing. I looked at my watch. It was ten o'clock in the evening. I was tired of the long waits until morning. Sleeping during the day meant you paid for it at night, alone with the agony of your wounds and the torment of your memories.

I hated the medic on night duty. When I was in pain and asked for sleeping pills, he condescendingly said that priority went to those wounded in actual combat. Normally, I would've floored the bastard, but even sitting up was an excruciating ordeal, so I couldn't even complain. A gecko was on a crossbeam of the ceiling, directly above me. I was worried he might fall. We were in a school building, which had been requisitioned for use as a hospital. My bed was near the hallway in a classroom filled with wounded GIs. The gecko mocked us with its cries. I reached down and touched the bandages on my side. The wound was warmer than I'd expected. *Fuckin' Jap!* I muttered to myself, triggering a memory of a conversation between a couple of fellows in my outfit:

—Originally, this wasn't part of Japan, said McCrory. So the natives weren't Japanese.

—So what were they? asked Kinser. Chinese?

—No, replied McCrory, it was an independent country called Ryukyu.

Kinser gave a slight nod, but he didn't show any further interest. I wasn't interested either.

After lying in bed for several days, I started recalling conversations and various incidents that had occurred on the island.

The island across the gulf was clearly visible under the afternoon sun. We'd finished unloading supplies from the cargo boats and were resting in the shade of a pile of crates next to the warehouse. Until three in the afternoon, we'd been conducting mop-up operations in search of Japanese soldiers hiding in the mountains, but we hadn't found any of them. After we came down from the mountains and were about to get some rest, we were sent to help unload supplies at the port. It wasn't a lot of work, but my three buddies and I were annoyed about being ordered to do extra chores. When we finished, we moved away from the others and sat chatting on the pier, while looking out at the sea.

—How about racing to that island and back? suggested Kinser.

Everybody agreed immediately, partly because we were feeling a bit rebellious. Even though we'd brought the island under US control, we knew it'd be dangerous to swim across without weapons. But at that point, we didn't care if we ended up being reprimanded. We threw off our sweaty fatigues and kicked off our boots. Then we dashed across the pier and dove into the ocean.

It was about three hundred yards to the island. Though calm, the current was moving out to sea, but not so fast as to make it difficult to swim. Besides, we weren't all that serious about racing; we'd just wanted an excuse to get in the water. Henry took the lead. He was a quiet fellow whom I could never read. Even after joining the same outfit, we'd never had a heart-to-heart talk. Until now, I never knew he was such a good swimmer.

The island had coral reefs along the coast on the opposite

side, but nothing blocked our approach from the gulf. Though we hadn't decided on any particular destination, the four of us naturally swam toward the beach. When I caught up with the last swimmer, I checked my position. There were only about a hundred yards left, so I started swimming all out. I passed McCrory and Kinser right away, but Henry was in a comfortable lead and reached the shallows about twenty yards ahead of me. As he was walking toward the beach, I saw a girl splashing through the water ahead of him. She looked about ten years old.

From the opposite shore, we had already noticed the girls wading in the ocean. Henry wasn't chasing the girl, but she looked scared as she ran to her friends on the beach. Three girls of about the same age as the first had gathered around an older girl of about fifteen. All of them looked terrified. We were the enemy, so that was only natural, I guess, but getting such a reaction irritated the hell out of me.

The girl running away steadied the bamboo basket at her waist and yelled to her friends. Henry strode past her and grabbed the older girl's clothes. The girl tried to get away while protecting her young companions. But then Henry wrapped his arms around her and covered her mouth with his hand. As I stood there in shock, Kinser raced past me, flung the younger girls to the sand, and grabbed the older girl's legs. Then he and Henry lifted her up and carried her off to the trees at the back of the beach.

—Don't do anything stupid! I yelled.

But my voice was drowned out by Kinser's squeals of delight and the girl's screams of horror.

I pushed off the girls pulling at me and dashed up the beach. In the thicket, Henry was holding the girl down. Meanwhile, Kinser was pulling down his trunks. The girl screamed and Kinser punched her in the face. Her head pitched back violently, and she fell silent for a moment. But when Kinser forced her legs apart, she screamed again. He started punching her in the face, but even then she continued to kick and scream. Infuriated, he punched her in the stomach and then wrapped his fingers around her throat.

—You make any more fuckin' noise, I'll fuckin' kill you! he screamed.

It looked like he'd crush her throat, so I knew I should stop him. But I couldn't do or say a thing. When Kinser loosened his grip, the girl, gasping for breath, tried to twist away. Kinser punched her in the stomach again, and she became motionless. After ripping off her top, he leaned over her small body.

—Son of a bitch! spit out McCrory, who was now standing nearby.

Repulsed by what Kinser was doing with his fingers, I turned around. The younger girls, huddled together on the beach, were crying and looking in our direction. Instinctively, I started to head toward them, but McCrory grabbed my arm.

—Don't try to run away! he said.

His words annoyed me. But I knew that if I left, they'd say all kinds of stuff to me later. Or rather, they'd *do* all kinds of stuff to me later. Panting heavily, Kinser stood up, and Henry took his place. He finished in less than a minute. When we got the signal, McCrory headed over immediately. Kinser held down the girl's hands, and Henry, who was pulling up his trunks while kneeling in the sand, flashed McCrory a smile. The girl's power to resist was gone.

Without the slightest hesitation, McCrory climbed on top of the girl, about half his size. As I watched, I realized I'd have to do the same thing. But I couldn't overcome my reluctance. It wasn't out of pity for the girl. I was scared that if I did what the others had done, something inside me would be destroyed, and I'd never be the same. As McCrory moved his body, Kinser and Henry kept glancing over at me and grinning. *Are you one of us or not?* they seemed to be asking. I knew I had to do it, but I wasn't sure I could.

McCrory took a deep breath and got up. Then he looked over at me and nodded. Mechanically, I stepped forward, pulled down my trunks, and spread the girl's legs, which had fallen to the side, the knees pressed together. I knew I shouldn't look, but my eyes moved down anyway. Blood and a milky liquid soiled the inside of her thighs, and a clammy odor rose from between her legs. I didn't feel any desire at all. When I pressed my unresponsive body against hers, the heat of her body and the chill of the slippery fluids repulsed me. Fighting to overcome my own reluctance, I pretended to have sex.

—We loosened her up for you! yelled Kinser. So put your big thing in her!

Then he and Henry started laughing hysterically. Maybe they'd seen through me, but I felt sure I'd be accepted for having come this far.

With my elbows planted in the sand, I kept moving until I figured I'd performed enough. When I started to get up, my eyes met the half-open eyes beneath me. Well, not exactly met. The girl was avoiding my gaze and staring at something behind me. I turned around, and there was that bright red fruit. Never in my life had I seen such a malicious-looking color. The finely divided chunks looked like clumps of blood. At that moment, something split open inside me. Once the thin membrane had ruptured, primal feelings erupted from deep inside and oozed through my body like a runny egg yolk. The girl's lips, distorted and covered with half-dried blood, were mocking me. Impulsively, I punched the swollen face with my fist. Someone whistled, but I didn't know who. *Son of a bitch!* I cursed to myself. Blood suddenly rushed to my penis. Oblivious to the gore and bodily fluids, I forced myself into the body beneath me. As I covered the girl's mouth and saw tears falling from the corners of her eyes, I moved my hips furiously, before I could figure out the source of my growing excitement: rage toward my buddies and the girl, self-loathing, or both.

—Check it out! jeered Kinser. He's finally getting into it!
The others laughed.

Fantasizing about shooting all three of them, I ejaculated.

Catching my breath, I brushed off the sand sticking to my sweat-drenched body and stood up, trying to act composed. The girl's legs remained spread open; she had lost the strength to close them. At the sight of the milky-white fluid dribbling from between her legs, a bitter liquid rose up into my throat. My hands dropped to my knees, and I started vomiting, only to be showered with laughter.

—You all right? asked McCrory, putting a hand on my shoulder.

I pushed his hand away and started walking toward the ocean. The girls huddled on the beach watched me spit numerous times. With my eyes averted, I had just reached the shoreline when I heard McCrory shouting:

—That's enough!

I turned around and saw him holding Henry, who was trying to go after the younger girls. The waves engulfed my ankles and washed away the sand burning my feet. The sunlight reflecting off the surface was so bright I couldn't see straight ahead. I dove into the ocean and let the water wash over my body. Pushing against the resistance of the waves, I began swimming toward the opposite bank.

I continued to sweat profusely, and my clammy back felt disgusting. I needed to wash my body in a mountain stream. The ocean water near the island never cooled, even at night. That's why I wanted to swim in the cool river in the woods near my hometown, back in the States. My entire midsection felt like it was on fire, especially near the wound on my right side. The red fruit lodged in my abdomen was scorching my insides like a hot iron.

—An inch to the side, the army surgeon had said, and you'd have gotten it in the liver.

He explained that the harpoon had penetrated to my bowels, and that the barbs got caught on my intestines when it was pulled out, causing some lacerations. Then he added:

—It's not too serious.

I sensed the hidden scorn in his voice. No, it wasn't even hidden; his sarcastic comment made his feelings obvious. The surgeons and medics looked down on me because not only hadn't I been wounded in combat, but I had been stabbed by a civilian while swimming unarmed.

Apart from getting angry and clenching my fist, there was nothing I could do. The gecko on the beam over my bed started to cry. Then another joined in. Even the geckos sounded like they were mocking me. Kinser said they were creepy and killed as many as he could. When McCrory told him to stop, he laughed.

—What's the big deal? We're killing bigger ones every day.

His forced laughter was just to make himself look big.

When we were driving to the village, he was laughing like that the entire time. He laughed when the men under that big tree recoiled in fear after we turned our guns on them. He laughed when we kicked that shoddy house's door down. He laughed when we dragged that woman out. And he laughed when he caught one of the men off guard and punched him in the stomach.

—They ring that bell every time we come! It's a welcome bell!

As we rattled along in the jeep, Kinser kept laughing. The driver was one of his buddy's from another platoon. Shouting over the engine noise, they took turns heaping abuse on everyone in the village:

—The men are as submissive as dogs!

—Yeah, and did you catch the look on that guy's face when we had his woman?

—The kids are like flies pestering us for gum and chocolate!

—That last bitch was too old.

—Well, find a younger one next time!

Now, they were probably joking about me. *Yeah, one of those submissive dogs did him in!* I could hear them talking behind my back, the bastards. What the hell did they know about friendship? I recalled the shabby-looking villagers watching us from under that tree. The guy who stabbed me must've been among them. *We should've shot every fuckin' last one of them when we had the chance!* Clenching my fist made my side hurt even more. Sweat slid down my scalp and down behind my ears. Outside were several of those trees with roots hanging down from the branches. I could hear the hooting of the owls coming from their direction. For a moment, the sound made me forget that we were in a war zone.

In less than two weeks, the Japanese army in the mountainous central area of the peninsula had abandoned their positions and fled. Though we still had to deal with small arms fire and occasional night raids, they were incapable of mounting any organized resistance. Their main army had retreated to the south, and it was our job to flush out the Japs hiding in the mountains. The village was already under our control, so we didn't take the disheartened men of the village too seriously. They were scared and cautious at first, but after we gave them food and medical treatment, they made a complete about-face and became cooperative. There was no denying that their new attitude had put us off our guard. I now regretted my carelessness.

✧ ✧ ✧

—Let's go, said Kinser.

The four of us walked over to the pier. We hadn't had any sorties into the mountains that day; we'd spent the morning cleaning our weapons and equipment, and we were free for the afternoon. After stripping down to our trunks, we dove into the ocean from the shade of some freight. Due to the sunlight streaming through the water, the ocean was a beautiful color. The water caressed our skin, even as our backs got scorched. This time, no one was interested in racing or betting, so we swam at a leisurely pace toward the island.

This ocean's the only thing of value here, I was thinking, as I took up the rear. Henry, who was in the lead, was signaling for us to look to the right. Someone was swimming toward us. Appearing out of nowhere, a young villager was about fifty yards away. I tensed up, thinking he might be an enemy soldier. But then he smiled, waved with both hands, and headed back toward the pier.

—Was that a fisherman? McCrory asked.

No one answered. But since the man was alone and appeared to be unarmed, we nonchalantly kept swimming toward the island.

Two or three minutes passed. Suddenly, something thrust up from beneath me. Before I could realize what was happening, the water around me was turning dark red. My hand instinctively pressed down on my side, and when I noticed blood gushing out, I fell into a panic. Kinser immediately swam over to support me. Meanwhile, McCrory and Henry swam after the attacker, who then hurled a harpoon at them. A black string shot up out of the water, and the spray sparkled in the sunlight. McCrory dodged to the side, but the harpoon caught him in the shoulder. The attacker dove into the water and disappeared. With Kinser at my side, I floated on my back while pressing down on the wound with one hand. McCrory swam back and supported me from the other side. Ignoring the blood flowing from his own shoulder, he encouraged me instead. Following McCrory's instructions, Henry started swimming to the pier to get help. Even though I was now pressing down with both hands, the blood still oozed between my fingers. Encouraged by my two supporters,

I somehow managed to stay calm, but I was terrified that I'd die right there in the ocean. I gritted my teeth, but I couldn't stop shivering. Though my face and chest burned from the sunlight, I felt as if I were freezing to death.

Later, I heard that the soldiers at the warehouse had sprung into action before Henry even reached them. Noticing something was wrong, they immediately sent out a boat. I remember being lifted aboard, but when they pulled my hands away to apply a cloth, I lost consciousness. When I came to, I was lying in a cot. McCrory, Kinser, and Henry took turns visiting and filling me in on the situation. They told me that the guy who'd attacked us had been captured in a cave in the woods and was now being questioned. Since he was being treated for gunshot wounds sustained during his capture, the interrogation wasn't making much progress, but apparently he had no ties to the Japanese army and had acted on his own.

—We should've shot him on the spot! snarled the usually taciturn Henry.

His unexpected comment pleased me. When I was lifted out of the boat and set on the pier, I had been as pale as a sheet and bleeding profusely. For my operation, Kinser and McCrory, who had the same blood type as me, both volunteered for blood transfusions. I could never thank the three of them enough. We were from completely different parts of the country, so if we hadn't ended up in the same outfit, we never would've known each other. I wanted to fight with them until the end, so I was bitterly disappointed to learn that I'd be the only one left behind.

❖ ❖ ❖

The gecko cried out in the darkness. I couldn't see him, and being in a silent sickroom late at night, the cry startled me. *How much longer did I have to stay here?* When I asked the doctor, he wouldn't give me a definite answer. But from my condition,

I knew I wouldn't be joining the battle in the south. My progress was unsatisfactory, and the doctor implied that I should be transferred to a proper hospital. That didn't please me in the least.

Last night, Kinser and Henry paid me a visit.

—We're being transferred tomorrow, said Kinser with a laugh.

He firmly gripped the hand I held out to him. He explained that our unit would be joining the rest of the army, which was closing in on the Japanese, fleeing to the south. Then he asked:

—So how's the wound?

I explained that it was a bit infected, but that it didn't hurt.

—You were unconscious when we got you out of the boat, you know. So we didn't think you'd make it. With a wound like that, you've made an impressive recovery, I'd say.

Unsure whether he was being sincere or sarcastic, I smiled. Suddenly, a sharp pain shot through me, and I grimaced.

—You okay? asked Kinser, leaning in close.

—Naw, I'm just acting, I answered, forcing a smile.

Kinser nodded and smiled back.

—Listen, Okinawa's gonna fall. And the war's gonna be over soon. Sure, you might be heading home early, but we'll be joining you in no time.

I couldn't say anything to that. Perhaps guessing that I was depressed, Kinser bawled out in a loud voice:

—Don't you worry! We'll kill every fuckin' Jap, and fry those damn rats hiding in their ratholes!

Then he pretended like he was spraying the area with a flamethrower.

As they started moving off, Henry, who'd been silent up until then, said:

—See you later.

—Yeah, see you back in the States, I answered, getting choked up.

The two appeared blurry as they left the room. When they were gone, I felt annoyed at myself for not being able to join them—all because of a stupid wound. I glared at the ceiling and cursed myself. *When that guy disappeared, why didn't I notice him coming after me? And why weren't we more cautious when we first spotted him?* I knew it was too late to do anything, but I felt thoroughly disgusted at my carelessness.

Heated up with anger, my wound throbbed with pain. I stared down at my body, which I couldn't even lift out of bed, and my anger turned to self-loathing. I was being sent home as a wounded GI. How pathetic! My family and hometown would praise me for my wound of honor and distinction. The thought depressed me. Not that I wanted everyone to know the truth. *I was stabbed swimming across a stretch of water to get women on an island. On top of that, the guy who stabbed me wasn't a soldier, but a young civilian.* If all that was made known, I wouldn't be able to show my face again. My family would be deeply shocked and disappointed.

Stuck in my cot, I could only escape these thoughts through sleep. As I endured the heat and pain, I waited for sleep to crawl across me like a snail and then wrap me in its protective shell.

Suddenly, pale light was streaming through the window, so I must've escaped into sleep. Memories of the island returned whether I was dreaming or awake, so I often felt disoriented upon awakening. This time, however, the fresh light and early morning chill offered the promise of a new day.

But then it dawned on me that the fellows were probably preparing for their departure. My feelings of shame and anger returned. I didn't want to lose that rare early-morning sense of invigoration, but I instantly became depressed. I didn't want to be sent home like this. I'm sure some guys in my outfit were calling me a coward behind my back. And I wasn't sure what Henry and Kinser were saying either. I pictured them laughing and joking with their friends. *He couldn't even get it up at first!* one would say. *At first?* the other would reply. *I bet he was faking all the way to the end!* The blood rushed to my head, and my face burned. But then I loathed myself for suspecting them, and the blood subsided. I remembered the look on McCrory's face when he warned me on the beach. *Don't try to run away!* he had said. Yet wasn't that precisely what I was doing by not going with them? My mind was starting to go in circles again. Unable to stop the unpleasant thoughts, I closed my eyes and took some deep breaths. Just then, I heard a consoling voice:

—So how are you feeling?

McCrory, in combat fatigues and with his helmet under his arm, was standing next to my bed. He had a gentle smile on his face.

—Sorry, I answered.

My reply puzzled him at first, but then the meaning sunk in.

—Oh, you were just unlucky.

If someone else had said that, I might've objected, but with McCrory, I just nodded meekly.

—I was busy yesterday, he said, so I couldn't come with the fellows. Still, I wanted to see you before we shoved off.

—Thanks, I said.

He smiled in embarrassment, and for a moment, we stared at each other in silence.

—Uh, I made this, he said.

From his breast pocket, he pulled out a black lump attached to a chain. Then he dangled before my eyes a pendant made from a harpoon tip.

—That's not what I think it is, is it? I asked.

McCrory nodded and said:

—My dad told me soldiers should keep any bullet or shrapnel that hits them. 'Cause they make great charms. When I fought in Saipan, several fellows made pendants out of bullets.

But needless to say, nobody made one from a harpoon. Sorry for the poor job, but I hope you like it.

McCrory handed me the pendant. He had filled the hollow part of the tip with lead and passed a chain through a tiny iron loop attached at the top. The lead made it heavier than it looked.

—How'd you get this? I asked.

—When the guy attacked, McCrory proudly explained, the harpoon was attached to his ankle with a string, and he still had it with him when he was in that cave. It was confiscated as evidence, but, uh . . . well, let's just keep that a secret. Actually, that's why I couldn't come yesterday. I was taking care of this.

McCrory flashed a mischievous grin and glanced at his watch. Then he became serious and said:

—Well, I better be shoving off.

We shook hands and promised to meet again.

After McCrory left, I stared at the handmade pendant. As I listened to the medics and wounded stirring in the sunlit room, I suppressed the sentimental feelings welling up in me. I squeezed the pendant in my hand, and the tip and barbs cut into my flesh. To punish myself, I squeezed harder, closed my eyes, and embraced the pain.

I don't know how long I tormented myself, but suddenly the room was quiet. When I opened my eyes again, the room was dark, and the light filtering in through the window had changed to pale moonlight. Had a full day passed already? I thought I'd just said goodbye to McCrory, but maybe it was all a dream. But it couldn't have been; I could feel the pendant in the palm of my hand. I was going to lift my hand to check, but I couldn't move. Thinking I was paralyzed, I took a deep breath to release the tension.

Just then, I noticed the red fruit hanging from the beam over my bed. A cold sweat broke out over my whole body, and I tensed up even more. The fruit was quivering and squirming. Peering through the darkness, I noticed it was covered with large red hornets. I tried to call for help, but I couldn't speak. When I tried to twist away, a sharp pain shot through my side, and my body went stiff. The more frantically I tried to speak, the more difficult it became to breathe. The large hornets, about half the size of my little finger, were jostling against one another. Suddenly, one dropped off and came flying straight toward me. A scream froze in my throat, followed by the sensation of a pebble striking me in the chest. Something slimy spread out over my skin. Then I realized that the hair on my chest was covered in gore. The fruit had transformed into a gooey clump of blood, and large drops were dripping down onto me. Flowing down my neck, along my sides, and over my belly, the blood slithered over me like a red snake pinning me to the bed.

At the foot of my bed, a girl with long hair was staring at me. I immediately knew it was her. Her eyes turned to the ceiling. The clump of blood glistened garishly in the darkness—and then fell. The blow to my chest knocked the breath out of me. As blood splattered across my face, I blinked and looked down. The clump was now twisting and turning. A newborn baby, covered in blood and still attached to an umbilical cord, moved its gaping mouth and tiny arms and legs. The heaviness and slime made me think I was going crazy. The girl reached out and pulled the baby to her chest. Then she stared at me with a vacant look. A deep sadness was frozen in the depths of her eyes. *This is her baby*, I thought. Then the baby shook its head and looked at me. At that moment, I knew everything that was going to happen. The tip of the harpoon in my hand cut deep into my flesh, and the blood dribbled down my arm. The baby began crying feebly. The girl pressed her palm to the baby's wet forehead and whispered something. After a while, the girl and the baby disappeared, but the whispers and feeble cries never left me.

BULLIED GIRL (2005)

I headed to the lunch pickup area, instead of my classroom. I had just left the auditorium, after listening to a speech about the Battle of Okinawa. The prefecture's June 23 Memorial Day was approaching, so our homeroom teacher had invited a college friend's seventy-year-old mother to talk to a couple of classes about her war experiences. Mina had told me to sit up front and pretend to listen, so that's what I did. Sitting right in front of the podium, I kept my eyes on the lady for the entire speech. I didn't have to pretend, though, because she was pretty interesting. I considered myself lucky to be able to sit up front, but I was so stressed out about what was going on behind me that I had a hard time concentrating. My classmates, apart from Mina and her group, would think I was putting on a show for our teacher again. Or Mina might spread such a rumor on purpose. That made me think something bad was in store for me later. I got so nervous I had trouble breathing. Trying not to hyperventilate, I concentrated on the speech for the entire forty minutes.

The chime rang shortly after she'd finished. As planned, our class representative expressed some words of thanks, which were read from prepared notes. I could sense the impatience of everyone behind me. Thinking that their frustration might be taken out on me later, I broke out in a cold sweat. I prayed that our teacher would be accommodating and wrap things up quickly. The lady received a small bouquet and said a few word of thanks. Then the other class representative gave the signal for all the students to bow. A moment later, I could hear the boys in the back pushing open the doors and rushing out of the room. The lady looked surprised but returned to her chair and sat down. As she waited for everyone to leave, she stared at the floor. I overheard our teacher thanking her for giving a moving and instructive speech. I sat with my head down and listened to my teacher and the noisy students. When I figured most of the students were gone, I lined up behind the stragglers at the exit.

The auditorium was on the second floor. I went downstairs, walked along the covered walkway past the faculty room, and headed to the pickup area near the school's rear entrance. Not many students had arrived yet. I opened the screen door and entered. Cases of bread, containers of food, crates of dishes and eating utensils, and other items had been divided up for each classroom. I lifted up several cases of milk cartons with both hands.

—You can carry those by yourself? asked the supervisor, wearing the usual food industry surgical mask.

I nodded and left. As I headed back along the walkway, I passed other students who were coming to pick up food and utensils for their classes. Suddenly, someone called from behind, and I turned around. It was the lady who had given the speech.

—Thanks for listening so attentively, she said with a smile.

—Uh, sure, I answered, looking down.

—That was my first time speaking in front of people, so I was pretty nervous. But having you listening at the front was a huge help.

I knew I should say something, but I couldn't think of anything and hung my head.

—My stories about the war must've been confusing. I'm sorry I was such a poor speaker.

From the movement of shadow, I could tell she was bowing in apology. *That's not true! You were easy to understand*, I muttered to myself, but I couldn't manage to speak up. My silence must've made her uncomfortable.

—Oh, you're on lunch duty, she said. Sorry to interrupt.

Then she started to move away.

Just as I was getting up the courage to lift my head, I heard footsteps dashing past me. Then I heard the three other lunch-duty girls calling out:

—Thank you for your speech!

—I'm so glad we had the chance to hear you!

—That was the most moving story about the war I've ever heard!

They had spoken in rapid succession, and I could tell the lady was at a loss. *You'd better get your ass moving!* said Mina's voice in my head, so I stared at the ground and headed back to the classroom. I could feel the lady's gaze on my back, but her good intentions were blocked by the three cheery voices, and left to shrivel on the school's grounds under the hot sun.

—You had such a painful experience!

—We all need to fight for peace!

—People are still suffering from the war, aren't they?!

They don't really feel that way, I thought. But then I hated myself for my pettiness and tried to make my mind blank. I climbed the stairs to my classroom on the second floor. The desks had been pushed together into groups of six. The students were talking in their seats or making noise at the back of the room or in the hallway. Beside the podium, the teacher was talking with the student council vice president and the broadcasting club member who usually read the announcements over the school's public-address system When the teacher saw me, she asked:

—You're not doing that all by yourself, are you?

—No, I answered, the others are picking up stuff, too.

I put on one of the aprons and started distributing the milk cartons. I was afraid the boys would start making sarcastic comments. As I placed their milk in front of them, I could hear them thinking, *I don't wanna drink anything from you.* But since the teacher was there, they just scowled. When I put down the milk for the volleyball team girls, Mina pushed her carton away with her index finger. She was the star attacker and one of the most popular girls in the school. The other two girls did the same thing, and then glared at me and laughed. To avoid their stares, I moved on to the next group. Some had their heads on their desks and others were chatting. Luckily, all of them ignored me.

Just as I finished passing out the milk, the other three girls and two boys on lunch duty entered with the food and dishes. The teacher said to call in the students goofing off in the hallway and to have everyone sit down. Then she went around warning students that wouldn't listen. Meanwhile, the lunch preparations continued. One girl ladled cream stew into small bowls, which I then distributed. I thought I was more likely to get comments about the stew, but the volleyball team girls just pushed their containers away like before, and everyone else ignored me. However, that meant something much worse was going to happen later, so I started to get fidgety. Once our jobs were finished, I took my seat and tried to hide my anxiety.

All through lunch, the other five members of my group chatted, boys and girls separately. But no one spoke to me. This started from the beginning of the school year, so it didn't bother me anymore. Actually, I was more nervous about someone throwing me off with a comment. The assistant homeroom teacher arrived and apologized to our teacher for being late. Then she carried two chairs to the groups at the front and sat in one of them. When our teacher told her about the speech, the assistant said she regretted not being able to attend because of other work. The girl sitting next to me mentioned that some of the girls had spoken with the lady on the way to the lunch center.

—What did you say to her? the teacher asked. Did you give your opinions about the speech?

The other two girls sitting in my group joined in, and the three took turns recreating the conversation. Everyone else became quiet, and our teacher listened with a big smile. I was so nervous about my name being mentioned that I couldn't even taste the cream stew, which I normally enjoyed.

Once the explanations were finished, and everyone started

talking again, I could relax and think about the lady and her speech. I regretted that I hadn't been able to give her a proper reply. The speech wasn't enjoyable so much as painful, but it left a strong impression on me. She talked about how during the US naval bombings and air raids, she ran away and hid in a cave; how whenever a bomb exploded, the ground shook and the sound echoed around them; how terrified she was of being blown into pieces or buried alive under falling stones; how twelve people from two families in another cave were buried alive after a direct hit, with only a six-year-old boy surviving; how the boy had crawled into a space created by a blown-up pine tree, and was able to breathe thanks to air seeping in through a crevice; how the villagers frantically dug up the cave, and the women cried when they found all the bodies; and how one of the dead bodies was her classmate, but that after the dirt had been wiped from her face, she only looked like she was sleeping. At that point in her speech, the lady paused and looked out at us.

—I was ten at the time. That'd be four years younger than you, right?

When her eyes met mine, I couldn't help looking down. I thought she might be checking to see if any of us resembled the girl who had died. Her story about people being buried alive was vivid, so everyone listened quietly, but during the other parts, there was an awful lot of talking. I couldn't turn around to check, but I could hear the two teachers going around, warning students to keep their voices down. I had to admit the lady wasn't a very good speaker. Sure, she was doing her best, but she was difficult to hear and sometimes stumbled over her words. And there were a lot of long pauses. She also talked about her childhood memories, such as going to the ocean to pick up shellfish and being terrified when she saw an American for the first time. During those parts, I couldn't really picture what she was describing. And she seemed to sense the poor reaction. As her speech continued, her smile gradually faded, and she started to look confused. Making matters worse, her voice grew fainter and fainter. It was painful to watch, and I wanted to look away. But Mina and her friends had ordered me to pretend to listen, so I couldn't.

After about thirty minutes, the lady stopped and stared out at us again.

—I'm really sorry, she said. I'm not a very good speaker, and I can tell that I'm boring you. . . .

She looked sincerely sorry.

—At least you know it! jeered a boy in the back.

A few seconds later, I heard the other class's teacher scolding him. Next, I heard several girls and boys giggling, and then a boy yelling at them to shut up and listen. After that, the laughter grew even louder. The lady stared at all this in silence. After nearly a minute, her expression grew stern. Finally, as one might expect, everyone quieted down. Then the lady continued:

—I was, uh, wondering, whether I should tell you about this . . . but since I doubt I'll have another chance to talk to you, I think I will. So, uh, please listen just a little bit longer. . . .

She gave a little smile, and her cheeks and lips stiffened. I could tell she was bracing herself.

—Hey! How long are you gonna eat! said one of the boys in my group. Start cleaning up!

When I raised my head, I saw that lunch was over. Everyone looked over at me, staring into space with my spoon in my hand. Half the class erupted in laughter.

—I'm sorry, I said, rushing to start cleaning up.

In my haste, I knocked over my bowl of stew, which was still half full.

—Eww! How disgusting!

—What a klutz!

—Hurry and wipe it up!

—You make me sick!

The comments were like slaps across the face. I ran out to the hall and grabbed one of the cleaning rags near the window.

Then I hurried back to the classroom and wiped the desk. As I was rinsing out the rag in the sink, I saw the other lunch-duty girls heading off with the used food containers and milk cases. I quickly wrung out the rag and hung it up to dry. Then I grabbed a crate of dirty dishes and hurried to catch up. On the way, I ran into them on their way back to the classroom. As I was passing them with my head down, one of them stuck out her foot and tried to trip me. I stumbled but didn't fall.

—So close!

—You almost got her!

The other two girls laughed. As the first girl was pulling her foot back, she scowled and said:

—Why didn't you fall?

—I'm sorry, I said, bowing in apology.

At that moment, our PE teacher happened to be passing by. When the girls saw him, they quickly wished me good luck and scurried off to the classroom. I didn't want to give the teacher a chance to question me, so I dashed off to the lunch center. After I dropped off the crate of dishes, I hurried back to the classroom to help with the noon cleaning.

—Sorry to be late, I said, entering the classroom.

I grabbed one of the brooms hanging on the back wall and began sweeping the floor. When I finished, I waited until the boys finished mopping the floor and then started returning the desks that had been pushed to the back. One group was in charge of the classroom; another was in charge of the hallway. Everyone worked very hard, even though they were talking at the same time. They figured that the sooner they finished, the more time they'd have for play. Personally, I wanted the cleaning to continue for a long time, but that wasn't meant to be. When I finished pushing all the desks back to their proper places, the nicest girl in the class picked up the trash bags and said:

—I'll throw these away, so you wipe the desks.

I nodded and said thanks. Then I picked up a cleaning rag

and got to work. Just as I finished wiping down about half the desks, Mina came over and started scolding me:

—You're wiping the desks with that rag? Isn't that the one you just used for the stew? That's disgusting! Are you doing that on purpose?

At first, I didn't know how to answer. Several girls rushed over, and one of them asked:

—What? What happened?

Mina answered in an exaggerated tone of voice:

—She used the same rag she used to wipe the stew to wipe our desks! And she did it on purpose!

—What the hell do you think you're doing?!

—You're harassing us, aren't you?!

—The smell's gonna get on the desks!

—Why don't you wipe your face instead?!

Battered with comments, I bowed my head and stood immobile. Suddenly, the rag was snatched from my hand and pressed against my face.

—Stop it! said Mina. The rag'll get dirty!

Everyone laughed. Another rag came flying and hit me in the side of my face. Then someone poked me in the back of the head and demanded an apology.

—I'm sorry, I whispered immediately. That was careless of me.

—We can't hear you! someone scolded.

I tried to speak louder, but the words got caught in my throat. Struggling to breathe, I ended up not being able to say anything at all.

—You always clam up like this!

—That's why everyone hates you! 'Cause you won't apologize even when you've done something wrong!

—We're telling you for your own good!

—Oh, don't expect someone like her to understand!

—That's true. Even when we're nice to her, she twists everything and blabs to the teacher.

About ten girls had gathered around, and the boys in the room were gawking. After somehow managing to control my breathing, I stood and prayed that the chime would ring.

—We forgive you, said the student council vice president.

—Yeah, we forgive you, said another.

—I guess she didn't really mean any harm, said Mina.

—Huh? Didn't you just say she did it on purpose?

The other girls laughed.

—I shouldn't have said that, said Mina, turning to me, so I'll give you the rest of my juice.

Then she pushed the orange juice can under my nose.

—But first, we'll put our friendship in it, so look and see!

Someone yanked my hair from behind, forcing me to raise my head. Standing in front of me, Mina raised the can to her lips and let some saliva dribble down into it.

—Disgusting! someone yelled.

Then Mina passed the can to one of her teammates.

—I'll put my friendship in, too, said the girl.

Just like Mina, she let her saliva dribble down into the can. A boy who had been watching yelled:

—Wow! I can't believe you girls are doing this!

Students in the hallway came in to watch, too. When all the girls had finished, the can was passed back to Mina. She gave the can a little shake and held it out to me.

—Here you go, she said.

When I resisted, someone grabbed my elbow and pushed my arm forward.

—Hurry up and take it!

Another girl grabbed my wrist and pressed the can into my hand.

—Don't you dare drop it! she said. Everyone's friendship is in there!

—No need to hold back! I'm sure it's delicious!

—You love orange juice, don't you?

—You're not gonna betray our friendship, are you? Hurry up and drink it!

—Why aren't you drinking? Get a move on it!

Bombarded with comments, I brought the can close to my face. But I couldn't manage to put it to my lips.

—Don't be shy! Here, let me help you. Jeez, you're so much trouble.

Saying this, Mina grabbed my wrist. Another girl grabbed my hair from behind, so I couldn't turn my head, while two other girls held me down, so I couldn't run away. Then Mina put the can to my mouth. Since my mouth was closed, the juice flowed over my chin and down my neck. But then a hand reached out and plugged my nose to force my mouth open, while another hand held my chin. This time, the gloppy mixture was poured into my mouth. My throat convulsed, and fluid from my stomach pushed up against the fluid coming down. There were screams, and then the sound of the can falling on the floor.

—Disgusting!

—Eww, it got on my uniform!

—Mine, too!

As I doubled over, I saw chunks of half-digested vegetables scattered throughout the orange-and-white-colored vomit. The sight caused me to retch again. I quickly covered my mouth, but the vomit gushed through my fingers. I crouched down, and as the tears came to my eyes, everything became blurry. *Don't cry!* I told myself. *That'll only make things worse!* Curling myself into a ball, I tried to make myself disappear.

—She's so disgusting!

—Yeah, and we just finished cleaning!

—We have classes in the afternoon, you know!

—If you're gonna throw up, do it outside!

—You, idiot! Don't you know it stinks?!

—You betrayed everyone's friendship! And we were so worried about you.

—She's dangerous, isn't she?!

Somehow, I managed to apologize out loud.

—Oh, you poor thing! said someone, squatting down beside me. Are you okay?

She wrapped her arm around me, and a split second later, I felt a piercing pain in my back. As I jerked back, a gold-colored thumbtack rolled across the floor.

—Jeez! And she was just trying to be nice! said the student in the broadcasting club.

As everyone laughed, the chime sounded.

—Mr. Tamaki's coming! someone called from the hallway, and everyone scurried to their seats.

Our social studies teacher entered the classroom and immediately sensed that something was wrong. He stopped the class representative from initiating the class greeting and looked out over the podium. When he noticed me crouched down at the back of the room, he walked down the aisle to check on me.

—What's wrong? he asked, putting a hand on my shoulder and stooping down to look in my face.

—Nothing, I said.

—Well, obviously something's wrong, he said, sounding a bit annoyed.

When I fell silent, he shook me by the shoulders and yelled:

—Tell me what happened!

—When she was drinking juice, said the girl in the last seat, she choked and spit up.

—Really? asked the teacher, turning toward her.

—Yes, really, said another girl. We were telling jokes, and she laughed so hard she choked on her orange juice.

—That happened before, too, didn't it? said a boy by the window.

—Really? cut in another boy. She puked before?

Some other students laughed. Taking his hand off my shoulder, the teacher stared at me and asked:

—Is that really what happened?

—Yes, I'm sorry, I answered.

—Why don't I take her to the school nurse? Mina called out. My body instinctively went stiff.

—Sure, would you do that, please?

As the teacher stood up, Mina hurried over to me.

—Let's wash your face, she said in a gentle voice.

She put one arm around my back, another under my arm, and pulled me to my feet. As we were leaving the room, I heard one of the volleyball team members calling to the teacher:

—I'll help, too! I'll clean up!

With Mina's hefty arm around my shoulder, we shuffled over to the sink in the hallway. As instructed, I washed my hands and face, and then rinsed out my mouth. I could feel the stares of not only my own class but of the neighboring class, too. I wanted to use the soap, but I just rinsed off and turned off the tap. When Mina held out her handkerchief, I hung my head.

—What's wrong? It's okay. You can use it.

When I still wouldn't take it, she said:

—Here, let me do that for you.

She wiped my face, and then my neck, too. When she finished, I stood there passively until she draped her arm over my shoulder.

—Let's go, she said.

As we headed to the nurse's room, I could feel students from every classroom staring at me. Halfway down the stairs, Mina pulled me tightly to her side and whispered in my ear:

—You tell anyone what happened, and we'll never forgive you. You got that?

—I won't say anything, I answered in a shaky voice.

When we arrived at the nurse's room, I gave the same explanation that had been given to my social studies teacher.

—Is that so? asked the nurse.

I nodded, then turned to Mina and thanked her.

—Well, she said consolingly, have a nice rest.

With my eyes turned down, I nodded. Mina returned to the classroom, and the nurse handed me a spare PE shirt and told me to change out of my uniform. After I said thanks and changed, she asked me to take my temperature. I sat down on the bed and put the thermometer under my arm.

—How do you feel? Do you still feel nauseous?

—No, I'm okay.

—Has this happened before?

—No.

—Do you have any allergies?

—No, uh, nothing at all.

—Today's lunch was cream stew, right? Did you feel strange after eating?

—No, not at all.

—Did you have breakfast?

—No, uh, I didn't.

—Do you ever have breakfast?

—No, not usually.

—I see. . . .

The thermometer beeped, so I took it out and handed it to her. She looked at the display and said I didn't have a fever. Then she stared straight at me.

—Did something happen in class?

—No, nothing at all.

—That's the truth?

—Uh, yes. . . .

—You've nothing to worry about. I'll keep any secrets, and protect you no matter what.

—Really, nothing happened.

—If you're telling the truth, that's fine. But I hope you'll let me know if anything's wrong.

—Okay. Thank you.

—Okay. So why don't you lie down and rest for a while?

The nurse sounded nice, but I couldn't trust her. If I told her what had happened, she'd certainly tell my teacher. And then my teacher would talk to the class, and I'd end up being accused of squealing. After that, I'd be bullied even more mercilessly.

I pulled the divider curtain closed, climbed into the bed, and pulled the thin blanket up to my chin. The air conditioner kept the room cool, but the thought of returning to class caused me to break out in an unpleasant sweat. The volleyball team girls who'd cleaned up my vomit were certain to harass me later. The smell undoubtedly lingered for the rest of the day. I knew that everyone's annoyance would be taken out on me later, and that made me feel more nervous. *Why couldn't I control myself? If I had to throw up, I should've gone out to the sink in the hallway.* As I started to blame myself, I recalled the gooey sensation in my mouth and pictured Mina and the other girls letting their saliva drip into the can. As my stomach started to churn, I fought back the nausea welling up into my throat again. Realizing I should try to think of something else, I remembered the lady who had given the speech in the auditorium.

Toward the end of her speech, the lady looked upset that students weren't listening anymore. She fell silent and seemed to be struggling to find the right words. After what seemed like an eternity, she began:

—It happened when we were searching for shellfish. The ocean was dazzlingly bright under the afternoon sun. . . .

Saying this, she squinted as if she actually were staring into the sun. Then she continued:

—There were five of us: me, three of my classmates, and a slightly older girl. We were searching for shellfish when four American soldiers came swimming across from the port on the opposite bank.

The lady's expression grew stiff, and her eyes began to wander. I looked down to avoid her gaze, but then I remembered what Mina had told me, and lifted my head. That was when our eyes met. Once they did, I couldn't turn away from her forceful gaze.

—The American soldiers . . . and this might shock you, but I'm telling you because I want you to know what happens during war. . . . Well, those soldiers raped that older girl. . . . And they destroyed her body and soul. . . . What made her even worse, though, was that her father beat her pretty badly. You see, he thought those Americans made her pregnant, and even though the girl was the victim, he told her that she was better off dead than giving birth to an American. After that, she did in fact try to kill herself . . . many times. . . . But she never succeeded. . . . In the end, she gave birth to a boy, but she could only be with her baby for about a month, because her father put him up for adoption. . . . Uh, that means someone else takes the baby and raises it as their own. . . . So anyway, her baby was taken away. And after that, she was even crazier, partly because she could never see her child again. . . . Her family couldn't bear having the other villagers always talking about them, so eventually they had to leave the island. After that, the girl lived quietly in her home in the south. There are fewer US bases there, compared to the north and central parts of Okinawa, so she was less likely to see American soldiers. . . . But before Okinawa reverted to Japan, there were a lot more Americans than now, so she couldn't risk leaving the house. . . . For more than ten years, she never went outside. . . . Even with her father still yelling at her every day, she gradually improved and became more mentally stable. . . . At that time, the family next door ran a dressmaking shop. They were really nice people, and they showed the girl how to operate a sewing machine. She was very skillful with her hands and could concentrate on her work for hours, so she improved very quickly. . . . When she started earning an income through her sewing, her father stopped yelling at her as much. She spent her thirties and forties like that, working all day at the shop next door and then walking home. She never even thought of going anywhere else. Even so, I'm sure those were the happiest days of her life. . . .

The lady paused and looked off into the distance. Then she cleared her throat and continued:

—But then things started to change. About ten years after Okinawa returned to Japan, big stores started springing up, and the amount of dressmaking work drastically decreased. The shop next door managed to scrape by for a while, by doing alterations on school uniforms for the local junior and senior high school students. But when the owners got older, they said the work was too demanding and closed the shop. . . . The girl became confined to the house again. By then, her father was dead, and her brothers had moved out, so she lived alone with her aging mother. They lived simply, relying on her mother's pension and some assistance from her brothers. . . . But one day, she suddenly went crazy again. She'd scream and yell, hide in the bathroom or closet and not come out for hours, or suddenly dash out of the house and run around. Up until then, she'd never gone anywhere except to the shop next door. Now she'd sneak out late at night and then be discovered sitting covered in mud in a park over ten kilometers away. . . . Her mother was nearly eighty years old, and even though she was healthy, she was completely incapable of looking after her daughter. Even so, she insisted on taking care of her. However, the brothers decided to put their sister in a hospital anyway, against their mother's wishes. . . . She's been living there for over ten years now. Her mother died recently, but she doesn't know it. Of course, she's much older now. Since she's on medication, she doesn't get violent like she used to, but she doesn't have anyone to talk to, and it's not clear whether she even recognizes her brothers. She spends her days drawing pictures by herself, or going outside when the weather's fine and staring at the ocean. . . . You know, sometimes I wonder, if war hadn't come to Okinawa, she wouldn't have been raped by those soldiers, and she would've led a completely different life. . . . In war, you see, it's not just that many lives are lost. The lives of the survivors are often ruined, too. For that girl and her family, the war still isn't over. . . . I'm sorry I'm such a poor speaker, but thank you for listening to the end. I hope we never have go to war again, and that none of you has to suffer such agony. I sincerely wish that all of you can be happy. And I want you to know that's how I feel.

After the lady had finished, she bowed, and the audience applauded. Then she smiled awkwardly and stepped down from the platform.

I hugged myself under my blanket and pictured that teenage girl, cringing inside a dark closet. As she waited in terror for the Americans to break down her door and drag her away, she covered her ears and curled herself into a ball—in a pathetic attempt to disappear. *Just like me!* I thought. *Always scared, never able to relax. And just like her, I'll go crazy and end up spending the rest of my days inside the house.* Tears streamed down my cheeks. *You're being overly optimistic! Do you actually think you'll make it to adulthood? Junior high lasts a long time, you know! Instead of worrying about the future, you'd better worry about the present!* The voices inside my head chilled my body, and the last remnants of warmth fell away with my tears. *If only I'd get colder and colder, and freeze to death.*

With my finger, I traced the scars on my wrist. Even though I'd cut deeply enough to cause some bleeding, I didn't have the courage to slash the veins. *Does that older girl living in a hospital and staring at the sea enjoy her life? When her baby was taken away, and she was locked up in her house, sitting in front of a sewing machine every day, was that fun? Wasn't life unbearable? I bet she wanted to die, but just couldn't manage to kill herself.* But I wanted to ask the lady who gave the talk to make sure. *Why is it necessary to endure so much pain?* I pictured the lady's troubled expression. And then I heard everyone laughing. *If you don't want to live, kill yourself. Nobody will care. And nobody will cry. But we'll put flowers on your grave. How about some white chrysanthemums? And a can of orange juice containing our friendship!* Everyone started laughing and jeering. I covered my ears and struggled, struggled, struggled to shut out the voices.

The chime for the end of the period sounded. A few minutes later, my homeroom teacher came to check on me. After drawing open the curtain, she called my name and tapped me lightly on the shoulder. I pulled down the blanket and feigned a smile.

—You got sick in class, huh? How are you feeling now?

I nodded and answered in my cheeriest voice:

—I'm okay! Don't worry!

I was used to fooling teachers. Most of them hated trouble and were more than happy to go along, so it wasn't all that difficult.

—Do you think you can attend the next class?

Instead of answering her, I directed a question to the school nurse, standing behind her:

—Excuse me, but would you mind if I rested a little longer?

—Sure, said my homeroom teacher with a nod.

—Yes, I think that would be best, too, said the nurse.

—Well, I'll notify your teacher for next period, said my homeroom teacher. I have class, too, so I guess I'd better get going.

As she started to walk away, I called her. For a split second, a look of annoyance crossed her face, but she quickly managed to hide it.

—Yes? she asked, feigning concern.

—Could you tell Mina that I said thanks? I said. Thanks for bringing me here.

—Sure, of course, she said with a nod and a smile.

Then she closed the curtain and left. Before long, several other students arrived, and the nurse became too busy to worry about me. I spent another hour in bed. By then, the final period and homeroom were over, but my teacher hadn't shown up again. I got out of bed and opened the curtain. The nurse, who was writing at the desk, turned toward me.

—How are you feeling? she asked.

—Oh, I'm fine now, I replied.

—Have a seat, she said, waving me over.

She put her hand on my forehead and nodded. Then she took my hand in hers and said:

—I won't tell anyone, so tell me the truth. You're being bullied, aren't you?

—No, I'm not! I said, breaking free. My classmates are very nice!

I stood up and flashed my biggest smile.

—Can I go home now? I have cram school.

For what seemed like a full minute, she stared directly in my face and looked me up and down.

—Okay, I believe you, she finally said, but if anything's going on, please let me know.

She handed me the paper bag on her desk. I opened it and saw that my uniform had been folded neatly.

—Take this, too.

She handed me a slip of paper with an e-mail address written on it.

—Please contact me if anything's wrong.

—Thank you, I said with a bow.

I left the nurse's room and headed back to my classroom. On the second floor, I edged my way along the wall and strained my ears near the door. Satisfied that no one was there, I entered. Before heading to my desk, I tore up the slip of paper from the nurse and tossed the pieces in the trash. As I was putting my books into my bag, a sheet of paper fluttered to the floor. I picked it up and took a look. At the top was written, "How would you feel if Puke Girl died?" Underneath were two columns, one labeled "happy" and one labeled "sad." Not a single tick mark was under "sad," but a couple dozen were under "happy." I crumpled up the paper and went to throw it away, but realizing that that might lead to trouble, I shoved it into my bag and rushed from the room.

I made a detour to avoid the playground and gym, and then exited by the rear gate. I was afraid someone might be there, but luckily, no one was. On my way home, I tried to stay near crowds as much as possible, even though that made the trip longer. I passed through the shopping district and then walked along the prefectural highway. It was a little over a kilometer to my house. When I'd made it halfway without meeting any of my classmates, I prayed that my good luck would continue for the second half. About two hundred meters from my house, I reached a cream-colored apartment building.

The eight-story building had been built about ten years ago. It was the tallest building in the area, and one of my classmates lived there. I looked up and saw a young woman looking down at me from the eighth-floor landing of the outside stairway. I passed through the nearly empty parking lot. Sensing the woman's stare, I stood at the bottom of the stairs and looked at the ground. The stain on the asphalt still remained, even though the custodian had scrubbed the spot for a long time. Three months earlier, a woman in her mid-twenties had jumped from the landing on the eighth floor. A passerby had witnessed her climbing over the handrail. I saw the passerby making the statement on TV and also read about the incident in the newspaper. The media agreed with the police that it was suicide. The bloodstain was now so faded that if you didn't know about the incident, you'd assume it was dirt. As I stared at the spot, I heard someone call my name. I looked up and saw the young woman leaning over the railing, still staring down at me. *I have to stop her!* I thought, and dashed up the steps.

I kept running until the fifth floor, but then I got worn out and had to walk. Finally, I made it to the eighth-floor landing. But nobody was there. From the railing, I could see the ocean beyond the rows of houses. Since it was slightly cloudy, the ocean looked more gray than blue. There wasn't any circulation in the stairwell, so I had worked up a sweat. But on the landing, I could feel a pleasant breeze. *Danger! Stay Away!* read a sign on the railing written in red letters. Beneath it was a bouquet of withering white chrysanthemums wrapped in a dirty plastic sheet. It looked like it had just blown there by mistake. I gingerly placed my hands on the railing and looked over. The railing came up to my chest, but if I jumped as high as I could, I could probably pull myself up. The thought made my feet tingle and goose bumps stand up on my skin. The sweat under my arms and on my back made me shiver. On the asphalt below, I could see a young woman contorted into a strange shape. After a few seconds, the shape turned into a black shadow, which then faded into the asphalt and disappeared.

—Hey! What're you doing there?

I turned around in surprise and saw a short man of about forty standing there with a phony smile.

—It's dangerous there, so come over here to me.

He beckoned to me, but his eyes weren't smiling. The railing knocked against my back, preventing my escape. Looking flustered, the man held out his right hand and moved closer.

—It's okay. Look! You got nothing to worry about.

My body went stiff, and I couldn't move. *Stay away from me!* I thought, but I couldn't speak. Slowly, the man closed in on me. When he was about a meter away, he threw open his arms as if to hug me. I instinctively jumped to the side and pushed him away. He staggered back two or three steps and then fell on his backside. I slipped past him and ran down the steps.

—What the hell are you doing, you idiot! I was trying to help you!

His howl of protest was hurled at my back. I thought I heard footsteps behind me, so I raced down the steps without stopping. When I reached the landing and turned around, I was relieved that there was no sign of him. As I was catching my breath, a lump of concrete smashed into the ground right in front of me and shattered into pieces. I looked up and saw the man with another lump of concrete held over his head. Shouting incoherently, he hurled it at me. I jumped out of the way, and the concrete shattered on the ground right next to me. A fragment struck me in the ankle. As I raced toward the exit of the parking lot, other chunks of concrete came hurling toward me. All of them missed, but with each piece that struck the asphalt, I could feel another hole opening in my heart.

I kept running, even after reaching the sidewalk. But after another hundred meters, I was out of breath. After making sure the man wasn't chasing me, I crouched down beside a roadside tree. I looked over at the apartment building, but no one was on the eighth-floor landing. While keeping an eye on the parking lot exit, I tried to catch my breath. Neither cars nor people came out, but it occurred to me that the man might be watching from one of the apartments, so I entered an alley that wouldn't be visible from there.

After checking several times to make sure no one was following me, I returned to the apartment where I lived with my mother. As I reached into my bag to get the key, I was still terrified that the man might suddenly reappear. I was so flustered that it took me a while to open the door. As soon as I got inside, I locked the door and collapsed in the entranceway. Hugging myself in the dim light, I somehow managed to stop shaking. Suddenly, I heard something deep inside my heart. It sounded like a piece of coral, being trampled on and breaking. *That's enough, isn't it?* I muttered to myself. Then I felt a gentle hand on my shoulder and pictured the lady who'd given the speech. *I sincerely wish that all of you can be happy.* As her slightly raspy voice reverberated inside me, tears poured down my cheeks.

TAMIKO (2005)

The cases of milk must've been heavy. The small, thin girl seemed to be struggling with her load. When I called her from behind, she cringed before her tiny steps came to a halt. Slowly, she turned around, her eyes widening in fear. This confused me because I really hadn't called that loudly.

—Sorry for calling so suddenly. Did I surprise you?

—Uh, only a little, she said in a barely audible voice.

Staring at the ground, she started to blush. She was extremely shy.

—Thanks for listening so attentively. That was my first time speaking in front of people, so I was pretty nervous. I know I'm not a very good speaker, so I apologize for being so boring. But having you there at the front really gave me the courage to continue. That was a big help.

After nodding, the girl blushed even more and kept staring down. What I told her was the truth. My speech had been okay for the first ten minutes, but then the students started to get bored. From the podium, I could see more and more of them starting to talk. The teacher at the back and the one along the side managed to quiet them down, but if it weren't for them, I'm sure the students would've just left.

I had agreed to give the speech because my youngest daughter talked me into it. Apparently, she owed one of her former colleagues a favor. But halfway through my talk, I was already regretting my decision. Suppressing my feelings, I pushed through to the end, but I told myself that I'd never do this again.

What helped me get through those forty minutes, however, was the girl listening at the front.

After my speech, I went to the principal's office with the two teachers. The principal was a woman of calm demeanor. As we were chatting over tea, she told me that her uncle had served in the defense forces and was killed in action, but that his remains were never recovered. After relating how her late grandmother had often spoken about the uncle, she told me that my speech was a good experience for the students. Then she politely bowed. I felt embarrassed since I knew I was inept at public speaking. The two teachers and the principal saw me off at the entrance, and I started walking toward the gate. That was when I saw the girl.

She was walking along the covered walkway, off to the side. I immediately knew it was the girl who'd been sitting in the front row. I hurried after her and called out when I got within reach. That's how happy I was to have had someone listen so intently. But when I saw her standing with her head down, I could tell I was being a pain.

—I guess you're on lunch duty, I said. Sorry to interrupt. I just wanted to express my appreciation. Anyway, thanks for listening.

When I was about to leave, the girl raised her head and looked at me. She was so nervous that her face had turned red. Just as her mouth opened to speak, shrill voices accosted us from the side.

—Thank you for your speech!

—I'm so glad we had a chance to hear you!

—That was the most moving story about the war I've ever heard!

The voices belonged to three girls who'd been sitting at the back of the auditorium. I remembered them passing notes and talking during my speech, so I was surprised that they were now praising me.

—I felt sorry for the girl rescued from the cave, said one girl, apparently in reference to the boy who'd been saved.

—War should always be avoided, right?

—How'd you go to the bathroom when you were in the cave?

The first two girls punched the girl who asked the last question in the arm, and then apologized and bowed. The girl who asked the question bowed, too. Their overreaction made me chuckle. Looking relieved, the three girls laughed, too. The shy girl, who'd been pushed off to the side, hung her head and began to walk away. I wanted to find out what she was going to say but didn't get a chance to stop her from leaving.

—What happened to that baby put out for adoption?

The unexpected question felt like cold fingers probing inside my chest. The tanned girl, who looked rather athletic, stared at me with an unconcerned smile. However, her question was difficult, and I couldn't answer right away. As I searched for the right words, the small, thin girl walked away. The three pushy girls stopped laughing, no doubt sensing my agitation.

—I'm sorry, I said. I don't know what happened to him, either.

The girls nodded in silence.

—Well, thank you for today.

—Please come again.

—Take care.

Extricating themselves from the awkward situation, the girls dashed off as if they were in a race. Their cheery voices and carefree movements were pleasant, but they also made me feel nostalgic, envious, and a little sad.

I looked down at the bouquet in my hands and then over at the building to where the girls had run. Then I started walking to the front gate again. As I listened to the lively voices echoing through the schoolyard, I pictured the shy girl with her head down. I regretted that I hadn't gotten a chance to talk with her.

She had alleviated some of the regret I felt about agreeing to give a speech in spite of my poor speaking skills. If only some of my words had reached her, and yes, some of the other students, too.

After waiting ten minutes, I boarded a bus and returned to the main terminal. The restaurant on the second floor was half filled with bus drivers and tourists. I ordered some Okinawa soba noodles and drank some water while waiting for my food. Suddenly, I felt overcome by fatigue. The air conditioning was so chilly that I thought I'd catch a cold, but the noodles warmed me up. I usually only eat about two-thirds, but this time I gobbled up all of them. Giving the speech must've made me hungry.

When I left the restaurant, exhaust fumes drifted up the stairwell with a lukewarm breeze. I hurriedly covered my nose and mouth with my handkerchief. About five minutes away by taxi was the condo where I lived with my youngest daughter's family. But there was nothing for me to do at home. When I got to the bottom of the stairs, I saw a bus that would be heading south, so I boarded without much thought. As soon I sat down, the engine started, and within a couple of minutes, the bus departed.

My sister lived in an institution in the south, on a hill overlooking the ocean. When the roads weren't too congested, it only took about forty minutes to get there, so recently I've been visiting her about once a week. From about six months ago, I started finding her in bed, even during my daytime visits. Before that, she used to watch TV in the recreation room or sit at a table drawing pictures. On sunny days, she used to go outside and stare at the ocean. But then, on about one out of three visits, I started finding her in bed. Before long, that changed to about two out of three. From about two months ago, I've been finding her in bed nearly every single time. When I shake her shoulder, she wakes up right away. Then, we usually watch TV or go outside for a walk. However, I've been sensing a growing frailty in her. She's been taking medicine for diabetes and high blood pressure, but her caregiver said those symptoms hadn't gotten any worse. Still, I knew she was moving into a stage of inexorable decline.

My sister wasn't the only one. I couldn't believe I was already in my seventies. Three years had passed since I started living with my daughter. Until sixty-five, I had lived alone in central Okinawa while working at a small delicatessen. But then my knees started hurting, and I could no longer work standing on my feet. Long ago, my husband died at the young age of forty-two in a work-related accident. He had been doing work for the military. After that, I worked day and night to raise my three children. With retirement, I lost my purpose and passion for living. When I'd been working, I didn't have much interaction with my neighbors, so now that I was retired, I didn't feel comfortable attending the local senior citizen group's gatherings. Instead, I spent most of my time confined to my apartment. My youngest daughter noticed this and asked me to live with her family in Naha.

My daughter had two boys: one in fourth grade and the other in second. Moving to such a lively environment cheered me up. But I couldn't get rid of the feeling that I was in the way. My son-in-law was generous and considerate. As for my grandchildren, the older one had stopped talking so much, but the younger one had grown attached to me. So much so that some of the neighbors called him a "granny's boy." Having entered old age in comfort, I knew it'd be selfish to complain. Still, I couldn't shake the idea that I should be living on my own in the north, in the town that I had made my home.

All three of my children were girls. My oldest married an oldest son and now lived with her husband and his parents. My second moved to Tokyo after graduating from high school. She was now married and living in Ibaraki Prefecture. Apparently, the three of them had decided that I should live with my youngest when I stopped working. That made me happy. So after I quit my job, and started to feel lonely and unsatisfied with life, I made up my mind to move in with my daughter. *But had I made the right choice?* asked a voice inside me. *Of course you did!* I muttered to myself as I stared out the window. *You're lucky! Some people don't have any relatives, and others can't live with their children, even though they want to. You've been fortunate. Expecting too much can only lead to trouble. You have three daughters. Compared to your sister, you've been very lucky.*

The face of the girl who'd asked about the adopted baby popped into my head. Surely, she didn't mean any harm. Even so, the insensitivity hidden behind her carefree expression now irritated me. I told myself that she was too young to know any better, but still I felt annoyed.

Outside, the bright June sunlight caused every object to cast sharply defined shadows on the ground. The people at the crosswalk seemed disgusted with the heat. As they waited for the light to change, they fanned themselves with their handkerchiefs or their hands. On the bus, the air conditioning had felt good at first but started to wear on me. Now I was wishing for the heat and getting annoyed at the bus, crawling along at a snail's pace.

I couldn't get the girl's question out of my head. *What happened to the baby?* All this time the question had remained buried in my heart. Now that that closed door had been pried open, I had to face the unanswered question. I pictured my family waiting for the baby in our dimly lit house.

When we first heard the baby's cries, no one smiled. My mother looked like she was going to cry. My father looked furious, with frown lines stretched across his forehead and around his lips. The sliding door to the back room opened, and the midwife came out with the baby in her arms. Gray and covered with slime, the baby cried feebly.

—Doesn't look like an American, does it? said my father.

The comment brought a flash of relief to my mother's face, and that made me feel relieved, too. But not for long.

—Must've been one of those sons-of-bitches here on the island! my father spit out.

The look of relief vanished from my mother's face, and from my face, too. My father climbed down from the front porch, put on the US army boots so ill-suited for him, and headed out the front gate. His comment had pierced my heart like an iron-tipped arrow. If I touched it, blood would've gushed from the wound. My mother took the baby from the midwife and called out in a loud voice, as if to encourage herself and my sister:

—What a cute baby! Now, let's get him washed!

Then she started washing the baby in warm water. I could see that she was fighting back the tears as she held the baby in her trembling hands. Suddenly, we heard a noise from the back room, and all eyes turned to the white hand on the sliding door.

—Oh, my baby! My newborn baby!

My sister had crawled to the doorway and was reaching out with her slender hand. A smile covered her sweaty face.

—Don't move! shouted the midwife. You've got to lie down!

But my sister didn't seem to hear. Suddenly, the baby started to wail. My mother had been about to hand him to my sister, but the cries seemed to jolt her to some realization, and she pulled the baby to her chest.

—This is so painful! cried my mother. To have to go through such misery!

With the baby still in her arms, she broke down in tears. As if on cue, the midwife grabbed my sister from behind and dragged her back into the room. My sister no longer had the strength to resist, but we could hear her feeble cries coming from the dark room.

—My baby! My baby!

✧ ✧ ✧

Moved to tears, I wiped my face with my handkerchief. But the scenery outside remained blurry. The bus turned, and sunlight came streaming through the window, bringing some warmth to my cheeks and shoulders. The glare hurt my eyes, but I left the curtain open and basked in the sunlight. Even now, whenever I recall my sister calling out for her baby, I have trouble breathing. The light burned red against my closed eyelids. It must've been to avoid such light that my sister remained confined to the back room. No, it wasn't the light. She was avoiding the villagers' stares and whispers—and their groping hands, stomping feet, and wagging tongues.

✧ ✧ ✧

Whenever I brought my sister her lunch in the back room, she was usually lying in the corner with a blanket.

—Sayoko, here's your lunch! I would call out to the curled up figure.

—Thank you, she'd say, turning toward me.

But she wouldn't get up to eat. I'd leave the door open and hurry back to help my mother in the kitchen, in terror that my father might say something. My two brothers, who still hadn't entered elementary school, would always whisper. If they ever accidently got too loud, they'd immediately look over to my father, to gauge his reaction. During my time on the island, I lived in constant fear of my father's explosions of anger. No, that fear continued even after I left. The dirty looks and whispers of the islanders haunted my entire family—not just Sayoko. That's why there was no respite from my father's anger.

Looking back, I could understand why he was so angry. His daughter had been raped by US soldiers, yet he'd been completely powerless to do or say anything. In frustration, he turned his anger against himself. But even though I now understood, I still couldn't forgive him for taking his anger out on his family just to distract from his own pain. Twenty years had passed since my father's death, yet when I recalled those days lived in terror, worrying about every word spoken and every step taken, in constant dread of another outburst, the anger welled up from inside me. And when I recalled how he mistreated my sister, I felt something tearing inside my chest, and anger and grief pouring from the wound. Sometimes, the anger was so intense that I became terrified of losing control.

I could still picture the scene clearly: my father storming out the front gate with the crying baby in his arms; my mother and grandparents scolding my kicking and screaming sister as they held her down; and my two brothers and I huddled together in the kitchen. I could also vividly recall my feelings: the hatred I felt toward the neighbors spying from the gate; the hatred I felt toward my mother for scolding my sister; and the murderous rage I felt toward my father for slapping me to the ground after tearing the baby from my sister's arms.

At the time, I assumed he was going to dump the baby in the woods or in the ocean. I only heard about the adoption many years later. When I entered junior high school, my mother told me that the baby had been left at an institution in central Okinawa and that later he had been adopted. *So the baby was alive!* When I first found out, I felt as if the arrow in my heart had finally been removed. *But what about my sister? How did she feel? When she heard the explanation from my mother, did she feel the same way? That was unlikely.*

Talking about the baby was taboo in our house. If any of us mentioned it, my sister would fly into a crazy frenzy, and my father would fly into a violent rage. Even my young brothers understood this. The implicit agreement continued up until the present, twenty years after our father's death. During the summer O-bon festival, the New Year holidays, and the Seimei festival (when the family gathered at the family tomb), I usually stayed with the older of my younger brothers, the one responsible for the family's gravesite and mortuary tablets. But we never mentioned the baby, even when talking about our sister in detail. *But what about my mother and sister? What did they talk about when they were living together? Did they ever mention the child that had been sent to foster care?* If the baby was still alive, he'd be sixty years old now. That was difficult to imagine. I could only hope he was leading a happy life, wherever he might be.

I gazed out the window at the sugarcane fields. The plants, still no taller than human beings, were swaying in the wind. In the winter, when their leaves turned silver, it'd be like entering the world of a fairy tale. Now, the plants seemed to be trying to get in some last-minute growth before the extreme heat and dryness of midsummer. I could almost feel their youthful vigor.

A schoolgirl in her uniform was walking along the sidewalk. Since it was too early for school to be over, I wondered if she was cutting classes. I again recalled the girl who'd asked about the baby. For too many years, I had closed my eyes to the truth that should never have been forgotten. Perhaps that's why I had reacted so negatively to her frankness. With this thought, I tried to settle down. But I couldn't.

After my father died, my mother and sister lived together in peace. I pictured my sister just after she turned sixty. She had light skin and few blotches or wrinkles, probably because she never went outside. When she was emotionally stable, she looked much younger than her age. I disliked that I looked so much older, due to the daily pressures of my life. On the other hand, I knew that I was the happier one, though I always felt guilty about that.

As soon as I graduated from high school, I moved out just like my brothers. Apart from O-bon and the New Year holidays, I rarely returned home. Though my father didn't yell as much as before, he was as unpleasant as always. I hated seeing him drunk and out of control. What I hated even more was how he looked at my sister. His look was a mixture of anger, disgust, scorn, hatred, and every other negative emotion you could imagine. Just thinking about that look made it impossible for me to remain calm.

My mother told me on the phone that my father's attitude changed after my sister had learned how to operate a sewing machine and started earning some money at the dressmaker's next door. I was happy to hear that, but when I visited for the New Year holidays, I could see that he hadn't changed at all. In fact, his hatred seemed to have increased.

At my father's wake, I lifted the white cloth from his face and looked at his closed eyelids. *I'll never have to see that look again!* I thought. Although I didn't want to admit it, I knew that I was secretly pleased. However, I was more of a coward than my father. He had never run away. Certainly, his behavior was unforgivable, but he had faced my sister and his own powerlessness every day. That's why he suffered and sometimes became violent. I, on the other hand, merely escaped. Pretending not to notice my mother's and sister's suffering, I buried my memories in my heart. Even after my father's death, I used the pressures of daily life as an excuse for avoiding them.

With my father gone, I no longer had anything to fear. Yet I never once visited my mother and sister. During O-bon and the New Year holidays, I scolded my children for wanting to stay there and took them back to our apartment in central Okinawa. Even when talking with my mother on the phone, whenever she asked if she should put my sister on, I always said no and avoided talking to her. One day, my younger brother called and said that he wanted to put my sister in an institution. He explained that our mother was growing old and our sister was mentally unstable, so my mother couldn't take care of her anymore. I had noticed the problem much earlier, but made excuses to avoid saying anything. I felt ashamed of myself.

My mother stubbornly opposed putting Sayoko in an institution. Saying that she'd look after my sister herself, she insisted that we call and cancel the admission application that my brother had gone to so much trouble to submit. This really annoyed us.

—What're you saying? said one brother. You can't even look after yourself!

—The place has nice scenery, said my other brother, and everyone will look after her with kindness. If she ever gets sick, she'll be in good hands. And if you want to see her, we'll be happy to take you. You've nothing to worry about.

With tears in their eyes, my brothers scolded and cajoled my mother. But no matter what we said to soothe her, she continued to berate us for sending her daughter away. Unable to control my temper, I yelled:

—Why do you only think of her? Always her, and never us! What more do you want us to do? You can barely even walk and can't even take care of yourself! When there's trouble, it always falls on us! Who do you think will look after her when you die? Don't you appreciate anything we've done? Have you ever considered us at all? We're your children, too, you know!

When I'd finished shouting, I broke down in tears.

❖ ❖ ❖

The bus passed through the gently undulating hills. Beyond the sugarcane fields, I could see the green woods, a few houses, and the ocean. I remembered hearing that sixty years ago the ocean was black from all the US warships and that this area now covered with sugarcane and houses had been scattered with the dead. That meant that beneath these green leaves fluttering in the breeze were piles of bodies. I could sense the foul odors and groans oozing from the decaying corpses and leaking out between the stalks. The smells and sounds reminded me of my sister's body odor and mutterings as she cowered in the back room.

I didn't know it at the time, but Sayoko had been talking to her baby. I first realized that about a month after giving birth to my first child. One night, my baby wouldn't stop crying, so I pressed my breast to her mouth to soothe her. *What if she were taken away from me?* I thought. For the first time in my life, I could imagine the extent of my sister's pain. And then I suddenly knew what sort of things she'd been muttering.

Tears flowed from my eyes. I took a handkerchief from my purse and wiped my cheeks. The kindergarten-aged girl leaning over the seat in front of me was staring in wonder. When I smiled at her, she whispered to her mother, sitting at her side. The mother looked over the seat, nodded in apology, and then corrected her daughter. That brought back the memories, as I used to do the same thing. The bus entered a commercial district, and the girl and her mother got off. I got off two stops later, at the bottom of a small hill.

At the top of the hill was the nursing home where my sister lived. Climbing the three-hundred-meter incline wasn't easy for an old lady like me, but the distance was too short for a taxi, so I always walked. This was my sister's third institution. She spent over ten years in the first one, a care facility for psychiatric patients. After that, she moved to an institution for the elderly. The staff wasn't very attentive, so she moved here about two years ago. There were many applicants, but my brother knew one of the administrators. Without that connection, our sister would've had a long wait. This facility provided around-the-clock nursing care and had ties with the nearby hospital, so we could leave Sayoko in their hands without worry.

Before her death, my mother had burned up most of her savings caring for my sister. After another several years, her money was completely gone. The construction company where my brother had worked for many years went bankrupt, and he now struggled to make a living as a security guard. My other brother owned some restaurants, so he provided the funds for our sister. After graduating from high school, he had started off as a dishwasher, but now he had three of his own restaurants in Naha. The financial burden of my sister must've been heavy, but he never once complained. Though my brothers never said anything, I knew they agonized over what to do for my sister.

Climbing the hill took about fifteen minutes, with two breaks to rest my aching knees. I entered the front gate and passed through the garden, abloom with well-pruned weeping forsythias. The entranceway was lined with planters overflowing with red, orange, and purple flowers. When I got there, I took another break. Then I passed through the automatic doors and entered the vestibule. The air conditioning felt nice, but the peculiar smell bothered me. It wasn't an offensive odor; it was that overly sanitary smell you find in hospitals. No matter how many times I came here, I could never get used to it.

I wrote my name in the visitor's registry and headed up to the second floor room that my sister shared with three other women. My sister's bed was under the window at the back. Today, rather unusually, she was nowhere to be seen. An old woman was sleeping in the bed on the opposite side, but the other two women were out. I went to the head of my sister's bed and looked at the three pictures taped on the wall. Shortly after moving here, she had started drawing at the suggestion of one of her caregivers. All three pictures were drawn in crayon with dark, somber colors. Dark green, blue, and purple had been layered to create the impression of being deep in the woods. The pictures were similar but had some subtle differences.

The top right picture was the cheeriest of the three. Bright green and yellow were scattered here and there, but a section stretching from the middle to the right had been colored over in black, forming what looked like a hole. As I stared at the tenaciously scribbled over area, I got the creepy feeling that it really was a hole, sucking up everything that drew near. It occurred to me that a similar hole was in my sister's heart—and in mine, too—always making us feel scared and nervous. Suffice it to say, the picture didn't cheer me up in the least.

The picture to the left was the most somber one. Thick lines of dark green, purple, navy blue, dark brown, and black covered the entire page. The section from the middle to the top left was filled with a dark red circle, corresponding to the black circle in the other picture. Dozens of spirals scribbled with a crayon, the circle at first reminded me of some kind of fruit. But then I thought it might be the evening sun, visible through the trees. After a while, however, it seemed to have transformed into the eye of a glaring serpent, or even a pool of blood. The picture was as creepy as the first one.

The picture below the other two wasn't there last week, so it must've been drawn and taped up recently. In this one, a horizontal blue line about two centimeters wide was drawn above dense woods of green and purple. The blue created a unique impression. In the bottom right corner were two strange figures drawn with a brown crayon. At first they looked like foreign letters, but on closer inspection, they seemed more like human figures, crouching and cuddled up to each other. At least that's what they looked like to me. *Were they hiding together in the grass? Were they searching for something? Or were they just trying to keep each other warm?* Drawn with small curves and crooked lines, the figures seemed to have wandered into the woods and lost their way. Assuming one was my sister, who was the other? *Was it her child, all grown up?* Considering that possibility, I gazed at the thick blue line. Suddenly, it occurred to me to look outside.

The nursing home was on the top of a hill, so the ocean

was clearly visible. The water looked gray because of the clouds blocking the sun. Beyond the sugarcane fields, stretching out along the coast, were beefwood trees that had been planted to protect against tsunamis. From this angle, the ocean was above the trees. I realized that the blue line, which I had assumed was the sky, was probably the ocean. As I stared down from the window, I spotted Sayoko standing on the edge of the lawn with her hands on the railing, facing the ocean. I placed the bouquet on the bed and hurried off to see her.

When I called out, she flinched and slowly turned around, just like the shy girl at the junior high school. Realizing that I had scared my own sister, I felt annoyed at myself for being so careless.

—Did I surprise you? I'm sorry about that.

As if responding to my voice rather than to my appearance, she nodded and smiled. Saliva dribbled from the corners of her mouth, filled with brown teeth. When I wiped her chin with my handkerchief, she thanked me in a quiet voice and started looking at the ocean again. In spite of the clouds, it was still quite warm, so I was worried about her physical condition. Who knew how long she'd been standing there, without a hat or a sunshade? Even so, I was happy to see her getting outside for a change, instead of lying in bed as usual.

—What're you looking at, Sayoko?

Without responding, she kept staring straight ahead. I stood next to her and leaned against the concrete handrail, which had been painted to look like a tree trunk. Then I looked in the direction she was staring. The sugarcane was gently undulating in the sunlight. The leaves and slender branches of the beefwood trees were swaying, too. White waves rippled along the coral reef, and I could hear the rhythmic rushing in the distance. We were the only ones in the yard, and the nursing home was as quiet as if everyone were fast asleep. My sister's short, gray hair was disheveled from the wind, which had blown over the sugarcane and up the hill. There was a twinkle in her eye, and then she smiled. Staring at her face, I couldn't remember the last time she looked so peaceful. Suddenly, her lips moved, and she seemed to say something.

—Huh? What?

Still staring at the ocean, she didn't answer. But her words echoed in my ears, together with the faint sound of the breeze.

—I hear you, Seiji.

ROBERT HIGA (2005)

Dear Mr. Arakaki,

I would like to express my sincerest appreciation for your kind letter. Actually, I already heard about Okinawa's plan to honor Japanese-Americans who served as interpreters during the Battle of Okinawa. About a month ago, one of my former army buddies called and told me about it. Like me, his parents were born in Okinawa, and we served together there during the war. He's excited about attending the awards ceremony and asked me to join him. I was pleased to hear that we interpreters will be recognized, but I couldn't give my friend an answer.

I'm deeply grateful that you'd like to submit my name as an honoree. But to tell the truth, I also feel embarrassed. Well, let me stop beating around the bush and get to the point: I can't accept your kind offer. I know it must sound as if I'm spurning your goodwill, but I just can't accept. I'm not being modest. I simply can't permit myself to receive such an honor.

Let me tell you my reasons, as it would be rude to decline without doing so. I should probably explain to my fellow interpreters, too, since my refusal might reflect negatively on them, but I'd like to ask you to keep this confidential. Please don't ever tell the others. If you can't agree to this, please don't read any further. I apologize for not leaving you any choice, but I trust that you will honor my request.

Both of my parents are from Okinawa, so I have a decent command of both Japanese and the Okinawan language. I made use of those skills to become an army interpreter, and as you know, I was sent to Okinawa. My work consisted of questioning prisoners, sorting through documents confiscated from the Japanese army, and translating anything that looked important. Another one of my duties was trying to convince Japanese soldiers and civilians hiding in caves to surrender. I've already spoken to you about these things.

But there was another important experience I had in Okinawa, which I've always wanted to tell you about, but never could. If this opportunity hadn't presented itself, I probably wouldn't have mentioned it. It's something I've never been able to forget, even though it's painful to remember. I've never told anyone and have kept it buried in my heart all these years. Just to let you know in advance, it's a long story. But I hope you'll read to the end.

When I arrived in Okinawa, I didn't join the battle in the south right away. For the first month, I was with a unit that landed in the north. As you know, the fighting in the north ended quickly. The Japanese forces stationed there were poorly armed and couldn't withstand our assault. However, with all the densely wooded mountains, we had a tough time flushing out soldiers who'd fled to fight as guerillas. Even so, they were hold-outs, poorly armed and lacking food supplies. As a result, they didn't have the strength to carry out any organized resistance.

Even after the battle in the north was over, an intense battle still raged in the central and southern areas. Units needed to be moved to the front lines in the south, so it was urgent that we speed up our mopping-up operations and secure the area. As a result, I became extremely busy with interrogations and dealing with villages and civilians.

During that time, an incident occurred in one of the villages: a young fisherman stabbed and seriously wounded one of our soldiers with his harpoon. I immediately went there to serve as an interpreter under the command of Lieutenant Williams, the MP in charge of the investigation. The fisherman had disappeared, so we questioned the leaders of his village. At the same time, we conducted a search of the mountains.

The villagers were unexpectedly cooperative. Pacifying the locals with medical treatment and food had obviously paid off. The ward chief took the initiative in organizing villagers to help with the search. Consequently, we easily managed to identify the cave in the woods where the suspect was hiding. The ward chief said the youth had acted completely on his own, without any ties to the Japanese army or the village. He told us that the youth's name was Seiji, that he'd been violent and mentally deficient since childhood, and that he was viewed as being crazy. He explained that the boy must've been trying to become a hero by copying other kamikaze attacks. He even apologized and said he was sorry that one of our soldiers had been injured. Such excessively cooperative behavior made us suspicious, but checking against the testimony of other villagers, it became obvious that the guy had indeed acted alone, without any ties to the Japanese army.

Our troops surrounded the cave where the guy was hiding. With about a hundred villagers looking on, I took the megaphone and urged him to throw down his weapons and come out. The ward chief also said some things in the Okinawan language, but the guy still wouldn't come out. On the lieutenant's order, a tear-gas canister was thrown into the cave. After about thirty minutes, the guy staggered out while supporting himself with his harpoon. Suddenly, he yelled and raised his right hand. When we saw he had a grenade, we threw ourselves to the ground. Several shots rang out, and the guy fell on his back. Luckily, the grenade was a dud, so we escaped unharmed.

We took the guy to our military post, where first aid was administered. He had been shot in the shoulder and leg, but his life wasn't in jeopardy. His eyes, though, had been seriously damaged by the tear gas. Because of the grenade, the lieutenant again suspected the involvement of the Japanese army and launched an investigation.

From this point, I'll refer to the young man by his name, Seiji. We interrogated Seiji to determine whether he'd acted alone or on the orders of the Japanese army. Seiji always mumbled and never gave a proper answer to our questions. He spoke in the Okinawan language, but in a different dialect from my parents, and since he didn't enunciate his words clearly, I usually couldn't understand him.

The lieutenant believed that Seiji was resisting. For that reason, the interrogation became rather brutal. We were in the middle of a war, so everyone, including me, got very rough with him. For Seiji, who was already wounded, it must've seemed like torture. Even so, he never submitted. To be honest, I was shocked by his stubbornness. At the same time, his appearance disgusted me. With his eyes swollen shut, he mumbled incoherently, as saliva and blood dribbled from the corners of his mouth.

Exasperated, Lieutenant Williams decided to question the ward chief again. With an escort of four soldiers, we rode in two separate jeeps to the village. After parking in the open space in the middle of the village, we went straight to the ward chief's house. He had been contacted through our patrols, so we weren't surprised to find him waiting out front when we arrived. The island had been spared most of the shelling, so many houses were unscathed. The ward chief asked us to sit in two wooden chairs under the low, thatched roof. The lieutenant sat down immediately, but I remained standing and told the ward chief to sit facing the lieutenant. He was reluctant to do so and kept urging me to sit there instead. The lieutenant asked what the heck he was doing. After I translated this, the ward chief finally realized he was being annoying and sat down.

When we asked if Seiji had acted on an order from the Japanese army, the ward chief reiterated that Seiji had acted alone. He explained that since all the Japanese soldiers had been taken prisoner, they couldn't possibly have issued an order. Sweat dripped down his face, and he sounded nervous, so the lieutenant began to get suspicious. His piercing gaze seemed to make the ward chief even more nervous. As he wiped the sweat from his face, he glanced over at the crowd of villagers and smiled awkwardly.

The villagers had started gathering as soon as we arrived. By the time we started our questioning, about thirty of them were at the wall on the edge of the ward chief's property. Our military escorts stood alert at the gate, but they didn't really try to control the villagers. It was hot and humid, but the ward chief's excessive sweating made us suspicious.

"You say he acted alone, but what was his motive?" asked the lieutenant. "Do you have any idea?"

When I relayed what the lieutenant had said, the ward chief wiped his brow, started to say something, and stopped. Then he looked at me and twisted his face into an unpleasant, obsequious smile. For me, who was from Okinawa, seeing that expression was heartbreaking. It was one of those servile smiles that attempt to hide both fear and resentment. Being disarmed in this way irritated me, and my anger toward him intensified.

"Just tell the truth!" I shouted at him.

The ward chief looked down at the ground. I loathed myself for scolding a man old enough to be my father. His knees were quivering.

Seeing this, the lieutenant snorted and said, "Tell him if he doesn't talk, we'll have to haul him in."

When I translated this, the ward chief became flustered and said, "I'm telling you! He was acting on his own!" Then he bowed again and again in apology. The lieutenant spit on the ground and stood up.

"Just tell them the truth!" a young woman's voice called out from the yard.

Standing just inside the front gate, a woman of about twenty was staring at us with a look of defiance. The ward chief started to turn red. The lieutenant asked what the woman had said, and when I told him, he beckoned her over. The small, dark-complexioned woman pursed her lips as if she might cry, but she walked over to us with confidence.

"Don't say more than necessary," said the ward chief in the local dialect.

I understood what he said.

"What's more than necessary?" I asked him.

He looked over at me in surprise and then turned his eyes away.

"Tell us your name."

"I'm Kana Matsuda," the woman answered in a shaky voice. However, I could sense the determination in the black eyes staring straight at me.

"What is it that you know? What's the truth you were referring to? Tell us everything."

She took a deep breath and began speaking in an energetic tone of voice.

"Four American soldiers attacked Sayoko," she said. "Seiji got angry and tried to get revenge. Those soldiers are the bad ones."

Struggling to keep up with what she was saying, I cut her off and asked her to speak more slowly. Then I translated what she had said for the lieutenant.

It was a horrible story to hear from a woman. Her voice sometimes cracking, she told us that a girl named Sayoko was searching for shellfish along the shore when she was attacked and raped by four of our soldiers. Afterward, the soldiers often came to the village and attacked other women, too. Seiji got angry and struck back with his harpoon. Sayoko was his childhood friend.

"The Americans were the bad ones," she concluded, "so please spare Seiji's life." Then she put her hands together and began to cry.

When I finished interpreting everything, the lieutenant and I didn't know how to react. The woman certainly seemed to be telling the truth.

"Is what she said true?" the lieutenant asked the ward chief.

The ward chief stared at the ground and seemed to be mulling something over. Then he glanced over at the woman and answered, "It's true."

The lieutenant glared at the ward chief, thanked the woman, and looked around at the crowd of villagers. Other than some children, none of them looked the lieutenant in the eye. The woman who had told the story, however, stared straight at him.

"Where's the victim now?"

When I passed this on, the ward chief answered in a quiet voice, "She's confined to her house."

"Where are the parents?"

"They're probably at home, too."

When I relayed this to the lieutenant, he told me to tell the ward chief to take us there, so we could hear directly from the victim and her parents. The ward chief stood up and said with a bow, "Sure, it's right nearby." He mumbled something to the woman who had testified, but she didn't react. The lieutenant ordered our escorts to move the other villagers to under the banyan tree, and then he followed the ward chief and me to the girl's house.

It didn't even take a minute to get there. The thatched-roof house, surrounded by trees, was right next to Seiji's house, which we had visited earlier as part of our investigation. In fact, the ward chief was the one who had guided us there. The lieutenant could barely suppress the anger he felt over the ward chief's never having mentioned that the victim lived right next door. But when we asked about this, the ward chief only bowed and muttered an apology.

The ward chief entered the yard ahead of us and called out to the occupants. A woman of about forty came out.

"This is the victim's mother," said the ward chief, introducing her to us. As he explained the situation to her, she glanced over at the lieutenant and me with fear. Upon hearing that we wanted to question the girl, she stared at the ground in silence. The ward chief took off his shoes and entered the front room, a wooden floor covered with straw mats. We entered with our boots on. The tall lieutenant clicked his tongue when he had to duck to avoid hitting his head on a beam. The sound seemed to scare the ward chief. With a deprecating smile, he slid open the door to the back room.

The room was so dark that we couldn't see inside. However, any occupants could probably see us. After a few seconds, a scream came from the darkness. Never in my life had I heard such a heartrending scream, nor have I heard one since. The voice ripped through me and pinned me to the spot. Neither the ward chief nor the lieutenant could move, either.

We heard footsteps on the floorboards, and then felt the vibration of the air. For an instant, I thought that some wild beast had been lying in wait and would come springing out with its sharp fangs and claws. I saw the lieutenant reaching for his holster. Then we heard a loud thud and saw someone tumble down into the yard on top of a broken shutter. What rose up outside the window was a girl, looking nothing at all like the beast I had imagined. Her long, black hair was disheveled, and her face was distorted as if by a drastic change in air pressure. Even so, her striking eyes and eyebrows, and shapely nose and lips, revealed her beauty at a glance. However, that impression vanished when another scream issued from her throat. Staring straight at the lieutenant and me, the girl screamed again and again, all the while scratching at her neck, breasts, and shoulders. With her kimono open, and her breasts exposed, she ripped into her flesh with her fingernails. Blood began oozing from the deep scratch marks across her chest. Then her obi came untied, and her kimono fell to the ground. Still staring and screaming, she began scratching between her legs and inflicting wounds to her genitals. Then she turned and ran out the gate.

The mother, who up until then was standing behind us, yelled and pushed us aside. Then she jumped through the window into the yard, picked up the kimono, and ran after her daughter. The lieutenant and I stood transfixed, frozen until the voices of the girl and her mother faded into the distance. The trees in the small yard created shade and a cool breeze. If it weren't for the fallen shutter, I'd never have believed that a girl had just gone crazy there. Her screams, however, reverberated in my ears—or rather, through my entire body.

In silence, the lieutenant climbed down into the yard, looked around, and headed toward the gate. As I hurried to catch up, I sensed someone behind me and turned around. I don't know where they'd been hiding, but the girl's younger sister and brothers were peeking out from the back room. A clear vision of how I was reflected in those innocent eyes flashed into my mind. To escape that knowledge, I ran off to join the lieutenant.

The villagers at the banyan tree were in an uproar. After seeing the naked girl and her mother run past, they probably assumed that we had committed some sort of outrage. When they saw Lieutenant Williams striding toward them, they stopped talking, and a heavy tension descended over the area. If our escorts hadn't brandished their rifles, we might've been attacked. Well, maybe not. Still, the icy stares turned on us were terrifying.

Walking just behind the lieutenant, I held my head high to hide my discomposure. On the way, he turned to me and said in a commanding tone, "Never tell anyone what you just saw."

I instinctively answered, "Yes, sir!" The lieutenant quickened his pace and headed to the banyan tree. The ward chief chased after us.

The lieutenant told the villagers to disperse and to stay in their homes until new instructions were issued via the ward chief. I translated this, and the villagers headed off in silence. After making sure the order had been obeyed, we boarded the jeeps and returned to base with the ward chief.

When we arrived, we immediately started questioning him. His testimony changed completely. Just as the young woman had said, he now stated that a girl had been raped by four soldiers, and that several other women had met the same fate. He went on to say that the women in the village were terrified, but that the men couldn't do anything since the soldiers had guns. He ended by saying that Seiji had probably attacked the soldiers to get revenge. In contrast to before, he was quite talkative. The lieutenant, looking so infuriated that I thought he might punch the guy, asked why the ward chief had remained silent all this time. Terrified, the guy merely apologized.

Once the lieutenant got a general sense of the situation, he leaned back in his chair, folded his arms, and stared at the wall while stroking his chin and lips with his fingers. His anger at being forced to deal with such an awful situation was obvious. The ward chief wasn't the only one feeling nervous. I thought the lieutenant's anger would explode at any moment. When the lieutenant finally slapped the table, the ward chief pressed his knees together and sat up straight.

"The village can continue as before," said the lieutenant. "I'll increase the number of patrols so that something like this doesn't happen again. The young man who wounded our soldier will be released as soon as he recovers. I'd like your help in maintaining order so that gossip about this incident doesn't spread any further."

When I finished translating all this, the ward chief stood up and answered, "I understand. I'll take care of it without fail." Then he bowed deeply.

The lieutenant stood up with a pained look and ordered me to accompany the ward chief back to the village and to check up on the situation. Then he left the room.

In the jeep on the way to the village, the ward chief looked like he wanted to talk, but I ignored him the entire time. I couldn't control my anger at him for having deceived us, even when we were conducting a search to capture Seiji. I was surprised at the lieutenant's lenient orders; I thought the guy should be harshly punished. On the other hand, I understood what the lieutenant might be thinking. According to proper military procedure, the four soldiers should've been court-martialed, but the lieutenant was trying to deal with the situation quietly. That's what I assumed, and I needed to proceed cautiously, in accordance with his wishes.

We arrived at the village in the early evening. Purplish light had begun to spread through the slightly cloudy sky. The open space was quiet, without the usual shouts of children playing under the banyan tree. The villagers were undoubtedly staying in their homes, as the lieutenant had ordered.

I asked the ward chief to repeat the lieutenant's instructions, and he reeled off what he'd memorized without the slightest hesitation. This obvious talent of his only made me feel all the more unpleasant.

After dropping him off at his home, I decided, after a moment's hesitation, to visit the girl and her family. I walked up to the gate and looked at the house. The shutters were closed. I pictured the parents, younger sister, and younger brothers huddled around the girl, clinging to them in the dark. The image prevented me from proceeding through the gate. I recalled the girl's piercing stare and the horrific scream that issued from the depths of her soul. The vivid memories chased me back to the jeep.

As I rattled along on my way back to base, the girl's intense stare and blood-curdling scream never left my mind. They were still with me after lights out. Though I hadn't done anything wrong, a feeling of guilt kept me awake. Was there anything I could do? Even if there were, I wasn't free to act on my own. The only thing I could come up with was to have some extra food sent to her family through the ward chief.

As expected, the lieutenant pursued the investigation in

secret. I wasn't present during the questioning of the four soldiers. Nor did I ever receive details about how the case was handled. Rumors never surfaced in our unit about what the four had done. Even if they had, it wouldn't have been all that unusual. I often heard such stories. Soldiers who'd harmed civilians were sometimes warned or punished by their superiors, but the rank and file hardly took notice.

One day, Lieutenant Williams informed me that the wounded soldier had been sent home and that the other three had been sent to the front lines. That wasn't a disciplinary action. Most units had been relocated to the south, and that included mine. Anyone who knows about the Battle of Okinawa would agree that the stabbed soldier who'd been sent home early was lucky.

There was one last job I was given before being transferred: escorting Seiji back home to his village. After finding out the truth, I deeply regretted how we had treated Seiji during our interrogations. Our medical team provided only minimal treatment for civilians who'd harmed Americans. I wanted to explain so they'd treat Seiji better, but I could only look on in silence. Surgery and antibiotics helped him recover from the gunshot wounds to his shoulder and leg, but his eyes were a problem. No doubt, this was due to the long exposure to the tear gas and the poor treatment that followed. There might've been other causes, but even after the swelling subsided, he never recovered his eyesight. Whenever I went to see him, he was always lying in bed muttering deliriously. I never did understand what he was saying.

I took Seiji home the day before I was transferred. He could now walk with the help of a cane, but since he was blind, I had to help him get in and out of the jeep. As we were driving to the village, Seiji muttered as incoherently as always. I drove into the village, passed through the open area, and parked in front of Seiji's house. His mother and father came running up and bowed many times while expressing words of appreciation. The ward chief had informed them of the day and time of Seiji's return.

I had planned to leave immediately, so that I could avoid any crowd that might form. However, I was worried about the family next door, so I walked over and looked through the gate. The shutters were open, and I could see into the front room, but no one was there. The girl might've been in the back room, and if she noticed me, there would've been another scene. I took off my hat, gave a slight bow, and started to head back to the jeep.

Just then, Seiji came up with his mother leading him by the hand. When I stepped aside, he stood in front of the gate and murmured something. Unlike his previous utterances, his words were spoken calmly. For the first time, I could understand him.

"I've come home, Sayoko."

From the side, I watched him take a deep breath as if inhaling some kind of fragrance. He had a gallantness I'd never seen in him. I now realized that the ward chief, the villagers, and I myself, had completely underestimated him. As Seiji stood straight and tall, tears ran down from his closed eyes.

I put my hat back on, saluted, and got in the jeep. That was the last time I ever saw Seiji, and I never visited the village again.

I've spoken with you many times about what I did in the south, so I won't repeat that here. To be sure, I helped to rescue hundreds of Okinawans hiding in caves. That's something I'm still proud of. But at the same time, I can't forget Sayoko, the girl Seiji tried to protect. When I recall how she stared at the lieutenant and me, and how she screamed as she fled, those proud feelings completely vanish. To her, I was just another terrifying American soldier.

Maybe you'll say that I'm overanalyzing everything. I've searched for vindication, and I've told myself that I didn't do anything wrong. However, the girl's stare and scream trump all my arguments, leaving me with unbearable guilt. As long as I have these feelings, I can't allow myself to accept your proposal.

This has turned into a long letter. It's taken me over a week to write. I've never told this story to my family. I've confided in you because you've been sincere in listening to and recording the stories of old veterans like myself. But let me repeat: please don't make this story public. It probably wouldn't cause any trouble if you did, since the entire episode ended sixty years ago. Even so, I want you to keep the story to yourself.

If Seiji and Sayoko are still alive, they'd be in their late seventies. I have no idea what happened to them afterward. But I'd like to believe that they got married and are living together happily. I know this is just a way to console myself, but I really do hope that that's how things turned out.

When you read this letter, I trust that you'll understand my feelings. I sincerely hope that you'll continue your work of recording the war and that you are rewarded for your efforts. I want the younger generation to read your record of our testimony so that such a war never occurs again. This is not a wish easily granted, I know. However, it remains this old soldier's fading but sincere hope.

Sincerely,

Robert Higa
(US Army Retired)

AFTERWORD

In the Woods of Memory by Shun Medoruma is an important work of Japanese literature for its combination of insightful social commentary, literary sophistication, and compelling narrative. Informed by Medoruma's intimate understanding of and exposure to the long-lasting psychological aftereffects of the Battle of Okinawa on the lives of his parents, the novel presents significant insights concerning war memory and trauma. It portrays not only the events of the war past, but also how the experiencing, perpetrating, and witnessing of wartime sexual violence traumatizes and haunts multiple lives across decades and disparate locations.

Additionally, the novel invites readers to re-evaluate their own understanding of Okinawa's contemporary social, economic, and political situation through the multiple interweaving narratives that draw from and comment on Okinawa's historical and ongoing relationships with Japan and the United States. Medoruma's skillful use of shifting perspectives and multiple focal characters, various narrative styles, and experimentation with the representing of a fractured consciousness through an Okinawan linguistic filter makes *In the Woods of Memory* his most complicated and sophisticated work of literature to date.

Although *In the Woods of Memory* is a work of fiction, it reflects historical facts and incidents of military rape and sexual violence against Okinawan women during and after the Battle of Okinawa that possess the potential to disturb and complicate narratives of the war that exclude or suppress such incidents. Medoruma has acknowledged that the core story is based on his mother's experiences during the war in which she saw American soldiers swim across the ocean and take women from her village away.[1] In addition, numerous accounts of wartime rape committed by American soldiers in Okinawa have been documented by both American and Okinawan researchers.[2] And, similar to the reluctance the characters in the novel have about publicly discussing the rape of Sayoko, survivors of the Battle of Okinawa have been reticent about reporting cases of rape. Although second-hand reports and rumors of sexual violence exist, first-hand accounts and detailed descriptions of rape and retaliation have been all but non-existent. The lack of first-hand accounts does not mean that such incidents did not occur. It rather attests to the constraining and silencing conditions of war and military occupation, to the pain and difficulty of recalling traumatic experiences, and to the social costs of disclosure. One example, the Katsuyama incident, where Japanese soldiers and village men worked together to kill a group of American soldiers who were repeatedly visiting an Okinawan village and raping the women there, remained a secret for over fifty years after the war; the details concerning the incident are still unclear.[3] Research on sexual violence perpetrated by members of the US military both during and after the war in Okinawa indicates a serious and recurring problem. Last year in June of 2016, a former US marine was charged by Japanese prosecutors for the rape and murder of a twenty-year-old Okinawan woman.

In the Woods of Memory's engagement with painful, taboo, and disturbing war experiences and memories contrasts with attempts by conservative nationalist groups around the time of the novel's initial publication to silence and erase critical narratives of the Japanese army's role in atrocities committed against Okinawan civilians during the war. When *In the Woods of Memory* initially appeared as a serialized novel between 2004

and 2007, various attacks on Okinawan war memory prac-
tices were launched, including the 2005 lawsuit against Nobel
prize–winning writer Kenzaburō Ōe for defaming Japanese
Army officers in his work *Okinawa nōto* (Okinawa Notebook,
1970) by writing that they had ordered civilians in Okinawa to
commit group suicides during the war. Additionally, in March
2007 the editorial board recommendations from the Ministry of
Education, Culture, Sports, Science, and Technology called for
the removal from high school textbooks of any references to the
military ordering group suicides during the Battle of Okinawa.

Large protests in Okinawa took place in reaction to the
recommended changes to the history textbooks, and Ōe eventually won the lawsuit filed against him. In contrast to these
public contestations over the acknowledgment of Japanese acts
of violence against Okinawan civilians, *In the Woods of Memory*
engages taboo stories not only of sexual violence against Okinawan women committed by the American military but also
those perpetrated by Okinawan men. Medoruma's critical gaze
severely scrutinizes Okinawan society and how it remembers
the war while sensitively situating acts of remembrance within
complex historical and social contexts.

The novel also portrays how the aging of the war generation and the context of the sixtieth anniversary (2005) of the end
of the war in Okinawa shape and affect how war memories are
recalled, expressed, and received. With the passing of sixty years
since the war, the war survivors in the novel are in the later stages
of their lives and Okinawan society is acutely aware of the aging
and passing away of the wartime generation. For Hisako, buried
and suppressed memories of war begin to appear in haunting
dreams, connected to the increasing isolation and loneliness that
the passing of her husband due to old age and living separately
from her grown-up children generate.

For some characters, such as Kayō and Tamiko, efforts
made by oral historians and peace education programs to

record and pass on the experiences of the war trigger painful memories that are difficult to share. In the third chapter, Kayō withholds information from the young researcher recording war experiences, presumably so Kayō can avoid disclosing his role in helping the American soldiers capture Seiji. Kayō even tells the young researcher not to go to the village for more details, attempting to keep his actions secret and at the same time revealing a possible way to uncover what happened. After the researcher leaves, haunting visions and the pain of being pelted with stones during the war assault Kayō. In the "Bullied Girl (2005)" chapter, at a middle school in Okinawa as part of peace education, during her talk about her war experiences, Tamiko reluctantly decides to share the painful story of Sayoko's rape. In the Woods of Memory highlights how agonizing experiences from the war that survivors want to forget or avoid remembering can be triggered by living conditions related to old age and society's desire to have the memories of the war passed on to later generations.

The novel also invites readers to consider how celebratory acts of commemoration for service during the war can be entangled with unacknowledged and unresolved feelings of guilt. The ceremonies mentioned in the final chapter to honor former US military interpreters, mostly nisei Japanese and Okinawan Americans, for saving Okinawan lives during the Battle of Okinawa, parallel actual commemorations held in Los Angeles and Hawaii as part of the 4th Uchinanchu Festival in 2006. Within Okinawa it is commonly known that Okinawan American nisei interpreters attached to the United States military used their knowledge of local language, dialect, and culture to save numerous Okinawans from committing suicide. Yet, the nisei soldier's story in the novel of haunting guilt for standing on the side of the rapists of Sayoko and his declining of the invitation to the ceremony of recognition contrasts starkly with the commonly known stories of lives saved and the award ceremonies of war commemoration. By exploring through literary narrative such private stories of guilt, Medoruma invites readers to think anew about how the Battle of Okinawa likely affected *nisei* soldiers in conflicted ways that have remained unacknowledged and hidden.

Medoruma also comments on the social and historical conditions of Okinawa by portraying how characters have been impacted by widely known historical incidents and how these are connected to the ongoing US military occupation of the islands, the Battle of Okinawa, and America's global military actions. For example, when Hisako sees the gate and fences of the US military bases during her bus ride to meet Fumi, she breaks out in a sweat and recalls the 1995 incident when a female Okinawan elementary school student was gang raped by US soldiers. Here Medoruma is associating the contemporary US military presence with Hisako's experience during the war, including her suppressed memory of witnessing Sayoko's rape, suggesting that this presence is a continuing source of trauma for Okinawans. Additionally, in the "Okinawan Writer (2005)" chapter, Medoruma links the Battle of Okinawa to the September 11, 2001, attack on the Twin Towers in the United States by having Jay, the grandson of the American soldier who raped Sayoko and was stabbed by Seiji, die in the towers during the attack. Medoruma additionally pushes readers to consider how ongoing US global military actions are connected to, if not extensions of, the Battle of Okinawa and the military bases on Okinawa when the character Matsumoto mentions that he couldn't help noticing how "the shape of the harpoon point began to look like one of those planes that flew into the towers."

❖ ❖ ❖

In the Woods of Memory is Medoruma's longest, most complex, and experimentally ambitious war-memory narrative to date. In the vein of his earlier prize-winning stories "Droplets," "Mabuigumi," and the critically acclaimed "Tree of Butterflies," the novel explores how survivors of the Battle of Okinawa have lived with unresolved war-related guilt, haunting visions, and trauma that have eluded public disclosure. Whereas these earlier works typically focus on a single survivor of the Battle of Okinawa, *In the Woods of Memory* engages multiple perspectives concerning an act of wartime sexual violence and its repercussions, revealing various character motivations, reactions, and levels of traumatization. The shifting perspectives in relation to an incident of rape may bring to mind similarities with Ryunosuke Akutagawa's "In a Grove" (Yabu no naka) or the Kurosawa film *Rashōmon*, which is based on that story, but, as Yoshiaki Koshikawa has pointed out, *In the Woods of Memory* differs from Akutagawa's "In a Grove" in regard to the core incidents of the rape—there is no doubt as to what happened to Sayoko in Medoruma's novel.[4] Additionally, as I have noted elsewhere, "In a Grove" only presents spoken testimonial accounts, whereas *In the Woods of Memory* additionally portrays the inner thoughts and unspoken memories of the involved individuals and witnesses.[5] The novel even extends beyond Okinawan perspectives to explore how the rape and Seiji's retaliation have affected one of the American soldiers who raped Sayoko, as well as the aforementioned *nisei* interpreter. Medoruma also includes transgenerational perspectives with his chapters focusing on the Okinawan writer and the bullied girl.

Although *In the Woods of Memory* reveals and explores war memories and experiences typically not shared publicly, it gestures to the issue of silence and lack of voice through the omission of a chapter from the perspective of Sayoko, the primary victim and most severely violated character in the story. Medoruma, when asked during an interview why Sayoko doesn't have a chapter in the novel, responded that Sayoko is unable to narrate her trauma, and that there are undoubtedly numerous war survivors who have never been able to talk about their traumatic war experiences.[6] By refraining from presenting how the rape has affected Sayoko from her perspective, Medoruma symbolically gestures to the extreme difficulty and even impossibility of narrating traumatizing war experiences that are too difficult to recall. Another interpretation of this omission is that by failing to give Sayoko a voice, Medoruma renders her a silent victim without agency. Alisa Holm insightfully demonstrates in her undergraduate thesis, however, that Sayoko's "voice" is her paintings, and that her rendering of her trauma through visual media is her way of expressing her experience.[7] Articulation through narrative is not the only mode of processing and expressing the traumatic.

The boldest literary and textual experiment Medoruma attempts in the novel and arguably his overall body of literary work, is the representation of Seiji's consciousness in the "Seiji (2005)" chapter. Primarily a mixture of multiple voices that constitute Seiji's memories, thoughts, and stream of consciousness, the chapter eschews visual description and places the reader in Seiji's sensory realm that relies heavily on sound. The translator, Takuma Sminkey, creatively utilizes bold text and italics to help mark some of the shifts in voices that Medoruma indicates in the original through various orthography, verb endings, and linguistic gender codes not available in English.

Medoruma's boldest experiment, however, lies in the extended passages written in a highly Okinawan-inflected Japanese presented with phonetic guides running parallel to the Japanese. The phonetic guides, what would conventionally be *rubi* or *furigana* in Japanese, however, are given not only for the *kanji* (Chinese) characters that may have various readings but also for the already phonetic orthography written in *hiragana*.

In other words, Medoruma uses the space next to the characters typically used to clarify the pronunciation of Chinese characters to present the actual sounds of the language Seiji is using itself, while the so-called main text is actually a gloss or translation for readers unfamiliar with the Northern Okinawan (Kunigami) language. In my personal conversations with literate native Japanese speakers unfamiliar with the Northern Okinawan language who have seen the "Seiji (2005)" chapter, the phonetic guides on the side are incomprehensible alone and become a nuisance in the reading experience. As Sminkey has explained in the Translator's Preface, conveying the linguistic difference of Northern Okinawan with the rest of the text within a translation proved to be too impractical.

Medoruma's attempt to write the Northern Okinawan or Kunigami Ryukyuan language through Japanese glosses, however, represents a significant, innovative, and provocative literary maneuver. Fiction writers from Okinawa who incorporate Okinawan words in their writing, including Medoruma, typically write their fiction primarily in Japanese, with brief moments of the Okinawan language used to represent the spoken dialogue of characters. In other words, modern Okinawa fiction writers such as Medoruma do not write in Okinawan or Ryukyuan languages but rather in Japanese for the narrative descriptions in their works.

The Ryukyuan languages have primarily been oral languages, with written forms of literature existing primarily in the Ryukyuan poetic form. Considering, too, that Japan's cultural and linguistic assimilation policies since the annexation of Okinawa in the late nineteenth century have meant the lack of a widely used written form for modern Ryukyuan languages, the absence of a modern work of fiction written primarily in a Ryukyuan language should not be surprising.

It is surprising, then, to see a Ryukyuan language used as the primary writing language for the narrative descriptive parts of a modern work of fiction. For Katsunori Yamazato, a native of the Motobu peninsula and native speaker of Northern Okinawan, the passages portraying Seiji's consciousness in the "Seiji (2005)" chapter represent a provocative and innovative attempt at writing Northern Okinawan using the Japanese language. At a colloquium on literature from Okinawa at the University of Hawaii in 2015, Yamazato said that when he first read the "Seiji (2005)" chapter it felt like he was reading his native language in written form for the first time.

While Medoruma's provocative use of phonetic guides to represent Kunigami language in textual form may be lost in English, the vast richness and complexity of the novel is still captured in Sminkey's translation. In other words, this loss via translation does not diminish the powerful impact the novel still delivers in Sminkey's rendering. The various elements of literary sophistication, critical social commentary, and compelling narrative that expand our understanding and knowledge of the personal and social costs, legacies, and ongoing repercussions of war make *In the Woods of Memory* a powerful novel and important work of literature.

Medoruma's thought-provoking and engaging works of literature, coupled with his social commentary and anti-base activism, have made him a public figure and brought him local, national, and international attention. His critical perspective on issues of social injustice in Okinawa and his work as an anti-base peace activist inform and enhance his literary writing. Yet, it is also clear that Medoruma's literary output has slowed immensely since the publication of *In the Woods of Memory* as his participation in protests and resistance to the construction of a new US military base in Henoko near his hometown in Nakijin has required his full attention.

In April of 2016 Medoruma made headlines in Japan for being taken into custody by US forces personnel and arrested by the Japan Coast Guard for paddling his canoe into a restricted area near the construction site. He was in the news again in October 2016 denouncing the Japanese riot police for using ethnic slurs against himself and other Okinawan protestors. For readers interested in reading more of Medoruma's work, although he has not published a full-length novel since *In the Woods of Memory*, many of his critically acclaimed and prize-winning short stories, such as "Droplets," "Mabuigumi," "Hope," "Taiwan Woman: Record of a Fish Shoal," and "Tree of Butterflies" have already been published in translation.[8] Two other provocative and finely crafted novels by Medoruma, *Fūon: The Crying Wind* (2004) and *Niji no tori* (Rainbow Bird, 2006), have yet to be translated, but hopefully will be in the near future.

Kyle Ikeda
University of Vermont

NOTES

1. See "Okinawa o kataru: shōsetsuka Medoruma Shun-san," *Okinawa Times*, May 8, 2016, page 2.

2. In English, see George Feifer's *Tennozan: The Battle of Okinawa and the Atomic Bomb* (New York: Ticknor & Fields, 1992), for mention of the rape of Okinawan women during and immediately after the Battle of Okinawa by US soldiers on pages 178, 338, and 495–99, and in Japanese, see Suzuyo Takazato et al., "Postwar US Military Crimes Against Women in Okinawa" (Okinawa Women Act Against Military Violence, 1998).

3. See Kyle Ikeda, *Okinawan War Memory: Transgenerational Trauma and the War Fiction of Medoruma Shun* (Abingdon and New York: Routledge, 2014), Chapter 5, for my discussion of similarities and parallels between the Katsuyama incident and the rape of Sayoko in the novel.

4. Koshikawa's review of *In the Woods of Memory* is available on the Japanese publisher's website http://www.kageshobo.com/main/books/menookunomori.html.

5. See endnote 6 in Ikeda, *Okinawan War Memory*, page 138.

6. See "Okinawa o kataru," *Okinawa Times*, May 8, 2016, page 2, for his explanation for Sayoko's silence.

7. Alisa Holm, "The Forest in the Depths of Her Eyes: Sayoko's Silence and Art-Making as a Reparative Force in Medoruma Shun's *Me no oku no mori*," undergraduate thesis, UVM, 2015.

8. "Droplets" appears in *Southern Exposure: Modern Japanese Literature from Okinawa* (Honolulu: University of Hawaii Press, 2000), edited by Michael Molasky and Steve Rabson; "Mabuigumi" appears in *Living Spirit: Literature and Resurgence in Okinawa* (*Manoa*, July 2011), edited by Frank Stewart and Katsunori Yamazato; and "Hope," "Taiwan Woman: Record of a Fish Shoal," and "Tree of Butterflies" appear in *Islands of Protest: Japanese Literature from Okinawa* (Honolulu: University of Hawaii Press, 2016), edited by Davinder L. Bhowmik and Steve Rabson.

TAKUMA SMINKEY (né Paul Sminkey) is a professor in the Department of British and American Language and Culture at Okinawa International University. He has been living in Japan for over twenty years and acquired Japanese citizenship in 2010. He received a master's degree in English literature from Temple University and a master's in Advanced Japanese Studies from Sheffield University. His translations include *A Rabbit's Eyes* by Haitani Kenjirō (2005) and *Ichigensan—The Newcomer* by David Zoppetti (2011).

KYLE IKEDA received his doctorate in Japanese from the University of Hawaii—Manoa in 2007 and is now an associate professor at the University of Vermont. He is one of the leading researchers in English on Shun Medoruma. His comprehensive analysis of Medoruma's work, *Okinawan War Memory: Transgenerational Trauma and the War Fiction of Medoruma*, was published in 2014.